CELESTIAL SPHERES BOOK #2

DRACA

LISA BORNE GRAVES

AUTHORS 4 AUTHORS PUBLISHING
Marysville, WA, USA

Published by Authors 4 Authors Publishing
1214 6th St
Marysville, WA 98270
www.authors4authorspublishing.com

LCCN: 2020941706

Paperback ISBN: 978-1-64477-062-7
E-book ISBN: 978-1-64477-061-0
Audiobook ISBN: 978-1-64477-063-4

Edited by Rebecca Mikkelson
Developmental and Copyedited by Brandi Spencer

Cover design ©2020 Brandi Spencer. All rights reserved.
Interior design by Brandi Spencer
Scene break icon by Lisa Borne Graves

Authors 4 Authors Publishing branding are set in Bavire and Milonga. Titles and headers are set in Mr Darcy. Handwriting is set in URW Chancery. All other text is set in Garamond.

CELESTIAL SPHERES BOOK 2

DRACA

SE DRACA

MONCYNNE

LISA BORNE GRAVES

Authors 4 Authors Content Rating

This title has been rated 17+, for older teens and adults, and contains:

- Brief sex
- Frequent graphic kissing
- Graphic violence
- Moderate language
- Frequent negative alcohol use
- Moderate fantasy drug use
- Indecent assault
- Domestic violence
- Discussions of rape

Please, keep the following in mind when using our rating system:

1. A content rating is not a measure of quality.

Great stories can be found for every audience. One book with many content warnings and another with none at all may be of equal depth and sophistication. Our ratings can work both ways: to avoid content or to find it.

2. Ratings are merely a tool.

For our young adult (YA) and children's titles, age ratings are generalized suggestions. For parents, our descriptive ratings can help you make informed decisions, but at the end of the day, only you know what kinds of content are appropriate for your individual child. This is why we provide details in addition to the general age rating.

For more information on our rating system, please, visit our Content Guide at: www.authors4authorspublishing.com/books/ratings

DEDICATION

To my brother, the original Jason Borne, who fostered this wild imagination of mine with our games, movies, and mutual love for books.

Works by Lisa Borne Graves

Celestial Spheres

Fyr
Draca
Bladesung

The Immortal Transcripts

Quiver
Fever
Shudder (February 2023)

Stand-Alone Titles

Apidae
"Dare"

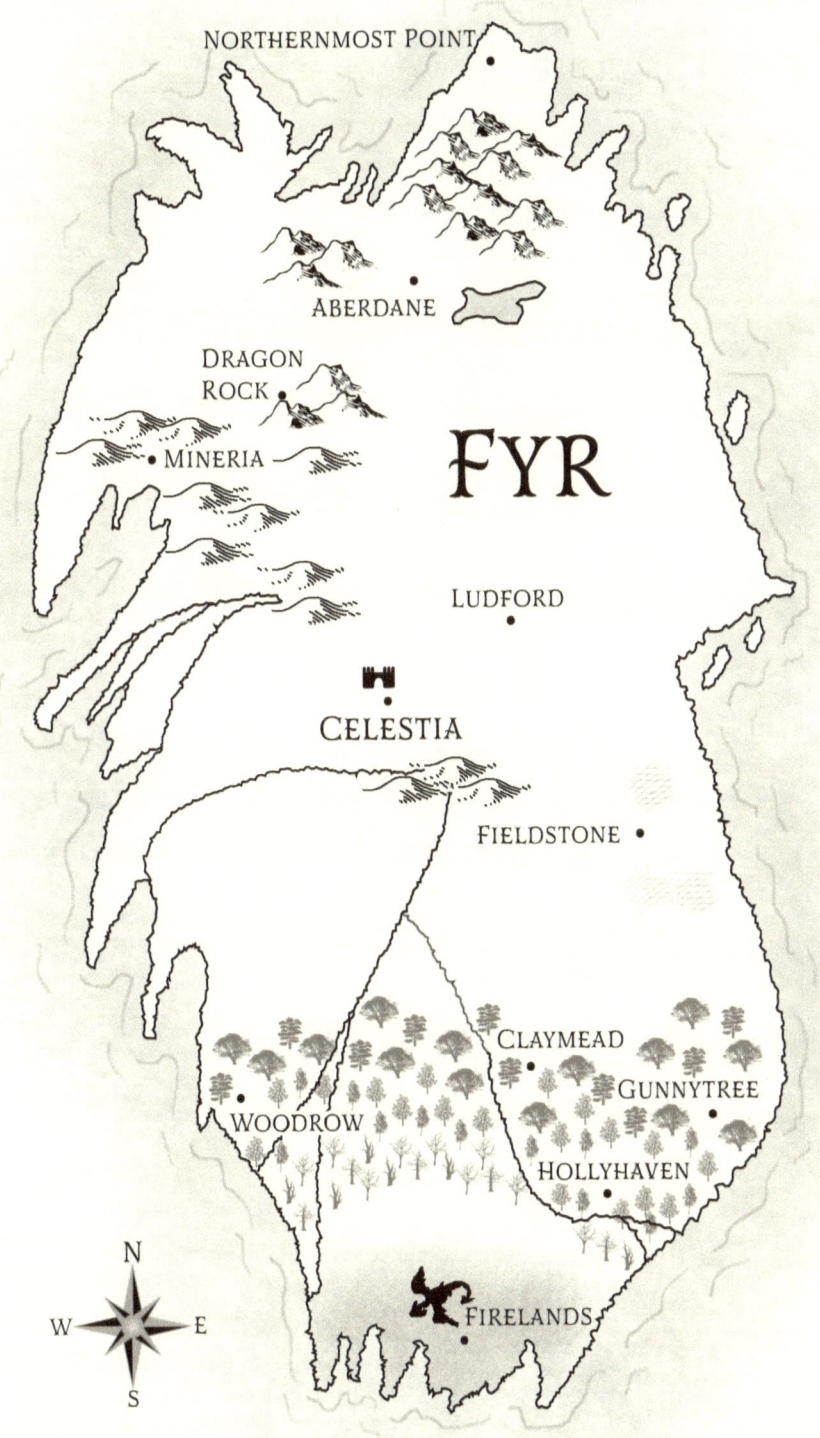

TABLE OF CONTENTS

1
SAPPHIRE

Toury Hematite was running from something, but she wasn't sure what. Her heart was hammering in her chest much too fast. Pains were radiating from it. Her breaths were quick, tight. She shuddered, her skin clammy and chilled. Was she having a heart attack? No, she had felt this way before: overwhelming panic. Running wasn't the cause. She knew that. There was this overpowering, compulsive sensation of impending doom.

The gigantic ballgown and the too-tight dance slippers were hindering her progress as she ran through the dark halls of the empty, cold castle. The castle was home, but it didn't feel that way right now. It was stiflingly oppressive, a dark prison of gray stone, with haunting shadows trying to consume her.

She stopped to look around, but she wasn't sure what part of the castle she was in. Something pulled her hair back as if Madge, her waiting maid-bodyguard, had twisted it up too tight. Her fingers went to her hair to touch a circlet like Princess Mary's. Attached to this circlet was some gauzy white material. She re-examined her dress. The embroidery with real jewels sewn into it showed she was wearing the best quality the land of Fyr could create: a wedding dress. It appeared to be extremely expensive.

None of this made sense. She and Alex hadn't set the date yet for their wedding. In fact, they were content with only being engaged for now. Things were still a bit shaky in their relationship after all that had happened.

Shivers ran down Toury's spine, and not the kind of pleasant chills elicited by Alex's fiery kisses. No, she was scared, trapped and hunted by some unseen presence. There was someone, or many people, in the shadows. Their eyes were on her. She wondered if they were the full necromancer black, devoid of color, open lids of obsidian darkness. She swore they reached out to touch her, but when she spun to look, nothing was there but shadows. Could she stop and create a ball of light? No, keep running. All she wanted was to get away. Get to a place where she was alone, safe.

She pushed herself harder, running so fast, she thought her lungs might burst. She almost fell when she saw Justine step out of the shadows, smirking. Toury halted and sharply turned left down another corridor. This couldn't be. Justine, her nemesis, had died when a magician tried to remove the dark magic from her. The girl had been so evil that there was no light magic left to sustain her. Fyr, the celestial sphere she had transported to from Earth, was made up of light and fire magic. But necromancers and dark evil threatened the kingdom—soon to be her kingdom if she married Alex Sapphirian, who had become king proxy overnight due to his father's deteriorating health. Toury had thwarted the necromancers' plans—or so she thought until she saw Justine. Had she reanimated herself somehow, brought herself back from the dead?

Toury had to find Alex. He would protect her. Did he know necromancers were in the castle?

She raced toward a rectangle of light, knowing that light was much safer than the encroaching darkness behind her. Her power came from light. She pushed through the pain slicing through her side, the corset constricting her every move. Breaths were so shallow, she grew dizzy. The room spun. Her throat tightened. She couldn't breathe or swallow.

The rectangle was a doorway lit by the sunlight. If she could just make it into the light, she was sure she'd be safe. The darkness was the enemy, its power and presence trying to kill her. She was the light they were trying to extinguish.

As soon as she reached the opening, someone slammed into her, cutting her off from her exit. The sooty, earthy smell unique to Alex enveloped her, and she relaxed into her fiancé's arms, or engagee as they said in Fyr. By his side was the safest place to be—so he had said—but then a tight feeling constricted her throat beyond the anxiety. The gauzy veil was quickly wound around her neck. Alex was choking her with a crazed expression on his face, his eyes inky black instead of their beautifully shining blue. She screamed for him to stop over and over again, and yet he wouldn't. Black dots clouded her vision, and she was about to lose consciousness...

Toury shot awake in bed in a tangle of hair and sheets, her breath coming quick. Alex was sitting on the edge of the bed in his robe, looking very different, and so were her surroundings. Alex had been choking her in what she now realized had been a nightmare. Here, in her bedroom, his face was concerned, and his hands were hovering in the air, hesitant to touch her. His sapphire eyes sparkled; the blackness wasn't in them. He went to touch her, maybe to tame her hair for her, but her instincts took over, and she scuttled back away from him until she reached the headboard.

She regretted it instantly. His crestfallen and guilt-ridden face made her heart sink. She had done it again.

"It was just a nightmare, Toury," he said quietly.

Only, that wasn't quite true. It had happened, just not in the castle. Justine had kidnapped her, turned Alex dark, and the necromancer version of Alex had almost killed Toury. She could not forget those black eyes full of dark magic, his grotesque and angry countenance, and his hands, which choked her almost to death.

"I know." She nodded. She was pretty sure he could tell she was lying. "It was...it was about Justine." There, that was some truth.

Then he sighed, reaching tentatively for her hand. She met his with hers and knotted their fingers together. "She is long gone, Toury. And it wasn't just about her. You screamed at me to stop so much and so loudly, I had to shake you awake lest Madge would come to filet me." He tried to make a joke about her bodyguard coming to the rescue, but it did not succeed for either of them.

"I'm sorry," she murmured, not knowing what else to say.

"No," he protested, moving closer. "Don't you dare apologize when you've done nothing wrong."

Alex closed the distance and pulled her into his arms, holding her. Her troubles and fears melted away in his warm arms. This was where she felt truly safe. She knew now that the curse was broken and he was free of the darkness. Alex was full of strong, powerful fire magic, and he was lighter in mood. A brooding darkness had lifted from him, although his intensity and serious nature remained. That, she was sure, must come with the station. He was king proxy now, ruling a kingdom in turmoil. Still, she saw he was happier, more full of life and energy than he had been before she'd broken the curse. Deep down, she knew he would never lay a hand on her again, but her subconscious was having a hard time forgetting about how he had hurt her. Then there was that troublesome voice in her head that told her he'd hurt her in other ways again and again.

"Toury, you know I would never again—"

"I know." She cut him off with a kiss.

He let her momentarily distract him before he pulled away. "Do you? Because these nightmares prove otherwise."

"I know it when I'm awake, Alex. I can't control what happens in my sleep." She surveyed the room and saw the doorway to her bedroom, where only two weeks ago, she had been taken from her bed and held hostage by Justine.

3

"How can I make it up to you? Anything in my power to give you, just ask. It's yours." It was a familiar speech. She knew of nothing, save turning back time, that would solve this. She wished it were as simple as asking him for some bauble or gown, but it wasn't.

She told him what she had countless times: "I have everything I could ever want. Time will make it go away." The former was true; the latter she worried might never be.

"Tell me about it, about the dream."

"Alex..."

"Don't make me order you," he teased.

She knew he would annoyingly persist until it was easier to simply tell him. "Maybe it's this room," she suggested, wanting to change the subject. She wanted to give him a solution to the problem, even if it might not work.

"Well, then, my future queen, we can solve that easily enough." Then he scooped her up and carried her over the threshold to his room. She was placed gently on the bed with care, and he scrambled in next to her, covering them both with the blankets. Still, she shivered a little.

"Ah, sorry," he murmured in her ear, lighting a fire in the grate just by gazing at it. Alex—being descended somehow from dragons—never got cold and pretty much could do anything with fire. Instead of igniting like it normally would, a burst of flames filled the entire fireplace and licked up the mantle. "Oops," Alex laughed. His gaze concentrated on the fire, and it retreated back into the fireplace. "Now, tell me about the dream."

"What was that?" She had never seen him lose control over his power before.

"Don't deflect."

"Right back at you."

He let out a breathy, amused laugh. "You win. From here on out, you always win." He pulled her in close, spooning her. "I'm having a few minor kinks in my powers since the...you know, since what happened."

"What kind of kinks?"

"Like that. I'm...more powerful, I guess. It's like I don't know my own strength. It's fine. I have it under control. Most of the time. I just need to remember to tone it down. Stop deflecting. Your turn. What was the nightmare about?" He was changing the subject again, but she wouldn't press. It was something Alex might have to work out on his own, much like she had multiple things she needed to deal with on her own as well.

The fact her back was to him helped her open up, for she wouldn't see the guilt on his face. Toury braced herself with a deep breath before launching into the tale that would break his heart. She could not lie to him, and the truth was, she wasn't sure she could ever marry him if she was subconsciously frightened of him. As she opened her mouth to speak, she thought to herself how she should've left him. Breaking their hearts once was surely better than this agonizing daily breaking of his and the slow deterioration of her self-confidence. She was becoming a shell of who she had once been and hated herself for it. More worrying was how, deep down, despite how furiously she loved him, she hated him for putting her in this situation. It was, after all, his fault. Throughout their relationship, he had made the calls, trapping her and taking away her choices one by one. Blaming his station and his gender was simply an excuse; it was Alex's nature to control and command. She wasn't sure she could live with that. Her guess was that this part of him hadn't had anything to do with the curse, but only time would tell.

2

A VILLAIN

It was the third nightmare in the span of seven days. Last week had been worse, seven for seven. Alex hated himself enough, and these reminders poured salt into his guilty wounds. When it came to Toury—the woman he loved and wanted more than anything—he was an utter villain. To rid himself of the necromancer's curse, he had put his people, his kingdom, and himself before her. He had told himself it was all necessary. Duty must come before personal sentiment, for the greater good of his people, to be the better man she deserved—free of darkness—but that was a lie. Sure, he felt different. When that curse had lifted, he was like a new man: more powerful, happier, and lighter. The curse had been this weight upon him, or valve that blocked his strength; he had gotten so used to pushing the fire power through the darkness that the same action now caused an enormous amount of power to burst from him. And it wasn't just this strength that had increased. The fact he realized now how much he had hurt Toury, emotionally as well as physically, told him he lacked empathy when he had been under the curse; this placing of himself in her situation was fresh now. He felt with so much more intensity than he ever had before. It was almost crippling to realize how much he had hurt her and how he could do nothing to help her heal.

Duty over love was a sentiment that had been instilled to him by his unloving, iron-fisted father, who was currently convalescing toward his death. But now the kingdom was Alex's to rule. There were many pressing concerns: gathering up the necromancers and ridding the land of darkness, delivering supplies to curb the famine and drought out east, and the draca he had foreseen in the flames wreaking havoc in the south. His sister, Princess Mary, could also see future events in the flames, as all Sapphirians could, and corroborated this vision. The when and why, Alex questioned. The dragons stayed in the Firelands, a place too hot for most Fyrians to enter, and they were docile creatures if unprovoked. Recently, he had also been given information he had previously been excluded from; there was an aftermath of his grandfather's Rebel Wars, bands of new-generation rebels who protested Sapphirian rule. This explained why his uncle and cousin had been absent from the palace—his father had sent them on a mission of intel. Alex hoped these rebels would disband now that he was cured, but his reign was still not secure. It would never be secure until he and Toury married and had an heir, among fixing all these other grievances that the rebels were upset about. These were problems created by his grandfather, worsened by his father, but he wanted to change all that. He wanted reform, and the world Toury grew up on, Earth, was far more progressive than his. But with Toury being afraid of him, he couldn't press her about marriage or dabbling in politics.

Out of all his problems, making Toury love him and not fear him was the most daunting of them all. He had broken a once-strong girl and knew not how to bolster her back to her former fighter status. What he wouldn't give to argue with her about nonsense again, instead of dealing with this subdued girl.

When she finished telling him about her nightmare, he said, "This dream sounds like you're not ready for marriage and that you still feel trapped by what I've done." More guilt. He had trapped her into the engagement in the first place by publicly breaking rules of propriety.

"No!" she protested, turning around in his arms.

He hated and loved when she did that. In a bed together, facing each other, her body so close to his, it made his blood afire with desire for her, and he could not cross this line of propriety with her for many reasons. He doused his inner fire with thoughts of things completely unrelated to her.

When he met her gaze again, he was somewhat in control of his thoughts; the fantasies drifted away as he tried to home in on her words: "I don't feel trapped. Yes, you were too impatient to await my decision, but I was just too stubborn to give in to my feelings. Imagine if you had not tricked me into the engagement. Where would we be now?"

He would've been forever dark and lost his kingdom and autonomy to the necromancers. She had paid the price, though, and that wasn't fair. She spoke nothing of how much he had hurt her. Her silent omission was enough to tell him she agreed.

"You know, in Fyr, dreams are seen as important windows to our souls. Yours is trapped, Toury. I will not marry you until you feel free and are unafraid of me."

She sighed, and it sounded like relief, making his stomach churn nervously. He had a gnawing fear she would leave him for good as she tried to do, just a week ago, before he had persuaded her to stay by confessing his love for her. The silly girl, never having known love on Earth—not even from family—couldn't fathom him loving her, but it wasn't enough. How could love not be enough?

"I will try to rid myself of these feelings, Alex. I thought time would help, but maybe I need more."

He mused for a minute. "Let's change everything possible that makes you feel trapped, starting by redecorating your room. Invite your ladies-in-waiting to help you. You haven't had your friends around but once. Go into the city with them. Visit their houses. You keep yourself bound here, and you know you're not. All I ask is that you take a retinue of a dozen soldiers for your safety." He hoped forcing space between them would help her. She needed to come into this on her own, gain mental strength, and then, he hoped, open back up to him.

Toury's lips quirked at the idea of redecorating; then she was beaming by the end of his speech. "I love you."

He smothered her with kisses before he could even say it back, and before he knew it, he was trying to pull her nightgown up. She froze under his frantic touch, and he knew his enthusiasm frightened her. He stopped himself and rolled off her, trying to calm the fiery blood pumping through his veins. "I love you too," he said and then added, "obviously."

She giggled, both of them dismissing the moment she had half cringed under his touch.

"Toury, I'd marry you tomorrow if you were ready. Don't." He stopped her before she could disagree. "I know you're not. You set the day, but no pressure." Then he kissed her quickly and slipped out of bed.

"Where are you going?" she playfully protested.

"To take an ice-cold shower," he told her with a laugh. He had to cool down his ardor for her somehow. Only, he knew it probably wouldn't work, for he never could be cold, and nothing—absolutely nothing—would make him stop wanting Toury.

She laughed.

He smiled and ducked out of the room, heading down into the bathing room. As he turned the dial to start the shower, he glanced into the looking glass. His smile faded. He should not be smiling. He did not deserve this happiness nor Toury's love, but how to earn it, to truly deserve it, was a perplexing atonement he could not figure out. By the god and goddess, he would win her back, no matter how long it would take.

The next morning, he slipped out of bed, sparing a quick glance at the peacefully sleeping Toury. Everything about her was calm, except her untamed hair. Interesting that she didn't have another nightmare while he was right there with his arms around her. Perhaps she truly was unafraid of him as she said and not simply trying to assuage his guilt. He did not wake her, but went down into the bathing chambers to dress, not bothering to call his valet-bodyguard, David.

When he later called the servant to their sitting room by the bell pull, David looked displeased. "Taking after your engagee, Your Majesty? Dressing yourself like some common Earthling." David snuck in as much derision as he dared, as he insisted on fixing Alex's attire to impeccable standards. Only after David tucked and tugged the shirt under Alex's doublet, and then choked him by fastening that insipid top button by his throat that Alex often left undone, did the overbearing servant give the impression he was pleased.

"Well, if she still readies herself, she does a mighty fine job," Alex said.

"No one would ever say otherwise."

Alex snorted. "Didn't think she was your type, David."

David turned a little red at that comment. "One can understand beauty, even if it isn't someone's preferred taste, Your Majesty."

"Oh, get that haughty look off your face. I was only teasing you. Do I have time to breakfast before the meeting? Most likely, it'll take me all day."

Alex opened the door and left, David following, racing after him and placing the King Medallion over his head. The thing was heavier and more ornate than his prince one had been, but at least it was the more prestigious silver.

"You may do as you please," David said. "They must wait for you to arrive at your leisure."

Alex gave him a leveled glare. "When, in all my years, have you known me to play such parlor tricks as my father and make people wait simply to exude my power and show who is in charge?"

"Forgive my bluntness, King Proxy, but the tricks started as soon as your path collided with a certain girl in a dress shop. Your direct manner left. I could hardly guess what you'd do next, and now the curse is gone. You are different. I do not mean in a bad way, Your Majesty. It's just, I don't know what to expect. I haven't truly known since you met her."

Alex hated when David was so candid, but he never stopped the man from speaking his mind, because Alex knew he needed to hear it. He pushed down the urge to argue with or yell at David and huffed out an annoyed breath instead. "Well, I won't deny the queen proxy-to-be is an exception to my composure, but I will not intimidate nor tolerate sycophants. I will earn respect through my actions. Get a servant to bring some food into the council chamber."

"Food...in the chamber?"

"Just because it hasn't been done in my father's reign does not mean it's wrong."

"I will send for the poison taster as well."

Alex was about to protest but then remembered Toury being poisoned by Justine when they were at school and simply said, "Do whatever you must to cater to my request, David." Alex's father rarely ate and drank with visitors around, due to fear of being poisoned. Alex had thought him ridiculous then, but now it didn't seem so far-fetched.

David paused in front of the doors leading into the chamber and whispered to the servant standing by the door, who then hustled off to get his breakfast. David was never to leave his side unless Alex was safely secured in his own quarters. David took this duty even more seriously after Alex had given him the slip to battle necromancers on a suicide mission. David even went as far as to obsessively watch over the door to Alex's chambers, as Alex found out one night when he decided to sneak down to the kitchen to get Toury some cake after a particularly distressing nightmare. He wondered when, and if, the man slept.

Alex took a deep breath and let it out as David opened the doors. Alex walked into the room, not sparing a glance at the almost empty table of the Sorcerers' Guild. Most of the men who had held the ranking positions—his father's men and friends—were necromancers who were awaiting trial or were already convicted.

Alex sat down and then surveyed the guild. Fifteen seats, and only six had men in them. The majority of this small group gazed at him with the same respect and reverence they gave his father, but two of the men gave Alex the same look they had given him when he was a child. He hated pissing contests, but it might need to be done until those two realized he was the king in every regard. Funny how little boys proving their worth by how far they could project their urine transferred into men wielding their power. He swore some of these nobles never grew up.

"I, King Proxy Alexander Rowland Sapphirian, call this emergency meeting of the Sorcerers' Guild to order. Right, so our first order of business is to get these seats filled. Let's get started."

"Your Highness." Lord Rhodonite laughed lightly. "You expect us to simply fill up these nine seats, just like that?" He condescendingly snapped his fingers.

The other dissenter, Lord Chrysoberyl, muttered in return, "Wouldn't need to fill seats if you'd free the innocent men locked up in your prisons."

The anger flared inside of Alex, the fire rising, wanting to lash out. Despite feeling more powerful, he squashed his rage quicker and easier than ever before. Everything was so strange after losing this curse, this lifelong damper over his entire being. He was free and in more control than ever—well, when Toury wasn't around. "Lord Rhodonite," Alex began politely. "It is 'Your Majesty,' now, as you well know. If you slip up again, I might assume it was on purpose. During my father's and grandfather's reigns, insults to the crown were considered heresy, punishable by death at the stake."

The man's face drained of color, his hard brown eyes widening in shock. He had expected a boy and was finding a man.

"And yes, I do expect the six of us to decide on nine nobles to fill these seats. Or, if it is too arduous for you, I can call upon *cynedóm*." Alex referred to the edict that allowed him to seize full power. "I can overtake this entire guild and appoint whom I wish, since less than half the seats are full..." He paused for dramatic effect. "But I was trying to peaceably work this out together.

"And Lord Chrysoberyl, if you believe the people in my dungeons are innocent, then perhaps you need to join them. They kidnapped Lady Tourmaline, Queen Proxy-to-Be, and tried to use the curse to control me and usurp the entire kingdom in hopes to turn it dark. You call these men innocent? It makes me wonder—actually, I think I can speak for the rest of us—it makes *us* wonder where your loyalties lie."

The man stammered, trying to speak but making no sense.

"David, summon Lady Edwina at once. I want to make sure one of the filth we call necromancers is not sitting at this table." As a Hematite, Toury's aunt also saw the darkness.

The lord suddenly was full of pleas for forgiveness and mercy. The others shifted uncomfortably. Alex hated begging. The man's snide and heretical comments either stemmed from being a necromancer, having rebel sympathies, or simply thinking himself above Alex. Any one of those notions was dangerous, and Chrysoberyl had to be made an example of.

"I haven't even had breakfast yet, so please stop groveling. If you have nothing to hide, the lady will clear you again."

"Your Majesty." Lord Spinel entered the conversation. "On no account should you delay your meal for us—"

"I would not have you wait. That is not the monarch I will be. I don't have time for parlor games. I will get things done."

The door opened, and a cart of food came in.

"Ah, here we are, men. Let us eat and weigh some candidates? I'm sure we can agree on a few."

Lord Spinel gave him a grin and a nod. Alex took it as a compliment, as the man was old enough to be his grandfather. They dined and discussed possible candidates, and Lady Edwina cleared Lord Chrysoberyl for a second time. At least the man was obedient and humble now, so the production of calling him out had been worth it.

Four hours later, Alex adjourned the meeting with all nine members selected. They grappled for more than half of that time over the last two slots. In order to get Cobalt's older brother Thomas in, Alex had to concede and allow in Lord Olivine, related to the Citrines through marriage. It made him wary, but diplomacy was full of allowances to get necessary results. Regardless, the guild was in his favor still. It was cleansed and rebuilt. Step one to undoing his father's damage completed. Feeling productive, he sought out his engagee for lunch.

3

LADIES

Even a full month after the battle in the north with the necromancers, Toury was only feeling a bit better. It was wrong to think she could get over all the trauma with time. Having her friends over, redecorating, and shopping were merely distractions, but they worked, at least while she was doing them. Alex even upgraded her allowance to a few silver Sapphirians—silver oddly being the most precious metal in Fyr as opposed to Earth's love of gold and platinum—but she never spent them. Madge tried to tell her it was simply a queen's allowance, the rise in her station, but the money felt tainted, as if he were trying to buy her forgiveness. Toury ended up buying little trinkets for other people with some of the money. She decided keeping herself busy was the best plan. In the mornings, she recommenced her physical training with Madge and her magical ones with her lightbearer uncle. Mary joined her in the combat training, which Toury thought would show her up, but Mary hadn't the inclination to learn to defend herself until the necromancers were in her own home. Apparently, Alex wanting Toury to defend herself was a progressive notion for women in the land. Even now, Mary joked around, not taking anything seriously, much to the dismay of Madge and Lucy—Mary's bodyguard.

Lunches were spent with Alex, who hoped to continue the tradition of eating most meals together, no matter how busy they were. Although she reached each meal with trepidation, the moment they were seated and chatting, she'd relax. He was a different person; a kinder, less commandeering Alex had been reborn in the old one's place. After lunch, she'd have tea with the queen, Mary, and her aunt, who had become completely compliant and a bit kinder now that she was not only invited back to court, but was also living there and using her light powers in the necromancers' cases. Toury would join the trials when she felt up to it, but she could not see their black eyes without having nightmares.

Sometimes at teatime, they would entertain other nobles, so Toury was meeting a lot of people—all who had nice clear eyes, thankfully, and not the necromancer black. They were beginning to accept her. The rest of her day she now filled up with outings with friends, shopping, or planning the redecorations. She was going to completely redo her bedroom and wanted to add her touch to their sitting room, making it less like a bachelor pad. Alex gave her free reign, although he warily asked her views on lace. There was already enough of it in the palace to make him cringe, thanks to the queen's love for it. It was a good thing for both of them that Toury wasn't a fan.

They ate dinner as a family, her aunt included, but sometimes they did not, for it wasn't the same with the king being unable to leave his rooms. Toury visited him once a week, but he never let her heal him. She understood he was done and that he no longer wanted to hold on, so she respected his wish, no matter how sad it made his family.

The evening usually consisted of Alex and her retiring early to their quarters, where he'd pore over documents about the land's problems aloud and go through outdated laws that he wanted to rescind, helping Toury dabble in politics. He always asked for her opinion, which made her realize how lucky she was in this patriarchal land to find a man who wanted a partner to help him, rather than simply a beautiful vessel who would give him children. He truly wanted her opinion, and the power she could wield over the land was flattering and left her breathless. If she could just conquer this fear deep down that he might hurt her, and realize that his actions and words now were promising a very different path than what it had been, she could marry him. Part of her wanted that more than anything. Another part of her wanted to shut herself away from the world and not face anything.

"You're woolgathering again," Lady Delphine Opal teased.

"Sorry." Toury shook her head.

"Thinking of your beloved king proxy?" Lady Henrietta asked.

Toury's face warmed.

"La! Look at her blush!" Lady Pearl giggled.

"I was, actually," Toury admitted, but it wasn't in the context they thought. Their giddy faces compelled her to play some part. She could not confide in them how she felt; she couldn't even talk to Mary or Madge about it. Maybe, just maybe, if she acted like everything was all right, it would become that way. "I was wrapping my head around trying to set a date for the wedding. It's been left up to me."

"Tomorrow!" The ever-outspoken Lady Deanna spat out.

Another girl smacked her, while another friend protested that they needed at least a month for the dress. The idea of a wedding gown brought back flickers of her nightmares, but she pushed them away, trying to focus on the voices of her friends. A couple others chimed in, debating on how long a royal wedding took to plan. There were too many voices, too much going on. She realized inviting all ten of her chosen lot was probably too much at once, but it did distract her.

"You're kidding? I would tomorrow, if I were you. Forgive me, Queen Tourmaline but—"

"Queen Proxy-to-Be, Lady Deanna," Toury corrected her.

"Queen to us, already," she retorted. "I meant it as no affront to the present queen."

"Forgive me for saying this, but your dreamy, beloved king is too delectable to leave untouched. Surely, you two are, you know, intimate," Lady Pearl said.

"None of your business!" Toury gasped but could not help but smile from Deanna's boldness. She threw a settee pillow at the girl, and they all erupted in laughter.

"She does have a point," Lady Lillian mused. "Tell us, what is he like in your private chambers?" She shimmied in a suggestive manner.

"You know we can't..."

"We'd never suggest that!" Lady Opal protested.

"But we know there must be some juicy details," Deanna pressed.

"Well, it's private, so I'm not telling." She inadvertently giggled from embarrassment afterward, which gave the wrong impression, inviting them to press her. They nagged her relentlessly, so she had to give them something. "He's an amazing kisser."

"That's it? C'mon!"

"Give us something!"

"Well, he is kind, compassionate, doting, and loving." Although she was still kind of playing some part, she wasn't lying about Alex. He was these things. When she compared him to the king—since her male acquaintances were limited, particularly of royalty or noblemen—she could see the superiority of Alex's character.

A few squeals frightened her back into silence. They were all leaning forward, wanting more. She did not want to share what she and Alex had with anyone, even her new friends. She was frightened she might inadvertently give away that there was this wedge between them, and even if she ignored that recent distance between them, what they'd had before was beautiful and private.

"What about his body? Have you seen it? He felt so muscular when he danced with me." Lillian sighed.

"He is strong, of course. He trains every day. Not that I stare at men's physiques often, but he is what I'd call chiseled but not too beefy."

One of the girls feigned a fainting spell.

The girls began debating on the correct amount of muscles, and Toury learned Alex was perfect in this land. Too many muscles proved to be working class; too little muscles showed weakness and laziness. It kind of made sense to her in a way, much different from Earth's girls she'd known who had a preference for burly muscles.

"Tell us more," Lady Pearl begged; the rest of the girls also egged her on. "Is he romantic?"

"Well, I'm not one for cheesy overtures. He tells me what is in his heart, and that, to me, is the most romantic thing possible."

The girls laughed and giggled. She did not find this funny and was suddenly self-conscious until she sensed a presence looming over the back of her and peered up to see Alex leaning down toward her.

He kept leaning and gave her an upside-down peck on her lips. He pulled away quickly, as the company was ridiculously fawning and simpering over them. "May I have a word, my love?" He took her hand, helped her rise, and walked her to the end of the settee where they came together closer.

She excused herself from her friends momentarily, and Alex led her into the hall, not saying a word. He had to be mad, although she could read no annoyance on his face. What king would want his personal life on display?

"I'm sorry, Alex. I didn't mean to say such things, but they were relentless. Everything I said was good, of course, but—"

Alex cut her off with a deep kiss and a moan, and they stopped walking. She found for the first time since the necromancers' attempt to overthrow the kingdom that she wasn't afraid. She wanted to kiss him. He pulled away too soon, and her lips followed his, refusing to stop the kiss until he pecked her away. "Toury." He took a deep breath. "Insecurity is not fitting for you. They are your friends. You are your own person, and you know that. Do as you will, and tell them whatever you please. They may tell others, but I couldn't care less. In fact..." He leaned into her, gently pressing her into the tapestry on the wall, and her breath hitched. He hesitated, searching her face for something—probably worried he'd find fear—but his mouth quirked, apparently happy with her expression. He kissed her soundly, pressing his body against her, fully awakening every nerve in hers. He plunged his tongue into her mouth, and her knees began to shake a little. Then he pulled away, staring at her with love and fire in his eyes. "...let them talk about that. I don't mind if everyone in the kingdom knows how much I want to marry you."

Then he pulled away, touching her chin.

"What did you really want, my love?" The pet name had slipped out, her having never said it before.

He smiled widely and leaned his forehead into hers and whispered, "I came because I just needed to see you, but now, I want to take you back to our room and kiss every inch of your—"

"Alex!" she scolded, trying to feign an affront, but she was sure he saw through it.

He pulled away with a reluctant expression and kissed the back of her hand. "Enjoy your friends. I will see you at supper in the main hall. Mother said to invite them to stay and dine if you'd wish."

She nodded as he walked away. "Mother," she pondered. He didn't say "my" nor call her the queen, but "Mother," as in both of theirs. Toury was family. She gave him "my love," and he gave her "Mother," and she now felt closer to him than ever. She realized, stunned, that her mind didn't at all think of black eyes, nor did her body cringe at his heated kisses. Perhaps she was finally conquering her fear.

She turned around to see the girls scatter back into the room, away from the doorway where they had been spying on them. Toury smiled to herself. The king proxy planned everything when in the presence of others, so the fact he'd let decorum slide meant something. It made her realize she could be herself and open up to her friends, and Alex would only find the positives in all of her actions. She could do no wrong in his eyes. This was something she could easily live with.

4

AN ADVISOR

It took weeks for the paper to report Alex and Toury were doing well, and how soon the wedding date would be was heavily speculated. The fact it took weeks was a testament to how honorable Toury's friends were. Most court debutants would run and instantly spread rumors like wildfire.

He had wanted the public to know. Maybe, just maybe the people would tip the scales, and Toury would want him again, be less frightened of him, and someday forgive him. Her forgiveness, he didn't care if it took his lifetime to achieve; he deserved it to take that long. If he could just get her to marry him, he could plan how to truly atone. He didn't want to pressure her, and yet they were edging ever closer toward the line of impropriety. He was a royal, and they were not supposed to act on their passions nor consummate them unless married. It was a rule a lot of noblemen ignored, but not Alex. Toury's effect on him made sticking to this rule extremely difficult.

"Where were you?" Cobalt challenged, making Alex come out of his reverie.

"I hardly know," he groaned, rubbing his eyes. "That woman is going to kill me."

"I can see that. If this is what love is, I never want to fall into it."

"You have to have a heart to fall in love, so you're safe," Alex taunted his friend.

Cobalt chuckled and sat on the edge of Alex's desk, formerly his father's desk and study. Alex hadn't altered it, hoping somehow his father might grace its walls again. It was a foolish hope, but he just couldn't redecorate it to his own tastes, not yet.

"I'd rather be heartless than brainless," Cobalt fired back.

Alex laughed. "Fair play, I suppose. What were you telling me?"

Cobalt's eyes sparkled with mirth, but then he stood up with a more serious expression. "I was merely updating you on the trials. We are working our way through the Magicians' Guild, but as you suspected, Your Majesty, there have been very few necromancers among them."

"Yes, the social divide between nobles and magicians has been going on far too long. I never could imagine the nobles would condescend to recruiting people they wrongly felt were beneath them."

"Wrongful, yes." Cobalt hesitated.

Alex knew it was a frictional area for his friend, who also had been raised believing he was better than others, just like Alex's father had tried to instill into Alex. His friend came through with logic in the end, making Alex confident about his trust in him.

Cobalt continued, "But the magicians are less powerful, less likely to attract people who are working with such complex magic. I imagine going against our fire, light, and energy instincts takes extreme power. So I've been concentrating our efforts on nobles. We don't want another Citrine incident; that entire family was rotten to the core. About half the suspects in custody have confessed, hoping for mercy, or have been confirmed guilty by the lightbearer and Lady Edwina. Your Majesty, we need to speed up the trials, and we'll need one of them to sweep other nobles who aren't part of the guild. We don't know how far this Black Order society goes. If the queen proxy-to-be could help—"

"No," Alex said. Her nightmares about him had started to dwindle this past fortnight. He wasn't about to jumpstart them by having her face the very people who had tried to kill her.

"King Proxy, with all due respect—"

"Cobalt, she isn't ready. She knows it would help if she assisted her family, yet she has shown no interest."

"Yes, Your Majesty." Cobalt suppressed his comments, even though it seemed to irk him. "Moving on, my father received a missive from your uncle. Your cousin Henry has gone missing, and your uncle returns to see what you wish to be done."

"Missing?" Alex was deeply disturbed by this. Nobles had stopped vanishing once most of the necromancers were imprisoned. Henry was a Sapphirian—one of the only ones left. Aside from Mary and himself, there was Henry's mother, Alex's aunt Anne, who had lost her mind when they were just boys. She had to be taken to Ludford and kept guarded, for she had tried to kill his uncle and burn the castle down twice. She was still living, and there was Alex's own father hanging on. His other uncle, Alfred—whom Toury's mother had been supposed to marry—died not long after Alex was born. Alex was next in line of course, but until he or Mary had a child, Henry was the last Sapphirian after them to stop their extinction. Henry was three years his senior and had married a beautiful debutant of the Topaz family, who died within a year of their marriage, along with their firstborn. Henry didn't appear to have plans to remarry, despite his father's persistence.

After a moment, Cobalt continued: "Nothing like we faced before, I'm sure. It points to him deserting his post."

Alex found this even more disturbing. What would make his cousin leave the protection of the army and venture out on his own? "Unlike him," Alex mused, for Cobalt awaited some kind of response.

"Not in my opinion. You always looked up to him, Your Majesty. You're family. I never trusted him. He's faultless outwardly, of course, but there's just something about him I never trusted. He seemed fake, lazy, entitled, and selfish."

"One could say that about all nobles, Cobalt."

"Not you or Mary. Mary is very affable and more giving than any noble I've met. She is one of the strongest women I've ever known. And you—although too serious for your own good—are generous, forgiving, and too damn good to live up to. You always do the right thing, no matter what you want personally."

Alex wanted to deny it because Cobalt was wrong in a sense. He said nothing because he knew Cobalt would back up sacrificing a woman to save the realm. Cobalt didn't know the bitter sting of love yet.

"Henry is a decent guy, though." Alex deflected the unfounded compliment.

"He's more of his father's son than a Sapphirian, but what would I know?" Then Cobalt sighed. "What are we to do with the guilty necromancers, Your Majesty? Death, banishment, snuffing? We cannot imprison all of them long-term."

"Snuffing seems easiest, and yet stripping them of their power doesn't prevent them from wielding arms against me. Death on such a vast scale will not please the people."

"But they are on your side, Your Majesty. They will support whatever you do."

"Not exactly, Cobalt. It isn't as easy as all that. This is my first sentencing as king. It will set the precedence of my rule. I have to think about it."

"But you need—"

"I will not commit a massacre as my first act!"

"But to protect yourself and your kingdom!"

"Stop!" Alex ordered.

"May I say one more—"

"No, you may not." Then he ran his hands down his face in frustration. Things couldn't be the way they were. He had always wanted his best friend to feel like his equal, but now that he was a ruler, this just could not be possible. Things had changed. "It's different now, or it must be. I am the ruler of this land. You cannot challenge me publicly, and in private, you cannot assert the same objection more than once. I heard you. I will take your advisement into consideration, but if I dismiss it, you must accept that without complaint."

"Yes, King Proxy," Cobalt said quietly.

Then Alex was filled with guilt for hurting his best friend's feelings and pride. "There are classified things I'm only privy to now. I have enemies other than the necromancers. The rebels were never fully squashed. A mass killing will only set them off into a possible revolution."

"You promoted me to your advisor. How can I advise when I don't know it all?"

"I was only informed of it recently myself. My father finally admitted I inherited his enemies. There was no meeting you missed, just a family nightcap when he told me."

"I should be informed of everything. Otherwise, how am I to truly help you?"

For a moment, Alex was stunned. He never thought his friend would take his job so seriously. He thought Cobalt would merely be supportive when he named him ealder advisor, a king's top counselor, one of the most illustrious positions for a lord. He was pleasantly surprised that his friend was ready to lay aside his cavalier ways and earn his keep. Alex had also made him the head inquisitor of the necromancer trials, with others under him to do the grunt work, but again, Cobalt took up the role with impressive vigor. "I understand your distress, but I did just inform you."

"I need to hear it immediately. I don't like..." Cobalt stopped himself and met Alex's gaze, a bit worried he had said too much.

"What?"

"Forgive me, Your Majesty. It matters not."

"Obviously, it matters to you, so speak," Alex growled, annoyed at this strange shift in their friendship. "I just meant not to challenge me incessantly. But always speak your mind."

"I miss everything important. I should be here, with you. I know I'm here a lot. I've always been as much here as I am at home, but what if something happens, and you need me, and I'm not here? My estate is over an hour away."

"So move in." Alex shrugged.

"Just like that?" Cobalt was taken aback.

"I'm not going to invite all courtiers, don't worry. You raised a valid point, and you were already half here anyway. Now you'll need to be here more. Take your guest quarters as your permanent residence. Do as you will to it, and send for your things."

Cobalt grabbed Alex's hand and shook it with enthusiasm. "Thank you, Alex—King Proxy. You honor me and dispel my worries."

"You're dismissed." Alex didn't like his friend groveling and wanted to cut that short.

Cobalt bowed his head and retreated.

Things had indeed changed. Alex had brought his friend into the fold better, but he no longer could fully rely on Cobalt for all decisions. He still worried Cobalt would want to influence him. Everyone wanted to influence a king for his or her own means, and although Cobalt was his best friend, Alex still held a slight mistrust.

Aside from his mother and Mary, Alex only fully trusted one other person, and his mind wandered to her. He could depend upon Toury for sound decision-making. Suddenly feeling a need for other counsel, he sought out the person who was his rock, his reason, his compassion, his strength, his everything: his queen.

Once he found her in their sitting room, he wanted to kiss every inch of her neck and rip the pins from her hair so he could run his fingers through the thick tresses. He shook the thoughts from his head and convinced himself that acting on these desires would ruin that lovely vision in front of him. He focused and debriefed her on the issue at hand.

She thought for a moment and then replied. "So, you must punish someone enough to please the people and to deter other necromancers from continuing their ways, but not go overboard to seem a tyrant to these rebels? The Citrines will have to go and any other heads of the movement. As much as the idea of burning people at the stake is awful to me, I understand that some must die. Can you banish that many people?"

"Yes, if we get permission from another sphere, but they'll have to be snuffed of power first. They'll end up being servants in their new spheres, which is fitting, I suppose."

"Would those who get their powers stripped survive? Or would they be like Justine, so dark they cannot exist without it?"

Her innocent question made him stop pacing and gape at her, stunned. "You have the greatest mind I've ever known." Then he kissed her soundly again and again until she pulled away laughing.

"I simply asked a question."

"Which sparked the solution. We kept what happened to Justine a secret, and I'm glad we did. We'll tell everyone the truth, have them publicly snuffed, and those who survive are not the greatest threat and can be banished. It's much more fitting than burning them, which as you point out, is quite horrific. It eliminates the threat without painting us in a bad light."

"Us?" She bit her lip.

"Everything I do as king proxy is 'us,' Toury. If you set a date, it'll be official."

For the first time, she did not shrug off the comment or ignore it. "How about your birthday?"

He was stunned, and it took a moment to find his voice. "That would be the best present you could ever give me." He kissed her madly with one objective: getting her into one of their bedrooms and kissing her until she begged to marry on the morrow instead.

5

DRAGONS

When Toury awoke, Alex was gone. He had begun to rise earlier and earlier due to his mounting responsibilities. He insisted it was only because he was planning, making changes, and that once the kingdom was his and change enforced, he could delegate better. The problem was, she well understood, whom do you delegate to, after finding out so many supposed supporters were actually planning to usurp your power?

She readied for combat training, feeling confident since she'd managed to truly disarm Madge yesterday. In some ways, she was almost as good as her bodyguard with a blade, but Madge was better at everything else. Toury was eager to catch up to her with a different weapon.

When they went to the courtyard, Alex was still there training. She entered the balcony and sat down to watch, not having seen him in action for ages. Cobalt and David were there with Alex, swinging swords at him, both at once, making Toury's stomach turn nervously. Alex was holding a sword in each hand. She knew firsthand how hard it was to use a sword with her left hand when she was right-handed, but astonishingly, he was holding them up as if they were made of wood and swinging them both accurately.

"Two against one," she said to Madge angrily. Surely, they could hurt him by accident.

"Don't interrupt them," Madge warned. Yes, it would be stupid of her to call out and have them accidentally lop off part of him, but she could hardly watch this.

And yet she did anyway. Her unease shifted to awe as she watched Alex expertly block each blow or evade by ducking and twisting out of the range of their swords. Alex moved a beat faster, most likely reading their body language. He beat David back, then Cobalt, and in one smooth move, at one point, Alex knocked them into each other.

They attacked, not taking turns but overlapping in their advances. He must've foreseen their moves. Alex defeated them at each turn with the gracefulness of a dancer and the strength and skill of two men. He wasn't even sweating, while the other men's white shirts were clinging to their bodies, wet hair matted to their foreheads. In one neat move, he twisted his sword to disarm David, and his other sword stopped an inch from Cobalt's throat.

Cobalt's eyes bulged, and he dropped his sword. "You weren't even looking!" he complained through his panting. "You could've taken off my head."

"I knew where you were." Alex smiled as he lowered his sword.

"That's it. Tomorrow, my trainer is joining us."

"Three on one?" Alex asked.

"Scared?"

"You wish."

Toury turned away from them to Madge and asked, "How?"

"The curse had weakened him. You lifted it. He's...a Sapphirian." The woman annoyingly shrugged, showing it should be a simple concept to understand.

"So what? He had suppressed superpowers or something?"

Madge's lips quirked at her Earth term. "That would be an apt analogy, yes. The fire magic is the strongest magic there is in this sphere. Compared to any other man, he tires less, is stronger, faster, and the fire magic comes easily. There are others who can work with fire, but only the Sapphirians can conjure it without a source. Add in the fact our planet from the outer core to just under the surface is all fire and molten rock, he has the strongest power of anyone. He can pull from the underground to use his powers on top of his natural abilities."

"Like I can conjure light in darkness."

"Hematites go back as far as the Sapphirians. Your ancestors are rumored to be traceable back to unwritten times. Ruby's strength most likely has put you up to Alex's level, if you learn to tap into it."

Toury balked at the thought. It had always disconcerted her that Alex's cousin Ruby had imparted her knowledge and power into the stone that brought Toury to Fyr, and when Alex had unlocked it, Ruby's knowledge and power were inside her. It was like a benevolent parasite at times, like when it helped her break the curse in the end.

Toury stopped thinking about the ghost of a girl inside her when she realized Alex was ascending the stairs to meet her. His cheeks were a healthy pink and his eyes vibrantly blue from the exercise.

"My love," he greeted her and gave her hand a kiss.

"That was..." Toury didn't know what to say.

He held onto her hand. "Impressive? Swoon-worthy? Amazing?"

Of course he would go the arrogant route to get a rise out of her, the brat. She knew he was joking, but she couldn't resist taking him down a notch. "Foolhardy, dangerous, and showing off."

Alex beamed at her, rubbing her hand with the pad of his thumb. He was flirting with her, and the way his eyes scanned her lips, she knew he wanted to do more. "I do have to prepare for all situations, Toury." He met her gaze. "But would you prefer it if I wore armor?"

Surprised that his flirty teasing gave way to an easy compromise, she simply nodded.

Cobalt groaned. "It's hot enough in here as it is," he grumbled.

"No one said you had to wear it, did they?" Toury fired at him.

Alex laughed, which made Toury join in, and Cobalt scowled, his gaze darting between the two, lost about what was so funny.

Toury made her way down the steps, but Alex called after her, "I'll see you at lunch!"

Lunch wouldn't be eaten. The moment Toury walked in the door after her combat and power lessons, Alex pulled her into his arms and kissed her. She knew what would ensue. Three weeks until the wedding had Alex wanting more than he was allowed to have at the moment. They would be kissing in one of their beds until one of them stopped their crazy make-out fest, and then they'd talk and plan in each other's arms until duty called.

Today, Alex was in rare form, and Toury had to stop him from undressing her. She wondered if his ardor had been cooled by the curse as well, because he was a force to be reckoned with now, and he went to great lengths to convince her they should marry immediately. Her willpower was much stronger than his, and she shut him down.

"You're cruel," he huffed, sounding very much like a spoiled little prince. His actions belied his words, and he lay back on the bed, tucking her head under his on his chest, where she could hear his exhilarated heart thumping wildly. "But you're right. Why does three weeks seem too far away?"

Toury said nothing. She did want to marry him, but to her, three weeks sounded too soon. She had no idea what she needed time for. She loved him, wanted to be his wife, but she was still apprehensive about his power and strength. He could hurt her even more than he had before.

"Because you, Your Majesty," she teased him by using his title, knowing he hated when she called him that, "feel everything so much more intensely without that curse."

He laughed, and it rumbled under her ear. Alex's hand was making unconscious circles on her back, giving her chills, despite the fabric separating his hand from her flesh. "When it comes to you, I've felt this way since the very moment I met you. I'm just more comfortable showing you now. Aren't you too? Am I too premature in thinking your nightmares have stopped and that you are no longer afraid of me?"

Toury didn't answer but played with the collar of his shirt, only realizing now that his doublet was discarded onto the floor with his boots.

A disappointed sigh left his lips.

"They have of you—the nightmares, I mean. But I still see other necromancers and events of that night, not you anymore. I'm not afraid of you."

"If you aren't ready to marry—"

"I am, and I think we have to soon. There are only so many times I can deny you."

"Is that so?" He pulled her on top of him and kissed her deeply, making her skin tingle from her scalp to her toes. The knock at their door disrupted what probably would've been another bout of kissing ending in morals and frustration. "A moment," he called.

She knew they'd eventually come to interrupt them, but normally, they had an hour for lunch. He slipped out from under her and climbed off the bed. Then he gave her a peck on the lips, his eyes regretful. He quickly lit a fire in the grate for her as he slipped back into his boots and donned his doublet. He would always be the king from here on out. Never a day off, nor her as queen.

"What is it?" he asked.

The door cracked open a few inches, and David, his eyes fixated on the cobblestone floor, said, "Your Majesty. I would never disturb you—"

"Unless it was an emergency or some dire news."

"Your Majesty, it's the draca. One has left the Firelands and is scorching the lowlands. The casualty count is climbing."

Draca! She had heard them mentioned now and then but never actually thought dragons were flying around Fyr. She never saw one.

"Do they know, male or female?" Alex asked.

"Female, they say."

"Get us ready to depart at once. You know what to pack for me, yes?"

"Yes, Your Majesty."

The door closed, and Alex leaned on it, his head down in thought or disappointment.

Toury broke the silence, "Do you have to go? You're the king proxy. Can't you, I dunno...delegate?"

"Only a Sapphirian can subdue them, so yes, I'm the one who needs to go. People are dying." He said it gruffly, but she knew his moods enough now to not take it personally. He was mad about the situation, not at her, and disappointment was etched on his face. He came over to her and sat on the edge of the bed. "I don't know how long I'll be gone. I fear the wedding will be postponed. I'm naming you and my mother equally in charge. That is, if you are ready?"

"Can't I come with you?"

"No," he said too quickly. His refusal stung. "No, draca hate sorcerers and magicians alike. They could kill you. Only we Sapphirian-blooded are safe. We are descended from them, remember? They see us as their babies. Fiercely protective and loving."

"You will be safe?"

"Yes. I'll have fifty or so dragons protecting me, and I cannot burn, so...odds are good. My love, are you ready for this? I could use your help in the investigation against the necromancers. You can see out my plans of snuffing them. Cobalt will guide you. Just make sure he...never mind."

"Make sure he what?"

"Nothing, just...he's a horrid flirt."

"I know. It was one of the attributes I disliked when I examined my suitor list." She laughed.

"You entertained the idea of him?" He gawked at her, shocked. "Now I really don't want to go."

"Alex." She pulled him close and kissed him. "There's only one man for me." Then she kissed down his neck to where it met his chest, making him hiss and back away.

"I really have to get dressed and go." He made his way to the door between their rooms.

"Couldn't your cousin go?"

"He's missing, and before you ask, no, I'm not sending Mary."

"Is it selfish I want you here with me?"

Alex frowned. "No, not at all. I want to stay, but this might be a good thing."

"How?" Why would he think it was good for them to be separated? Things were finally starting to get better between them.

He took her hands in his. "Don't take this the wrong way, but my absence will be good for you. Toury, you were upended from the only planet you knew, and then I absconded with you to my castle. Then I...did a terrible thing. You need to find yourself, your place in Fyr. This might let you figure things out without me distracting you, without you depending on me."

They were silent for a moment, and she avoided his gaze.

He tipped her chin back up until she was forced to make eye contact with him. "I've taken so much from you and don't know how to give it back. I want you to be who you were always meant to be: that girl in the dress shop who told me off for staring, the savior who took on necromancers, that girl who stole a heart and took over a kingdom."

"What? What do you mean?" She stumbled for words. "That last part."

"I'm powerless when it comes to you," Alex whispered at admitting a self-conscious fault. He leaned his forehead against hers. "I am yours, so the kingdom is yours. Know this: you are the most powerful woman in all of Fyr. I just want you to feel that way again." Then he kissed her softly and pulled away. "I've really got to go. You will do this? Take charge with Mother's help?"

She nodded and let him go. She knew he was right, that distance and time would help her grow stronger, but she didn't like it, and she didn't believe she could rule a kingdom. "Alex?"

"Yes, love?" He turned in the threshold of their adjoining rooms, and their eyes met, maybe for the last time for she knew not how long. She tried to memorize every detail.

"Why would a dragon leave and go on a rampage?"

"They are normally docile creatures. The males, for the most part, only attack over territory, but not the females. There's only one reason a female would do this." He stared into the flames in the fireplace as he said it.

"Why?"

His intense gaze snapped to meet hers. "Someone killed her mate. They mate for life, Toury, like us." Then he turned into the darkness of his room and shut the door.

Of course, the dragon would kill everyone and everything in revenge and anguish. If anyone hurt Alex, she might just do the same if she could.

She quaked at the thought of what havoc Alex might unleash if anyone ever hurt her.

6
TRIALS

It took almost a week for Toury to receive a letter from Alex. He was busy, and mail was slow; she understood that. She had worried over him to distraction, so much so, she had only been observing the trials from a side room through spyholes so far. She felt spineless and weak since Alex was off dealing with dragons. She tore the letter open at once and devoured its contents.

Dearest Toury,

I miss you beyond what justice any words could give. I do wish I had caved and brought you with me, except it has been too dangerous for you here. I could've used your healing abilities for all these poor souls.

Rest assured, I am fine. The draca situation is now under control. I wish that was the end of it and I could be with you. In fact, I'm perpetually tempted to transport to you, even just for a moment, but I cannot give in to such desires and lose focus.

I have captured one of the villains, which is a whole other situation I must tell you about, but I long to do this in person. There are things about my powers, too, that alarm me, but don't worry. Most likely, Madge was right in what she said about the lifting of the curse freeing my true potential. I have a lot of loose ends here to finish up. As soon as those are completed, I will be with you again, and I am counting the days until I return.

Till we meet again, my love,

Alex

Toury selfishly wished he would transport to her, only for a moment. Transporting—or dragon's trapdoor as Fyrians called it—was the fire-magic way Sapphirians could manipulate matter to disappear and reappear wherever they envisioned. He could come to see her and then leave, but she would not ask him to. Alex had not asked about the trials. She was glad for that because she would have to tell him how slack she had been about getting her feet wet. Sure, she helped the queen with daily tasks, grievances, and other boring matters, but she had not entered the courtroom of the trials. Alex would be disappointed. She decided it was time. She had to, and Alex's letter gave her the confidence needed to get her through such a daunting task. She would be Queen Sapphirian one day, so she had to be strong. This was going to be her life, and Alex had promised her equality, a partnership. He admitted she had more power over him than he probably liked. Refusing to take part in the necromancer trials would be tantamount to embracing patriarchy, like telling Alex she wanted him to command her. After she had fought tooth and nail to be treated fairly, this would be a grievous sin on her part.

The next morning, Toury walked into the courtroom with a dozen guards flanking the room for her protection. Cobalt sat beside her, giving her a reassuring smile. She understood why Alex had asked Cobalt to head the trials. He would do what was necessary and best for the kingdom, while Toury would not be able, in her heart and conscience, to condemn anyone to any horrific fate. Together, they would balance out the scales of justice and exact what measures Alex would have done if he were present. Cobalt was Alex's might, and Toury was Alex's moral compass.

Cobalt leaned in close and whispered, "It will be all right. No one will hurt you, and don't let them know how you can tell. Your aunt and the baseborn have hidden the ability well." He nodded toward the door. Her Aunt Edwina and the lightbearer baseborn—he had to be called something else, this wouldn't do—were in the next room to observe through a mirrored glass to confirm Toury's suspicions or to interrogate anyone Toury saw as innocent.

"I know," Toury told Cobalt, appreciative of the reassurance she desperately needed. She took a deep breath.

"Try not to let them see how scared you are of them."

"I'm not scared." The moment it came out, she realized how weak it sounded.

Cobalt gave her a measured look but didn't call her out on her lie. "It's okay to be. Some of them scare the daylights out of me, to be honest. If you must, just squeeze my arm, and I'll sort it out and order a break. Toury, you are doing the right thing. The only way to get over something is to face it head on."

"Sage advice," she said a bit sardonically.

Cobalt's mouth quirked up, the hint of a smile upon his lips. "That's more like the Toury we all know."

"I'm ready," she said more to herself than to him.

"Bring in the first prisoner," Cobalt commanded with an authority she couldn't muster.

They dragged in a dirty and unkempt girl, chained like an animal, who was younger than Toury herself. Of course, they would test Toury with the task of condemning a child. She had a feeling Cobalt had chosen this girl on purpose. Toury schooled her features to betray nothing, to not give away her hesitancy.

"Lady Fiona Beryl," the guard said. "Queen Proxy-to-Be." The guard bowed his head in reverence. She was not used to this distinction yet.

Cobalt read the charges against the girl aloud. She had been pointed out by other necromancers as being one, was present in the northern battle against Alex's men, and slew several soldiers through the use of dark magic.

"How plead you?" Cobalt asked, his face solemn and calm.

Toury's heart was racing along with her mind. How could such a young girl be influenced to do such wrong? She was sure it was the fault of her parents and not her own, for her parents were on the condemned list, her aunt having seen terrible darkness in them.

"Not guilty, my lord," she said in a hint of a whisper.

Cobalt asked her to repeat herself louder. The girl said it slightly louder but didn't look up. Cobalt's gaze shot over to Toury's, and she raised her eyebrows at him, unsure of what he wanted. A ghost of a smile threatened to take over his features, which was completely inappropriate in this situation. She had no clue what he found so amusing. She leaned over to whisper, "Get some emotion out of her, or I'll have to get closer to her, and wipe that smile off your face. This is serious business."

Cobalt's face sank, and his posture straightened, a bit annoyed at being scolded. His anger was taken out on the prisoner; his questions attacked the girl relentlessly, alluding to her being promiscuous, unable to think for herself, and being jealous of Toury. That last one, or the combination of all three insinuations, hit the mark, and she burst out in a fit of rage, eyes going black as night. She was one of them.

The sight of it was jarring, and the image of Alex's face—eyes black like hers, face screwed up in eerie aggression—shot forth from her subconscious. She pushed the thought away, but too late. She must've paled or flinched, because Cobalt instantly ruled the girl guilty. He ordered a guard to take the girl to the dungeons.

"You, Queen Proxy-to-Be, must control your expression as well," Cobalt bantered back. Instead of reprimanding her as she did him, he teased, wanting to get a rise out of her.

She did not take the bait, but asked for the next prisoner. It had been difficult to see those black eyes for the first time, but she would get used to it.

The next prisoner was a man who leered at her, eyeing her appreciatively, which unnerved her. His eyes were black without Cobalt needing to egg him on. He pled guilty straight away, obviously proud of himself. "We are not finished. We will rise again! You won't live to become queen!" he threatened as they struggled to get him through the doors.

"That is a direct threat to a royal-to-be. Add that to his charges!" Cobalt shouted.

She was taken aback. Toury just had her second death threat, and the fact it had come from a stranger and not the jealous Justine was even more unnerving.

The prisoner was lugged away, leaving only the soldiers, her, and Cobalt. She took a deep breath to calm herself.

"Are you okay?" Cobalt asked kindly, touching her hand. The gesture would be innocent from most people, but from Cobalt, it was laced with oddly placed flirtation. Stranger yet, his touch made her feel at ease, somehow channeling calm into her. She withdrew her hand from his, wondering what his power actually was. All her studies had thus far focused on light and fire magic, so she ought to start learning more about stone and blood magic.

"I'm fine," she said coolly. "I heard the dungeons were overly crowded. I think we should plan the public snuffing in a couple days."

"We're going to kill them, Lady Toury. If I have to wait for Alex's return, I will. He would want them dead, not given this merciful second chance."

"Alex and I agreed to this. He told you and the queen of it. We will honor his wishes and leave no mess for him to come home to."

"Lady Toury, he only said that to make you happy. He didn't mean it. He feels guilty and will do whatever he can to please you. He knows the best way to protect himself and you is to execute them all."

"You realize the snuffing will kill a lot of them, don't you?" she stalled. Surely, Cobalt was wrong, yet he and Alex were best friends, and Cobalt was Alex's advisor. Alex probably shared everything with him.

"Yes, but—"

"Did the King Proxy say this directly to you?"

"No, he doesn't have to. I know him, Lady Toury, as well as I know myself."

"Contrary to how well you think you know him, I know he would not instruct me to do one thing and expect us to do something completely different. We will obey his orders."

"Lady Tourmaline," he said, frustrated, as if she were too simple to see his point.

"Let's put it this way. You disobey *my* orders, you will be removed from the trials," Toury spat out. She had to assert herself, even if it was awkward.

Cobalt's expression froze, and his complexion blanched. His eyes met hers, and she glared at him in challenge. It took a moment for him to look away.

"Yes, Queen Proxy-to-Be," he choked out, his jaw clenching. "I hope you know what you're getting into."

"I do know. Alex wanted this."

"I meant with the marriage. He will not let you dictate much of anything after you marry. He always must be in charge, the dominant one."

"That's not the Alex I know." Although she knew it was somewhat true, she had to defend Alex. Yes, he had to be in control, be dominant. Part of it came from his station, and part of it she attributed to the curse. Ever since she broke it, he was treating her more as an equal. He even admitted she wielded power over him, but she questioned the validity of that. Was Cobalt right? Did this power only come from Alex's guilt about what he had done? His guilt would eventually fade. Would he then assert power over her? Take from her and ignore her wishes as he had before?

"Men say things when they want things, my lady. Don't believe a word until after you're married." His implications were thick, and she easily understood he was hinting to Alex being weak with want, and once they consummated their marriage, he would change.

She wanted to believe love was stronger than lust and that Alex would never go back on promises, but she wasn't sure of anything anymore, except the fact they wanted to be together. Her world had been upended time and time again, and now Cobalt's assertions were weakening her remaining trust in Alex. However, she didn't want to give Cobalt the pleasure of seeing how his words affected her. "Lord Cobalt, from the talk I hear from my court ladies, you seem to be describing yourself rather than Alex."

"Precisely. I know what I'm talking about."

She was not expecting that candid answer. "Well, you don't know Alex, and you don't understand love."

"He trapped you into an engagement to use you for his own benefit. How is that love? How can you defend him?" Cobalt growled under his breath, being careful to keep his voice down to not be overheard by the guards. They shifted uncomfortably; most likely, they could tell Toury and Cobalt were arguing.

"That is how you see it, of course. I see it differently."

"He trapped you!"

The guards tensed after that comment.

"At first, but his reason behind that was not all selfish. He loves his people, Cobalt. I understand why he did what he did. And he loves me—"

"He tried to kill you!"

"That was the curse, which is gone. He was right all along that I would break it."

"I can't listen to this. You're a victim defending the perpetrator."

"Then don't start the conversation in the first place. Let me remind you that the king proxy will not look kindly on your negative opinion of him. He is your king, not a perpetrator."

Cobalt floundered, realizing he was on a thin line of expressing his opinion versus committing treason. He appeared to be confusing his role of friend and advisor. "I did not mean to insult the king proxy. I simply believe you deserve to be treated better."

"You tell me nothing Alex doesn't know already nor that I'm ignorant of. There's a thing called forgiveness, Cobalt. You ought to try it," she snapped. She justified Alex's actions, although deep down, she had to force herself to. Part of her completely agreed with Cobalt, and that opened a chasm of self-doubt.

"You should just know, there are other nobles out there who would treat you like a queen, even if you are not queen in title," he whispered.

"Bring in the next prisoner!" Toury shouted, completely done with Cobalt and his suggestions. She had to stop the conversation because she was quite sure he'd tell her he would be the man to do the job.

The rest of the day, she kept calling in the prisoners to avoid any breaks where Cobalt would dare to discuss something other than the trial. As they worked through prisoners, he grew angrier to the point he was yelling at them. That's when she called it a day, having had enough of the entire process. More so, she'd had enough of him.

She couldn't understand him. Was this another head game Cobalt was trying to play, pretending to be some hero to rescue her, or was he competing with Alex in some womanizing feud? Was he simply jealous of their happiness? She had no clue what his motivation could be in speaking badly of Alex.

When she left the trials, she declined Cobalt's invitation to talk over the trials in the princess salon. She was so done dealing with or speaking about necromancers. Only, before she could even make it back to her quarters, a servant intercepted her with a summons to the king's quarters. The queen would've sought Toury out in the orchard or summoned her to the queen's room, not her living quarters. It was the king demanding her presence. Perhaps he wanted to be healed? If not, she had no idea what she was walking into.

When she arrived, the queen let her in and led her into the king's bedroom. Toury grew nervous. Had something happened to Alex? Was the king going to banish her in Alex's absence? He had started to warm up to her, but it could've been for show. A dozen other possibilities flittered through her head, becoming increasingly less likely as her imagination ran wild.

The king was propped up in the bed with lots of pillows for support, and Toury could tell it took effort for him even to sit up. He looked unwell—skin yellowing, purpled under his eyes—and he had lost some weight, which was not good, considering she had seen him a couple of weeks ago, and it was a notable difference.

"Lady Tourmaline," he greeted her.

"Do you need healing?" She grabbed his hand.

"No." He firmly shook her off.

"But while Alex is gone...you have to hang on," she pointed out.

The king sighed. "If it comes down to it, when the healers can do no more, I'll let you heal me until I can say goodbye to my son. But not now, not for anything else."

"I understand. I'm sorry I presumed. I didn't know why you sent for me."

"I wanted to see you, talk to you, to see how the trials are going."

"They're going. It was only my first day."

"I know. Are you okay?" He sighed and cringed. "I can't imagine what it's like. To see the evil in them. Such a blessing to have you in the family. I just worry the trials could take their toll on you."

Toury was not used to this caring and concerned king. She was wary, suspicious. How she wished Alex were here with her to take the brunt of his father's attention, for even though it was kind, it was intense and intimidating nonetheless. "I managed. And with me in the fold, we can speed things up, protect the kingdom."

"You will make a great queen."

Toury had no response to that and avoided his gaze.

"I know it may seem strange coming from me. I'm a dominant being, needing no queen."

Toury watched the queen bustle about; she gave no reaction to how she felt. Toury tried to mask her irritation at how such a comment must affect the queen.

"I can read your expression, so like Alex, unable to mask your emotions. My lifemate knows it's true and that I really mean I *want* my queen rather than need her, but my son is not me. He is sensitive, weak—the curse has wounded him permanently, I believe. He needs a strong woman to have his back if he wants to survive this world. He could not choose better than you."

A rage flared up in Toury that was bigger than any she had ever experienced before. She wanted to tell off the king, insult him, tell him Alex was ten times the man he was. It was no curse damage, but the fact Alex's mother showed him how to love, how to have a heart—things his father lacked. But she would never dare. Feeling like a coward, she nodded. Was she betraying Alex by accepting the compliment to her and the insult to Alex wrapped in one?

Thankfully, he shifted subjects, and her anger faded to a mild annoyance. He asked her about her tutor and her aunt, and she kept her answers short, knowing he was prying, trying to find a way to cast them out. She wanted to talk about the curse and her parents so badly but couldn't muster the courage to ask more than he had given. She doubted he even knew more than what he had already told her. Instead, she told him inane things about finishing her redecorations and her lessons about her powers. He seemed happy to hear it and was smiling so broadly, she realized that he liked this silly, girly side of her. For all the strength he applauded her for, he truly preferred docile, subordinate women in his household. It irked her, but she reminded herself he was dying. She should let it go.

Although the first day was difficult with Cobalt's and the king's words sticking with her, one good thing came from forcing herself to face the necromancers: by the end of the day, their black eyes did not bring images forth of Alex. Their faces now haunted her, and she could no longer remember what Alex had looked like with his cursed eyes. More importantly, she felt stronger than she had in ages. She knew Alex would let her—no, would *want* her—to be strong, to state her opinion, to rule with him. He would want the opposite of his father's sentiments.

7

FAMILY

Toury reread Alex's letters, trying to settle this dreadful inclination that something was slipping or shifting away from her. Alex was gone physically, but mentally, she worried their bond was fraying. The letters had been short and vague. The first letter had been short but sweet. The second letter was even more worrisome in its abruptness.

Dear Toury,

I wish there were somewhere to direct a letter to me, but I'll be on the move. If you wish to write, send it to the Post Inn in Gunnytree, and I will have someone check regularly. Please apprise me of the trials and, more importantly, how you are. I hate not knowing how you fare and if all is well, but perhaps your letters are on their way to me as I write this. I hope the necromancers aren't unnerving you and that the nightmares are kept at bay. I'm rambling now, hoping that my silly letter gives you some kind of joy or comfort as I know any word from you, no matter how mundane or short, will give me the strength to get through anything to get back to you.

Love,
Alex

She couldn't help notice the lack of endearments his morning notes had always included like "dearest" and "my love." The third letter was even worse.

Toury,

Things are taking much longer than I expected. Your last letter concerned me, and I have written at length to Cobalt that you are in charge, and you know my will, and he must abide by it.

If he does not listen, remove him from the trials and have your
aunt take over the inquiries. She has a knack for intimidation. If
you ask me how I know, I might tell you. Until then.

Yours,
Alex

Only three letters in two weeks. Toury folded the letters back up and placed them down. The first letter he had sent lifted her spirits, but then, the second was shorter, until the last couldn't qualify as a letter.

A knock sounded on the open door of the princess salon. Her uncle stood awkwardly in the doorway. "You summoned me, Queen Proxy-to-Be?"

Toury slipped the letters into an ornate keepsake box—one of Alex's non-stop gifts—and stood and greeted him. "Please, come in and sit. I wished to speak with you."

She offered to ring for tea, but he declined. She wrung her hands, not knowing how to start. He watched her dubiously but let her gain her courage.

"The time has come for me to know about my parents. I cannot enter this marriage without knowing what they have done. It cannot come back to haunt us after Alex and I marry. So please, I beg you. You will not be punished. I will see to that."

"Lady Edwina should know."

"She speaks of forbidden love and no understanding. She is biased and angry. The king is even more unfair in his retelling, I'm sure. I want to know what actually happened. I am ordering you to do this, by the way, so you cannot deny me."

He sighed, thinking. "I was not present. I can only give you rumors and conjectures."

"That's more than anyone has given me."

"Where to start," he mused. "I believe the King blames your father for the curse put upon their family."

"He does. Could my father have done it?"

"Your father was great at curse removals. Putting a curse on someone is just the opposite. Pulling the light out of someone is just as easy as pushing it in."

"Do you think he was guilty?"

"Would you pull the light from someone to let the dark in?"

"Never," Toury said, "not even my worst enemy." Then she thought of the necromancers they were going to pull darkness from, but that wasn't the same. Light magic was intended for only good purposes.

"No, I don't think he did it. Your father wasn't a foolish man. At least not until the end," her uncle said.

"What do you mean? I know they ran off together, which broke off her engagement with the king's younger brother. The king told me that part. And that I must've been the reason for them fleeing."

"Yes, that is probably true, but it was foolish for more than running away to be together or marrying due to a child. They allowed the king to blame them and didn't come forward to defend themselves. That omission is enough for the court to assume them guilty of murder and jilting."

Toury swallowed hard. Her father, if he were still alive, would be seen as a murderer and her mother, perhaps an accomplice. No wonder they'd abandoned her, yet surely Earth would be safe enough for them. One of them should've stayed with her.

"If the king and Alex were cursed, why is Mary not afflicted? Or the cousin? They are the ones in line after Alex."

"That is a great question. I think the answer, if ever discovered, would lead you to your culprit. Most assume the cursemaker was trying to wipe out every Sapphirian but could not finish the job. That the curse stopped after your father's departure from court did not help his case. You see, if King Craig had perished before King Proxy Alexander was of age—and he was a newborn then—next in line would be the sister, Princess Anne, followed by Prince Alfred. The laws were changed only years prior to King Proxy Alexander's birth to allow the princess to rule before her younger brother, Alfred. This was by no means a progressive move, but one to keep Alfred from gaining the throne. Alfred was a horrific person, devoid of all emotion and morality, a boy who found pleasure in torturing animals and then people. Princess Anne, however, was ultimately deemed unfit to rule. Alfred died, the curse affecting him the worst. When Alfred was discovered dead and Alexander cursed, his Aunt Anne went mad. She was always a fragile person, but Alfred's death hit her hard. Presently, after Alexander, Mary comes and their cousin Henry after her. With his sister Ruby dead, Henry is the end of the Sapphirian line. Someone stopped the curses for some reason.

"Regardless of the line of rule and our family's fall from favor, both Edwina and I were brought in to attempt to remove the curse from

Alexander. Neither of us could do it. She was banished for her failure, so they said, but really more likely due to her relations. I—never being at court—was allowed to crawl back to my home out west. Until the prince—now the king proxy—sent for me, I had no clue until I arrived at the palace who you were."

"Your niece?" she finished for him.

"It does not work that way."

"It does so if I wish it to be. I will be queen, and I can do as I see fit."

"Lady Tourmaline, you honor me but..."

"Well, from here on out, you will be known as Gareth Hematite or, to me, Uncle Gareth."

The man stared at her in shock and didn't say a word.

"Of course, I should clarify, you will not inherit or have a claim to anything in the Hematite estate or fortune. You shall only have the name. I understand, in this land, a noble stone name is everything and will elevate you. This is my reason for doing this, and the fact it is what is right. In a land so fixated on blood magic at times, it seems they fail to see the advantages of...extended family."

"You may want to rethink this. You cannot be sure."

"I am sure. I had the paperwork drawn up already this morning. Madge?"

The servant snapped to it from her stiff pose by the door and brought over the paperwork.

"I don't know what to say." Gareth's hands shook as he took up the quill Madge handed to him. He perused the parchment, which basically said he was a Hematite by law but not in estate.

"Don't say anything; just sign."

"But Lady Edwina signed..."

"I demanded it of her after she admitted she knew you were her half-brother. Of course, with her high airs, she's not pleased, but don't worry about her."

"Thank you," he said quietly as he signed. "You are a remarkable young lady, and you will make an excellent queen."

"I will strive to be the best I can be, with your help, I hope."

"I'm at your service."

Toury wondered how Alex would take her legitimization of her baseborn uncle. She hadn't asked, and even though he usually accepted all her whims without a flinch, she worried something this major would upset him. No one—except maybe a father needing an heir his wife couldn't bear—made a baseborn legitimate. She knew this was huge, but whether the kingdom saw it as progress or an affront, only time would tell.

Mary entered, which gave her uncle an excuse to leave. Toury was glad, because he was overwhelmed by what she had done for him and her many questions. Mary sat down and ordered tea.

"My mother and your aunt are the best of friends now," Mary said.

"Oh dear, we're doomed." Toury played into Mary's melodramatic tone.

"They're shopping."

"It is nice for your mom to have a peer, though, who is in the castle. And my aunt is so happy to find favor again. I think it was her only ambition in life."

"That's tragic."

They laughed. Mary caught her breath and sighed. "At least it means we don't have to entertain tonight."

"Between the training and the trials, this is a nice break."

"And your gaggle of girls," Mary scoffed.

Toury thought she detected a hint of jealousy. "You could hang out with us, you know. I think you'd like quite a few of them. Maybe not all ten at once. That has been a mistake."

Mary didn't respond. She appeared preoccupied, unable to be still, tapping a scroll on her knee repeatedly. She poured herself an ample glass of firespice whiskey, ignoring the tea Toury had ordered. Toury pursed her lips, but Mary gave her an I-dare-you-to-say-something glare.

Toury switched tactics from a scolding remark that had been on the tip of her tongue to inquisitive concern. "Is everything okay, Princess Mary?"

"We'll be family soon, Toury. For the millionth time, drop the blasted title, please." She huffed out a breath but said nothing more.

Toury waited and picked up her sad attempt at embroidery to pull out the stitches to try again.

There was another sigh followed by, "And no, I'm not okay. My mother is relentless about me cutting down my suitor list. She can't prepare for your wedding with all this dragon nonsense taking Alex away, so she's turned her attention onto me."

"But you don't want to cut it?" Toury assumed from her tone.

Mary unfurled her crushing grip of the creased scroll and offered it to her. Toury examined a list of over fifty suitors, half of them crossed off.

Most likely, every unattached man in the kingdom vied for her hand in marriage. Toury examined the list and saw some notable names on there. It was the best the land had to offer, but the princess appeared unhappy. "So, you made your first round of cuts; that's good."

"I'm supposed to cut it down to five soon, according to Mother. And I know it is wrong to give any man false hope, so I should cut it down." Mary met Toury's gaze. "I know what you're thinking, probably exactly what my mother was trying to tell me. I can't explain it. I gave the men I couldn't stand the cut, but none of these men, none of them, could I imagine a life with."

Toury sighed. "I understand. I didn't want to marry. People marry so young here, compared to Earth. I fell for your brother, despite everything. I don't think I'd know my true feelings if everything hadn't happened with the necromancers."

"So, what? Am I supposed to enter some death-defying mission to see if my suitors rise to the challenge?" Mary's snarky remark rubbed Toury the wrong way.

With a regal air of displeasure, Toury retorted, "I wasn't giving advice, but simply sharing that anything can change the way you feel about anyone at any time."

"Wow, you've changed." Mary's mouth dropped, and her eyes went wide.

"No, I haven't."

"I meant it as a compliment, actually," Mary began. "You'll make a great queen." Then she gave a dramatic woe-is-me moan and slouched in a way that was far from the princess posture they had drilled into Toury during her short stint at the refining school where she and Mary had met. "I'm sorry I'm so ornery. I just cannot resign myself to any of these men."

"Because something else is holding you back?" Toury inquired.

She saw from Mary's shift in posture that she had hit the mark.

"Do you want some advice? Or do you just want my sympathy? You can have both."

"Do you have any sound advice? Lucy is worthless," Mary glared at her servant, who stood quietly inside the doorway, Madge on the other side.

Lucy gazed at the ground, taking the scolding to heart.

"She's a human being, you know. You should treat her with respect. I'm sure she has given you plenty of information about these men. It isn't her job to make your decisions for you."

"Pah! I'm in no mood for a scolding. If you weren't destined to be a queen, you'd make a good headmistress."

After that remark, Toury wanted to continue to chastise her, but when Mary met Toury's gaze, her expression was sad and lost. "Maybe delay things," Toury suggested. "Over the next month, invite each of the suitors here. The one-on-one time will definitely help you cross some off, you'll iron it down to your necessary four, and your mother will be ecstatic to see you try. Meeting her halfway on this might buy you some time."

Mary smiled. "I think I could handle that, thanks. It might take more than a month to see all of them once. Maybe I can stretch it to two months? But Toury, you realize it is five suitors, not four."

"Oh?" Toury raised her brows. "I thought you might leave one open for a last-minute entry. I won't pretend to know who he is, but I think you have feelings for someone not on the list, which is making this so difficult for you."

Mary looked at her, aghast, and then glanced into the flames flickering in the grate. What Toury would give to know what the Sapphirians saw there, particularly when it came to Alex. His letters were hardly informative, and it was strange to not see him and know what was going on with him daily.

"You don't have to tell me. I'm not trying to pry, but you must do something. Before you're forced to choose someone else, you need to tell the man you like him. He needs to have a choice."

"It's silly, really. I just developed this stupid crush off things I saw in the flames that may or may not come true."

"Your foresight. So you know who he might be." Toury spoke her thoughts aloud. She was dying to find out too, but it would be utterly rude to further press Mary. Then her interest in futures shifted. "Did Alex know it was me all along?"

Mary smiled happily at the change of topic. "I knew from the moment he met you, but the flames showed so many different things back then because the outcome of decisions could've drastically changed."

Toury glanced at the fireplace, wishing she could see their future or even just the present to see that Alex was okay.

"It's all you now. You'll be happy, Toury, and make me lots of nieces and nephews."

Toury blushed, then looked away. She and Alex were far from being happy and having children. A large part of her missed him, but a bigger part was relieved that she wouldn't have to see the guilt on his face every day or fear going to sleep and dreaming memories of him hurting her.

"Oh no, what's wrong with you? Out with it," Mary pressed.

She could not deny Mary her confidence after Mary was opening up to her again. Things had been a bit awkward after Mary returned from school; Mary probably was still trying to find her footing when it came to being left out of the Alex-Toury dynamic. It had to be hard when your best friend and brother were in love. Now that Alex was gone, maybe Toury and Mary could get back to the closeness they'd had at school when they'd only had each other.

"Things aren't the same with Alex and me, after the, you know...necromancer business."

Mary scoffed and took a sip of her drink. She tossed her scroll onto the end table carelessly. She gave Toury a leveled gaze. "Obviously. You walk around all quiet and mopey. He's a different person now without the curse—strong and happy—but when he sees you, it's like the curse steals over him again. I know the curse is gone, but it used to be the opposite. He was all lightness and happiness around you. He feels guilty for hurting you, putting the kingdom before you. I hate what he's done to you Toury, but I can't lie to you. He did the right thing for the good of everyone in this sphere. I could never. I'd let my heart get in the way, and I'd bring this kingdom down in shambles. This is why I never wanted to rule. Every decision he makes, there is a price to pay; no matter the choice, he will never win."

"A Catch-22," Toury mumbled to herself.

"A what?"

"Oh, nothing. An Earth term."

"I would buckle under that pressure," Mary continued.

Toury wanted to stop her. Toury wanted to scream out that she was the one paying the price.

Mary's gaze lingered on her but wouldn't meet her eyes. "It might feel like you are the only one who has suffered through this ordeal, but one look at Alex tells me otherwise. Please, Toury, don't let this scare you off. There's only one way to right this now."

"How?" The word came out in such a desperate moan that Toury hardly recognized her own voice.

"You marry him as soon as he returns, and you make his life hell until you're satisfied he's paid the price."

"Mary," Toury chided, annoyed at her jokes at a time like this and depressed there was no amazing solution. Toury wanted to come first. She wanted Alex to not gaze upon her with guilt, but only love. And what she wanted most was to not fear him or resent him. Even though she loved him, deep down in the buried recesses of her mind, those hindrances were still there.

"I'm serious. No, listen." Mary stopped Toury's upcoming protest by raising her regal hand. "Neither of you will be happy until his guilt is gone, when you both can forgive him."

"I don't think—"

"Just think it over." Mary picked up her scroll again. "You can help me cross off a couple of these tomorrow night, maybe?"

"What's tomorrow?"

"A dinner party."

"Ugh." Toury sipped her tea, wishing after Mary's comment that she had poured herself some firewhiskey. Toury didn't like talking to nobles without Alex there to take the attention off herself.

"My mother demands our presence. You are on eyeball duty."

Even worse. She could get no break from these necromancers. She had gone through every single employee, then the necromancer trials, and now she was to go through the rest of the nobles. She pushed aside her annoyance. This had been her idea. She had wanted to help. She was being utterly selfish not to help and stupid if she wasn't trying to oust those who wanted her dead for her talents.

"Your Highness," Lucy said quietly, "you wanted me to remind you to catch up in your correspondence before dinner."

"Thank you, Lucy," Mary said kindly. "We shall retire to my quarters in a moment, as now we need to write invites to the most suitable gentlemen." Then after a sip of her drink, she said quietly, "And, Lucy, I'm sorry."

The servant bowed her head, returned to her spot by the door, and continued talking to Madge quietly. There was a lightness to her as though Mary's apology made her day. Toury felt great. If she couldn't fix her situation in the meantime, she could help Mary's.

8

EMERALD

Toury was painted, dressed, and her hair done to look her best, although she felt far from it. She was paraded around the room by Cobalt, who was arm in arm with her and Mary, in Alex's stead. Apparently, this meal was for the uncle Toury hadn't met yet.

Toury talked to noble after noble with Mary, who relayed messages in whispers through Cobalt about who was approaching. Madge trailed them, as well as Lucy, making Toury feel safe. She was exhausted. Every moment of her day was taken up, and the Queen urged her to lighten her load by dropping all the intense lessons, but she couldn't. She needed to stay busy. It chased the dreams of black eyes away and helped her miss Alex less, but the loneliness seeped in every night when she went into their quarters, when she slept alone, when she woke up to no note from Alex, who had always risen as early as the sun. She had slept in his bed the first week, enveloped in his sooty scent. Now, she loathed his room, which had stopped smelling of him a fortnight after he left. In her room, she always ordered a fire at night, the warm glow reminding her of him. When she would wake in the morning, it would be out, but the sooty smell that remained reminded her of Alex, allowing her to wake with a smile. He had believed distance would strengthen her, but it wasn't working. Alex had destroyed the Earth girl, and in her wake was a shell of a girl filled with power and austerity.

Cobalt nudged her subtly, and she realized the man sitting across from her during dinner, who had been fawning annoyingly over Mary, was now watching Toury expectantly. Mary tried not to laugh. She was no help. Cobalt leaned slightly into Toury and whispered subtly, his lips barely moving to say, "The trials."

Without another beat, Toury launched into a polite and vague description of the trials for the man, Lord Pearl. Then he mentioned Alex, wanting to know details. When she hesitated, Cobalt cut in, saving her. She was grateful for his presence. The last thing she could confidently talk about was Alex. First, his letters were short and seldomly sent. Second, she was so conflicted about him that she wasn't sure what would come out of her mouth. She missed him desperately and yet was angry he was gone and pushing her into this role of queen. She had only wanted the crown so she could be with him in the first place.

Half listening, she realized Cobalt knew more than she did about Alex's whereabouts and happenings, which had to mean either Cobalt was getting more letters, or more detailed ones, about what was going on, or he was making it up to impress everyone; Toury couldn't figure the guy out. Cobalt worsened her mood.

"What will the king proxy decide when it comes to the necromancers? It must be a difficult decision. Nobles have rarely been staked, allowed the dignified death," Lord Emerald said, punctuating with a slicing motion to his neck.

"Uncle," Mary protested, but she stifled a giggle.

"Truly, Humphrey." The queen shook her head.

"Sorry, Your Majesty."

"How is Anne?" the queen asked.

The man was taken aback and fidgeted with his napkin. "She was doing well; one of the gossiping servants told her Henry is missing, so she's had another fit. I had to lock her in her quarters. I've put out notices again for any fireproof folk, but it appears to be a rare talent these days. Not enough Sapphirians sowing their seeds elsewhere."

Mary's mouth dropped. The queen became furious.

Then Lord Emerald scrutinized Toury for the first time with interest. "Unless my nephew is up to it now?"

Toury wanted to throw her goblet of wine in his face but refrained. She simply fixed a cool gaze upon him and an austere smile that made his face sink. He wanted a reaction out of her, to break her, and she wouldn't let him win.

He examined her again, staring her down, measuring her up.

"Alex's aunt is ill. She went mad years ago. They have to lock her up during her fits, or she'll burn everyone and everything," Cobalt whispered.

This was the aunt Alex had told her about who lived in Ludford, not far from her aunt's estate. No wonder she went crazy, being married to a man such as this, who lacked tact, decorum, and had such empty green eyes. She refused to look away. Finally, the lord gave in first and turned his focus to the queen.

"Your successor has some pluck."

"My son has done me proud. I think he's chosen the most powerful and worthy girl in the land." The queen spoke with warmth, but it unnerved Toury to be discussed as if she weren't right there hearing them.

"And the prettiest, I'd say," the man added, making her queasy. From the depths of her subconscious—or Ruby's pool of information and sensations—Toury knew she shouldn't trust this man at all. Considering Ruby had been his daughter, Toury grew even more uncomfortable. At least the man's eyes were still green. That was something.

"Stop, you make our queen proxy-to-be blush," Lord Diamond said. He was an elderly man with scars across his face and a rigid posture. Ex-military. "Back to these necromancers, if you don't mind. Dignified death might be too kind. Their crimes were so atrocious."

"My son will see to a fitting solution," the queen answered dismissively. "But I believe he gave his specific instructions to his betrothed."

Throwing her under the bus. She didn't think the queen capable of such underhanded tactics. When the surrounding people all focused on Toury, she realized the queen was giving her a chance to assert herself. She was trying to help. The queen was weary. Lord Emerald's rudeness was taking a lot out of the woman. Alluding to her husband and son as philanderers to make fire-proof baseborns was pretty hard to ignore.

Toury mustered her strength, and again a strange relaxing energy rolled over her in waves. It was coming from next to her where Cobalt sat. Cobalt stone had the properties of lifting moods and inhibitions and stimulating creativity and peace; Ruby's bank of knowledge explained, so Ruby was still with her. It was a warning of some sort, which was strange because she remembered Cobalt had been Ruby's suitor. Why would she warn her, and what was the warning about? Cobalt was helping her, not harming.

Cobalt wasn't speaking up, but using his stone magic to bolster her. They all wanted her to be the queen she needed to become.

"Yes," Toury said, buying a moment to organize her thoughts.

Cobalt nodded at her with a smile. Mary glared at Cobalt as she drank firewhiskey.

The strange glare and her concern over Mary's drinking problem momentarily distracted her. "Um, yes. His Majesty has plans to snuff them all."

"Snuff?" Lord Emerald said, aghast. "That's it? He'll let them live?"

"No, Lord Emerald, we found—"

"And I had such high hopes that he would follow his father's example. Evil must be squashed—"

"Yes, but you see—" Toury tried to interject. The man kept trying to silence her and paint Alex in a bad light. She hated this odious man.

"I think the queen proxy-to-be is trying to explain if you would only—" Cobalt tried.

"Snuffing? Did I hear that right?" Lord Pearl asked.

"We found out that—" she raised her voice, but the men raised theirs too.

"He's a fool, then. He won't last long on his throne unless he strikes the fear in every eye that covets the throne," Lord Diamond joined the conversation.

Toury's strength waned, and yet she boiled inside at the cavalier way they discussed Alex. They didn't know him at all.

"No, not a fool," Lord Emerald said, looking at Toury salaciously. "He's thinking with something other than his brain. Women make men soft. He should've had an arranged marriage. Love has no room at court."

When Toury's gaze alighted on the queen—Toury was shocked she hadn't put a stop to this—she saw the queen's head bowed down and eyes blinking back tears. They were hurting the queen. Mary's mouth was agog; Cobalt was rigid, but neither appeared ready to defend Alex.

"Yes, too true. Beauty is distracting—" Pearl began.

"Silence!" Toury commanded.

The entire table stopped talking, even people at the other end, who had no idea what the conversation was about at her end of the table. The three men inspected her: Pearl shocked and frightened by her outburst, Diamond's eyes narrowing at her severely in challenge, and Alex's uncle smirking as if he had won. He was trying to set her up to misstep, to offend someone or to make a fool of herself, but it was too late to back down.

Since she had gone this far, she would keep going and hope the queen or Cobalt would stop her before she destroyed the monarchy. "You insult your king, your nephew, berate him like a love-sick puppy, make cheap innuendos at my expense—your future queen, let me remind you—and cut me off before I can get a word in to answer the very question you asked of me!" When she realized her rant had no point to it but to call them out, she added, "Who do you think you are to say such things without rebuke?"

The men said nothing. Pearl turned that very color, his flesh paling whiter than his eerie pale gray eyes. Diamond's glare softened into what one might see as pride or admiration, but Lord Emerald was creepy. He lost his jollity and stared at her with an empty, cold stare that gave her chills.

"I am the king's brother—" he began.

She cut him off just as he had her several times. "Through marriage. I believe no one has the right to challenge the king proxy's decisions. Not you, not I, not even our infirmed king. Am I wrong?" she asked Cobalt demurely.

"You are quite right, Lady Tourmaline, Queen Proxy-to-Be." Cobalt backed her, despite the fact she had formerly chastised him for doing the same.

Toury wanted to continue to threaten some kind of punishment, and yet she wasn't sure what she was allowed to do or what Alex would do in the situation. He would wound them with words, but she knew nothing about these men, nothing she could use against them. She glanced at Cobalt. He gave her a slight nod.

"I have half a mind to—" she began.

"Queen Proxy-to-Be," Cobalt cut in. "Please. Do not let your anger at their foolishness make you do anything rash. I do not think they mean what they say."

Pearl started groveling with apologies. Diamond stuck his finger in the collar of his doublet to pull it away to breathe better, which was the only sign of his discomfort. Emerald raised his eyebrows as if he was onto their act, but she didn't think he'd go as far as to challenge her again.

"Very well," she said, giving them looks that could kill, trying to ignore all the eyes upon her. More of that mood-enhancing energy emanated from Cobalt, and she was thankful he took her inhibitions away. She was herself again, whole, unbroken. "What I was trying to say was, the king proxy decided to snuff the necromancers first."

There were a few murmurs, so she raised her voice to drown them out. "Justine Citrine"—she purposely left off any distinction from her name—"died when Tobias Firebrander pulled the darkness from her. You see, there is no room in a strong necromancer for the fire, light, stone, or blood magic. They become wholly dark, and without the darkness, they cannot survive. This snuffing of dark power will kill all necromancers who are too powerful to live, as they would be a threat. They would turn this world dark. The flames would dwindle, the light would go out, and Fyr as we know it would cease to exist. We need to stop them. This is the best and most humane way—to use their own darkness against them, to have evil destroy itself."

She paused, and a few "Hear! Hear!" shouts echoed through the room.

"Those who survive will be traded in servitude to other spheres."

People were nodding and regarding her with what she could only describe as the reverence Alex garnered wherever he went. It was a heady feeling.

Toury stood, too exhausted, too agitated, too on display to remain at the table. "And as for love, which you so believe to be beneath court politics, well, that is a magic stronger than any magic on any sphere. It's what saved your king proxy, and it is what will make a kingdom flourish. Love kills hate. The necromancers cannot fight what they'll never understand."

With that, she swept from the room, Madge shadowing her. Toury knew very well she should've asked the queen to be excused as propriety demanded, and she knew she'd just offended three nobles, but she couldn't care less. Alex promised her the world to set ablaze, and she had just begun. Toury was back.

9

COBALT

Toury was elated, almost high on power. She had done her first act as queen proxy-to-be, faced the men's patriarchal derision with strength and dignity, and silenced them like the children they were being. The dinner party was just a warm-up. The next day, she entered the square out front in the queen's stead, as the queen had requested, and announced to the guild members, both magician and sorcerer, her sentencing of the necromancers. Cobalt had given her a good mood-enhancing pep talk and backed her when Lord Quartz presented similar objections as the other men had last night.

They were afraid of change. She knew that. They would've liked it more if it had come from Alex. They didn't trust her or fully believe that she was fulfilling Alex's wishes. They would learn to listen to her, or Alex would give them hell when he returned. They would learn to embrace her as Alex's equal eventually. Today, however, they behaved just as the men had at dinner: murmuring with a bit of annoyance and yet eyes full of interest.

She gave them a moment to digest the information and then ordered the snuffers—magicians with the ability to separate magic from beings and release it back into the atmosphere—to begin. Toury had lately learned that snuffing was a blood magic trait, and she noted she must learn more about this power.

The men's objections halted when they saw how the Citrines all died without their darkness. When they got to the young girl Toury had sentenced, she could take no more and left, having done her duty for the punishments. On the way out, Tobias nodded to tell her he would do his duty and take the survivors to another sphere.

Once inside, she started to walk away in haste. Her thoughts were to hide in her room and cry at the thought of killing others, even if they were utterly evil. Before she could get away, she heard footsteps behind her.

"Toury!" Cobalt called after her and hustled to catch up. "You okay?"

She sensed that pleasant magical vibe rolling off of him, which took away the tears prickling the back of her eyes and dislodged the lump that had been forming in her throat. He was pretty handy after all. She didn't even want to reprimand him for forgetting her title.

"I'm fine. I just didn't want to watch all of it." She led him to the princess salon, sensing he wanted to talk about it. Maybe it would be good to talk about it and get it out of her system.

"We need some drinks to celebrate." Cobalt surveyed the princess salon. "Say, where's the firewhiskey?"

"People are dying, Cobalt. Hardly a time to celebrate."

"Not dying, being executed. They would kill you, Toury, and Alex, and everyone in this castle. I don't mean we should celebrate their deaths but that justice was served, evil eradicated. Where is the blasted whiskey?"

"They are still being killed. It feels wrong to celebrate."

"What?" Cobalt looked at her, distracted. "Oh, no. Not the death. I want to toast to your success. You conquered the nobles at dinner and vanquished evil from the land after breakfast. The people love you, Toury." He gave up his search. "Seriously, is there no firewhiskey in here?"

"The queen banished it from the room. Her attempt to control Mary's...habits."

"She'll just drink in her room alone. Better to do it in front, where people can monitor it," he muttered.

"Better that she kicks the habit altogether," Toury amended.

"True, but she goes through such pressure that you and I could never understand."

"I am living with very similar pressure, thank you very much."

"You don't have to."

"I don't like this conversation. Weren't we celebrating?"

"You there!" Cobalt motioned toward Madge.

Madge came forward, looking at him perplexed. Toury realized no one else—aside from Alex and herself—ever noticed Madge.

"Fetch some firewhiskey if you will."

"She's not a servant, Cobalt," Toury protested.

"Relax, she'll delegate," he said as Madge, a bit flustered, left the room.

"The point is, she's never to leave my side for my protection."

"Don't tell me you think I'd ever hurt you, Toury. That would break my heart."

She laughed at that. "Don't be so melodramatic."

When she gazed upon him, he seemed genuinely put out, almost hurt. He crossed over to her; his demeanor she couldn't place, but it made her a bit uncomfortable.

He touched her shoulder and gave it a friendly squeeze. "That's what is so great about you, Toury. No overtures, no fine speeches needed, just facts, the truth. I see how easy it must've been for Alex to bewitch you."

Actually, it had been quite difficult, in her opinion, for Alex to capture her heart. Then he pulverized it, left her behind to chase dragons, and barely wrote to her. "I'm not bewitched. In fact, I'm quite angry he hasn't explained things in detail."

"You don't know what is going on?" Cobalt touched her other shoulder to steady her. "Why is he shutting you out? I got a pretty detailed letter just yesterday in response to mine updating him with the trials."

"What?" Her shock quickly turned to anger. Why would he ask Cobalt for an update and not her? Did Alex have something to hide? Was the news bad? "What did he say?"

"Boring stuff you wouldn't care about, like tracking down rebels and questioning one of the dragonslayers. No mention of his return, but he never even asked about you. Did you two have a fight?"

Fight? They had to communicate to have that. Alex was not good at communicating whatsoever. Oh, she could just kill him. Toury yanked away from Cobalt and turned her back to him. Her breaths came quick and shallow. Her anger was turning inward on her since it could not have its intended target: Alex. Her pulse spiked. Her eyes stung, and her throat started to constrict with an overwhelming feeling of furious helplessness. She blinked back the tears and swallowed the invisible band around her throat. She bit back words that would get her in trouble if anyone heard her slander the king aloud. It was building too much. The anger needed out, and for as long as she remembered, it had made Toury cry more often than shout. It was his birthday, and not a word. He was a piece of shit.

And tears began to spill over, as did sobs of rage.

"Oh please, Toury!" Cobalt said with emotion in his voice. "Don't cry! I can't handle that." He had spun her around, and when his face beheld hers, his eyes were soft, kind, and full of sympathy. He pulled out a handkerchief and dabbed her eyes with it, his hands pulling her in for a hug. Feeling utterly bereft after Alex had forsaken her for the umpteenth time, she hugged him back, needing the comfort and attention. She couldn't remember the last time she'd had any physical contact with someone, even a hug. Then that magic of his, soothing and curling around her, lifted her mood, taking the sadness away. She remained in his arms longer than she should've, that feeling intoxicating, but once she realized it crossed lines of propriety, she backed away.

Before she could fully leave his arms, they tightened, bringing her back. Only, instead of him pulling her head onto his shoulder in comfort, their faces met. Her breath caught as he pressed his lips against hers. Then he captured hers again. Her mind was blank, her tears dried, and her lips moved against his. She was of two minds. Toury knew it was wrong on so many levels, including how she felt nothing for him, yet she was starved for any kind of attention, and that pulsating magic that promised happiness and peace lulled over her like a drug.

Their lips met in tandem. Then, his tongue slipped between her teeth, and he moaned, pressing his body, every firm bit of it against her. The act was like dousing her with cold water. Shock and repulsion made her shove him away. Eww. *Eww.* What was *wrong* with her? What had she been thinking?

"Toury," Cobalt breathed out, his breath quick, his eyes wide, and his...well... Toury had to look away as her face flushed up in mortification. In comparison, Alex had so much more self-control. Alex! Oh no, what would he think? What would he do?

Cobalt yanked her back to him by the nape of her neck a bit too violently.

She shoved him away. "No. That was a mistake. I didn't mean—"

His lips cut her off. She shoved at him again, keeping her mouth firmly shut, but he was latched onto her in an octopus-like grip. His pleasing powers were piercing her almost painfully in their desperation, and she let the light magic bloom in her, which began to repel whatever he was doing with his magic, like an inner shield.

Toury gave a closed mouth scream and pushed him away as hard as she could. Images of Justine, the black-eyed Alex, and the necromancers filled her head, but instead of panic, she was full of fury.

Cobalt staggered back, gawping at her. Perhaps it was the first time a girl had been able to fight him off. "Toury—"

"Stop!" she shouted. "How dare you?"

"Dare I? You thoroughly enjoyed that. Don't pretend to be a prude. Look, I know you're scared, but we could leave here, you and I. We could go back to Earth and be together."

Her heart lurched. Earth would mean no Alex. Despite his silence and neglect of her, she loved him. She could never leave Fyr. Never. Of course, she would never leave it for this dipshit who took advantage of her with his bewitching magic while she was vulnerable.

"Get away from me."

"Toury—" He made another grab for her.

"Don't touch me!" Then she pulled her arm back and swung at him, smashing her fist right into his eye. Part of her hand hit bone, and it smarted terribly. "How dare you take advantage of me!"

He was stunned, seemingly more by her words than the punch. He didn't move, and Toury was about to have another outburst.

"My lord, you should do as she commands," Madge said. She entered, carrying firewhiskey, and put herself between her mistress and the man she argued with.

Great, they had an audience. A few other servants stood frozen in the doorway, most likely brought there by the commotion. And Mary, whose expression was distraught, disappointed, and angry, stood there, the look on her face revealing that she was upset about more than just a betrayal for Alex. Toury realized now whom Mary wanted man number five on her suitor list to be. An overwhelming guilt washed over her.

With a bitter glare, Cobalt stormed out of the room. Mary's face screwed up in tears after he brushed by her without a glance.

Toury released a pent-up breath. "Please everyone, as you were," Toury managed to say to dismiss the servants.

Madge went and placed the bottle of whiskey onto the table.

Mary's tear-filled eyes glared at Toury.

"Mary, I'm—"

"Don't." Mary transported, Lucy diving to grab the hem of her gown to follow her at the last second.

Madge cut into the awkward silence. "Sorry, my lady. I shouldn't have left you. By the time I returned, you were holding your own."

"It is no one's fault but that insipid flirt's." And hers. Toury was to blame too. "Cancel my day. I'm in no mood for anyone right now. I will retire to my quarters."

Once in her room, Toury flopped onto the bed. Cobalt—the scoundrel—had gotten a letter yesterday, so Alex had been able to write. Toury hadn't heard from him. Not only was it his birthday but also their missed wedding day. She had foolishly believed he would've written ahead some kind of apology or at least mention missing something as important as that. Perhaps it was for the best right now. She could no longer write him back either. How could she pretend in a letter that all was well? Toury had been longing for Alex's return, but now she was absolutely dreading it.

10
A TOWN

The day Alex left Toury was awful. The two additional days it took to travel with his men, painstaking. His military would not allow him to transport there with David and a couple others. They thought it was a trap, that murdering a dragon was a ruse to get him there. It very well could be.

When Alex approached the town of Hollyhaven, all he could see were the outline of a couple buildings and smoke. It was dying ember smoke, but it was still burning. He'd need his soldiers to later clear some debris to really put it out. There was something in the air in addition to the smell of burning wood; it was acrid and sharp like the burning of meat and of feathers or hair...bodies. A sinking feeling grew in the pit of his stomach as they neared. He recognized that awful smell from executions, where they burned people at the stake. Instead, these had been innocent people murdered by a dragon, not criminals. When they approached, the sign was decimated, and he stopped his horse. David stopped by his side, and men halted behind them. He knew they were as stunned as he was and needed a moment to grasp the sight.

In short, the town was gone, wiped off the map. There were two buildings left on Broad Road, the central cobblestone street where there once had been shops, smiths, pubs, an inn, and many jewelers. What had been houses on the side roads were nothing but a few fragmented boards and ash. There were no signs of life, except a now stray dog rummaging for food he probably wouldn't find.

"My god and goddess," David breathed out.

"How many lived in Hollyhaven?" Alex steadied his voice.

"About a thousand, Your Majesty," Captain Agate said, his voice soft for the normally robust lord.

"Look for survivors, tracks to see where they fled to. Send a few scouts to Claymead and Gunnytree to search for survivors. We will recompense them, at least monetarily, for their dwellings and belongings. There's nothing I can do about the people they lost."

The captain took his orders, and then his soldiers all spread out to search the rubble, four men veering off for the other towns. Alex and David kept riding slowly, assessing the damage. When they turned the corner, he called to Agate again, who hurried his horse to catch up. Alex wordlessly pointed at the stone fort that the town had built for the very purpose of hiding from dragons or any type of threat. The heavy wooden doors were still closed, the windows shuttered, the stones by the roof charred and smoking.

Alex sent his horse over at a gallop and watched as the first soldiers reached it. He dismounted and tried to force open the doors. They appeared to still be barred from within. And when they didn't get a response, he knew it was the worst situation possible, and there was nothing for it. He went over to Agate. "I will open it."

"No, Your Majesty. Too dangerous," The man protested.

"There is no danger in there for me," Alex returned.

"I will go with you, Your Majesty," David announced, drawing his sword. Alex nodded, and as David's other hand clasped his traveling cloak, they vanished in flames, transporting inside.

They appeared in the main hall, right in front of the door, for it was the only thing Alex could envision—having never entered this fort before. David put his sword away, seeing there was no threat, and worked to lift the wooden bar.

Alex stared at all the huddled, immobile bodies, all darkened and ash covered. He looked up to see the gaping hole where the wooden ceiling had been. He hadn't seen the damage from outside, but the fort was broken and vulnerable. It hadn't been updated like the palace had been, with its stone rib-vault ceilings, but why would they? Draca never left the Firelands, and the town was not wealthy like Celestia to be able to make such expenditures. This was an oversight of Alex's grandfather and father, and Alex himself would suffer for it.

"Your Majesty?" David prompted him.

Alex turned away, feeling ill, and noticed David couldn't lift the charred bar alone. With Alex's help, they lifted it up and threw it aside. David opened the doors.

Alex turned back and walked down the line and heaps of bodies, his people, estimating how many were dead. Then he saw two figures, a larger one holding what appeared to be a small child, one barely out of leading strings, just able to walk on his own. He thought of Toury and how she'd react to seeing a child, barely out of infancy, turned to ash. He swallowed hard but could not stop himself as he walked closer. The child's eyes were shut, the mother hunched down, trying to protect it. Their hair and clothes were all gone, bodies blackened. He touched the child's head gently, thinking of how sorry he was for this needless suffering. The child's form began to crumble and fall apart until both child and mother were a heap of ash and bone. He had never seen the result of dragon's fire on a human being before, how the fire turned them to detailed sculptures of ash, frozen in time, rather than decimating the bodies into oblivion. They did not do this to hunt; when they hunted, they cooked the meat and consumed. This was revenge, intentional, using the blunt force of its magical fire to instantly kill.

He turned to see all the soldiers standing behind him, helmets in hand out of respect, staring at the pile of ash that had once been people. Some of their stoic faces were sinking into despair. He had to bolster them for this.

"Search for survivors in the dungeon. Once the ceiling gave way, they'd go downward. Search every cell and the escape tunnel."

The men snapped to it. David urged him outside, away from the sweltering room. Alex hadn't noticed the heat, never did, due to his dragon's blood, but David was covered in a sheen of sweat. He went outside so David could cool off.

"What now?" David asked him.

"We talk to any survivors here, I hope, or in the other towns, and find out where the body of this male dragon is, find out what happened. More importantly, I have to find her and get her home."

"Will you put her down?" David cringed in reference to the female dragon who had done this.

"Not unless the people demand it. Someone killed a dragon, knowing what would ensue. They are the guilty culprits, and I think the people will recognize that." Draca were the emblematic creatures of the land, the last remnants of living gods. The people would never kill a god, except the fools who had done this.

There was some bustle as the guards rushed out in pairs, carrying something. Alex and David ran over to see them placing some drowsy or unconscious people down on the ground. A few moaned; some were burned, but their rising and falling chests were a glorious sight. More soldiers poured out with people as the former ones ran back in. There must have been a lot of them. He dared to hope.

Snapping back into the commander he needed to be, Alex ordered a dozen soldiers to set up tents. The healers ran to their patients, ready to do what they could, although he knew what they needed most was water.

"David, grab a couple soldiers and send them to the well!" Alex ripped his canteen off his horse and went to the first person he found awake.

It was an old lady, who greedily gulped from the canteen. He held her head up so she could drink properly. Then she stopped with a sigh, and her eyes focused on his. They grew wide, and her mouth dropped. "Thank you, Your Majesty."

He placed her head back down gently. "Can you tell me what happened?" he asked her softly, for she seemed uninjured and the most lucid.

She gave a tired sigh. "Yes."

Alex pulled up the little girl who lay next to the woman and tried to get some water in her mouth, despite her being out of it. The girl choked awake and then drank.

"Four strangers came to town, stayed at the inn, and were asking questions about the Firelands. Next thing we know, we saw one of them selling draca blood, so we knew one was slain. No shop would buy it—we're not stupid, you know—so they moved on, but dragons don't know innocence, do they? She came midday, when everyone was out and about. The fort sounded the alarm, and most got indoors or took to horses, fleeing. As you saw, she broke through the fort after torching the town. Then the men pushed us down into the dungeons until there was no room left. Half the stored food burned up, so it didn't last long, and the water barrels ran dry yesterday. The beams your men removed had us trapped, and we had no idea if we'd ever be saved."

Alex noted it was almost all women and children. All these children most likely lost one or both parents. They would need places to stay, people to raise them.

"These four strangers, what can you tell me about them?"

"Not much, Your Majesty. I never saw them, but I was told they were a family. Two adults, a young woman, and a little boy. They were cunning folk who gave the name Cursebreaker."

"Thank you for your help."

He continued to give the people water and question those who were coherent. He didn't learn much about the culprits, but he did learn what direction the dragon flew and where the male dragon's body was. He knew, despite what he was told, that they weren't commoners. Only a powerful and skilled sorcerer could take down a dragon.

As he and David readied to leave, Agate came over to him. "Your Majesty, what am I to do with these people?"

Alex surveyed the group, estimating three to four hundred survivors. "When they can be moved, take them to Gunnytree. Set up a place for them to convalesce, and get their names down for any family to retrieve them. Send the lists out all over Fyr. Those without places to go or who do not have family can come to Celestia. I'll send wagons for them later."

Agate nodded and gave Alex a small smile. The captain had been with his father for a long time, his hair silver with age.

"Why do you smile?" Alex demanded, still a bit insecure in this sudden leadership role and annoyed Agate might be mocking him.

"Sorry, Your Majesty." He bowed his head. "I could not help but smile at our good fortune to have such a king in his father's stead. Forgive me for saying, but you rule with your head and heart, which is most noble. Although your father was a mighty ruler, he ruled with an iron fist."

"What would he have done in this situation?" Alex asked, worried he was making poor choices.

"I believe he would force Gunnytree to take them in without much assistance. It would be their duty to do so."

"And then the old, feeble, scarred, and children would beg on the streets until they died," Alex said hotly.

"Forgive me, Your Majesty; I'm not being clear. I often did not agree with your father's 'only the strong deserve to survive' motto. I do not wish to speak ill of our infirmed king, but truthfully, I believe you will be the finest king Fyr has seen since the Sapphire Age."

"I see," Alex said uncomfortably. "As you were, Agate." He did not know what to do with that compliment, but what it did, without him outwardly acknowledging it, was bolster his self-confidence. He knew he could be a great king. With Toury as his queen, they'd reform Fyr into a place that had no room for rebels because everyone was satisfied.

With the people tended to, he selected a few brave men and rode out of town in search of a dead dragon and his widow, who would most likely be nearby.

11

A WIDOW

They found the dead dragon exactly where one of the women told him it would be. Flies buzzed about, but he had yet to decompose enough to stink. From feet away, he looked like he could just be sleeping, yet there was no internal glow. Alex felt as bereft as he had when he'd seen his people burned to cinders. A human—well, four of them—had done this, caused all this death and destruction. He would never understand the brutal nature of man. If he could do anything in his lifetime, for his kingdom, he wanted to grant peace.

Alex approached the dragon, inspecting him. His hide was gray and colorless. Normally, they emitted light, and you could see the fire brewing in their bellies, and it lit their opaque-gem-colored skin. He could tell this one had been red, due to the faint glittering specks he saw reflected in the sunlight. The color was how he could tell them apart: He had been known as Sir Draca B.

It was no easy feat to kill a dragon, with their almost impenetrable, glossy-stoned scales. He noticed a hole in the dragon's wing, so he climbed up onto the massive corpse—about the size of the great foyer of the palace when lying down like this—and used most of his strength to lift the folded appendage. There were several holes scorched into it. The rest of the body was not burned at all. They had purposely felled it from the sky with impeccable aim. Alex dropped the wing and slid down the back of the dragon.

His men stood a good distance away, watching the sky, apprehension on their faces, some shifting idly. Alex rolled his eyes and turned his attention back to the poor creature. The other wing was mostly folded under the body, but he saw more holes. He grew wary at the idea. Fire could not slay a dragon, only energy or light. Few people in Fyr could conjure balls of light or energy; to light up a projectile with magic and try to catapult it would not be as accurate as this attack had been. There would be more damage to the landscape, magic thrown astray, forests burned down, yet there was no evidence of these culprits missing their target. They were extremely powerful and able to conjure magic, instead of merely pulling it from the planet's energy.

"They knocked him from the sky by taking out his wings. Look for the place he crash-landed." Alex had to project his voice for his cagey men to even hear him.

His soldiers spread out, happy to move away from the body. In the meantime, he ran his hand over the dragon's hide. Its scales were like cold glass. Dragons always ran very hot; he remembered that—although it had been almost a decade ago—from when his father took him to meet the dragons. He smiled to himself. It was one of the only happy memories he had of his father. He would not let that happen with his children. He would do things differently, better, with everything, just as Agate had told him.

Alex found the deep slash marks under the dragon's throat, where they had drained the blood from him. The hide was impenetrable, but when a sword went against the grain of the scales, the flesh underneath was vulnerable. This is exactly what the murderers did. The ground was stained with dried blood, so this was where he had died, poor creature, suffering in the last moments, growing weaker as they drained him. Gallons of it were probably sold, gallons he'd have to track down and seize to stop these people, necromancers or rebels or—the god and goddess forbid—a new enemy, from drinking to become momentarily as powerful as him. It was most likely another plan to usurp him. If only they'd give him a chance to prove himself first.

Some dried blood around the dragon's eyes drew his attention next. With dread, he lifted the lid but did not see the blue eyes with reptilian slits. His eyes should have been deep blue and glittering like a sapphire, like Alex's own. Instead, he saw a socket full of pulpy tissue and a spearhead snapped off in it. They had blinded the poor creature. So much torture and death in one day, and for what? Money? Power? What bothered Alex most was, he didn't understand the motivation behind it. They had drained the dragon quickly and fled, not attempting to try to get off the hide or carve the dragon's meat—both very difficult and time-consuming tasks. There was no way they'd risk lingering, or his mate would've caught them.

Alex heard a whistle from one of his men. The soldier repeated the call until they were all congregated by him. They ended up gathered a ways into a forest—if you could call it that, since the trees this far south were bereft of leaves. They looked like cypress, but the heat withered most leaves, and the dragons took care of the rest, so it was hard to tell. In the area his soldiers stood, the trees were all knocked down or broken in half. A couple trees were stained dark red, as well as the soil around them.

"He crashed here and must've been impaled or injured a lot worse," Alex said aloud what they all were probably thinking. They followed the path he hadn't noticed on the way in: three-toed prints of the dragon. He studied them. "He must've hurt his left side. The prints show he was dragging on that side. This must be where they blinded him," Alex mused, for the pattern of prints had become erratic and disordered.

When they rounded the corner, they were back to the corpse. A quarter mile of agony, not to mention how long the culprits had chased and attacked the dragon while he was in the sky. Alex couldn't ignore the fact the cruelty of the death was a metaphor for what they wanted to do to him: an illustrated insult.

His men gasped, and that's when Alex peered up to the sky. Descending over them was a large female dragon—the widow. He recognized her as Dame Draca B, having memorized all fifty or so when he was young. Like memorizing houses of nobles, he had memorized drawings of dragons and their differentiating coloring patterns. Since dragon tongue could not be translated into man's English—it consisting of a series of hisses, growls, purrs, and such—his ancestors gave them names in the old language, each beginning with a different letter of the alphabet. Well, only the male ones got names back then, of course; it had been a very different time, and the females were given their lifemate's name, the same with the offspring. Then his great-grandfather shortened the dragons' family names to simple letters since no one truly spoke the old language anymore. They didn't like the name changes too much, so honorifics of sir, dame, and squire were added for the males, females, and offspring, respectively. It had placated them, not that they spoke to Sapphirians often. "Stay still," Alex hissed at his men.

She landed between her dead lifemate and them, protecting him even in death. It struck a chord in Alex. She roared so loud at them that he could feel the sound reverberate around them. He took a tentative step forward.

"Your Majesty," David choked out in fright.

"She will recognize me and won't harm me," Alex said. "For good measure, though, do not draw a weapon, no matter what happens, and slowly lower yourselves to the ground in deference."

Alex took another step, and she cocked her head to examine him, bearing spiky, narrow teeth three rows deep. He steeled himself. He could not show fear. He had lied to Toury, just a little, about dragons being harmless. Sure, he could not catch on fire or be burned, but she could rip him to shreds with her claws and teeth. That had never happened to any Sapphirian, but one of his great-great-uncles had been crushed by one during the battle of Lyft when the air sphere had tried to invade. It was purely accidental on the dragon's part and one of the many reasons dragons were no longer ridden to battle.

I know you're upset, Alex thought. Dragons did communicate through roars but mostly through thoughts, and a Sapphirian could tune in. They were fairly intelligent creatures, but communication had to be simple for them. It's not like dragons were well-read in man's language. *I know your heart hurts. Mine does too.*

You know nothing of feelings. You're man.

No. I am draca man.

She roared, calling him out as a liar and glared at him, the serpentine pupils enlarging. She was going to test him. First, her tail lashed around, and he leaped over it in time.

He tumbled back onto his feet right away. *Dame Draca B*, he thought hurriedly. *Come, come. Peace. I will find these people and kill them for you.*

Nooooo! her mind wailed. Fire shot forth from her mouth.

Alex was blasted by the flames, but he stood his ground, unflinching. *Are you done?* he demanded, trying to assert his power over her now that she must know who he was.

Not a boy anymore.

No, a man, and king now.

Humans grow fast, she thought. She relaxed and folded her legs under her body in a feline way. She placed her jaw onto her dead mate's head. *He breathes no more.*

I know. I am sorry. You had your revenge. You killed lots of innocent people, children. You must go back to the Firelands. I will bring him back there for you so you can have your pyre. His spirit will then be at home.

But I didn't get them.

I will get them.

Can I eat them? Her sparkling sapphire eyes were pleading.

I'll think about it, he mused. Would serve the people right to feed them to her.

Will you end me then? She bristled a little and then rose. Dragons mated for life. Without her mate, she would want to follow. The question threw him off, but he quickly realized she had something else to live for.

No. As long as you kill no more. No more people ever again.

I will never go near people again. I hate them.

He scoffed. *Thanks.*

I like you. You're our flesh babies. You're not man, but draca man.

Come. Let me take him back. He stepped closer.

She wrangled into a defensive position, growling in her throat. It was instinctual. She was very dangerous in her weary grief.

I cannot hurt him. I will transport him.

She reluctantly stepped aside. Her eyes were full of attitude, telling him she didn't like being ordered around by a "flesh baby."

You go on ahead, he thought, not trusting to leave her alone with his men.

She gave a heart-wrenching cry as she took off and then was flying south.

Alex let out a relieved sigh, not realizing he had been so tense during the exchange. His men were silent and staring at him in awe. He felt strangely on display. "To the Firelands with haste. David, you know where to wait."

They snapped out of their wonderment and hustled to their horses. When they were out of sight, he leaned against the corpse of the dragon. Never had he attempted to transport something this big, but without the curse weighing down on him, he knew he could do it. He had to do it, for the power had been building up inside him for months, and the physical and magical training sessions only relieved so much of his pent-up magic.

Alex closed his eyes and let the fire roll out of his fingertips over the broad beast and himself. He closed his eyes to imagine the Firelands, and when he opened them, he was there. On the first try.

12
A Dragon Slayer

Alex reappeared in the sweltering lands, which were devoid of greenery and had only remnants of charred vegetation. He stood there for a moment, pulling his fire back in and marveling over how he had miraculously ended up here with the massive body of the male dragon in one attempt. He took in the scene. In the distance, he saw the fireproof cottage, more like a shack, where he and his father camped out while Alex was tutored about the draca. Ashes, tree stumps, stones, and bone fragments from animals dotted the scenery. Most likely, they were the remnants of the dragons' favorite meals—goats and deer, which had been rampant throughout Fyr, but to deter these animals' overpopulation and to keep the dragons hunting in the south, there were shepherds who herded them southward. These Firelands were the home of the dragons, their communal nest with eggs warming somewhere on molten rock and fire. Something felt off, wrong, like something was there that shouldn't be, and the lack of draca in this area was not normal either. His instincts sensed a bigger problem.

Then he saw a person. He transported away from the dragon's body and reappeared behind a boulder that was clustered with charred tree stumps to hide from the figure. The person was a she. He could tell by the slightly graceful walk and short, thin stature. She was covered from head to toe by a cloak, and he wondered if it was enchanted to prevent her from burning or if she had drunk copious amounts of dragon's blood after she slew the poor creature. For she could not be a Sapphirian, and yet no one could walk in these lands without some kind of powerful fire magic.

The woman stopped short when she saw the dragon's body. Then she whirled around, searching all over, frightened. He knew right then that she was guilty. She knew the body of the dragon should be elsewhere. She backed up away from the corpse.

Alex was about to come out of his hiding spot when a bleat and the sound of claws on gravel stole his attention. A bearn, a baby dragon, not yet a year old from the looks of him, trotted up to the body, its glassy red hide matching the draca of the B family. This was the child of the dead dragon.

The bearn scrambled like an uncoordinated skink to his father's side, nudging him, his blue reptilian eyes expectant for some kind of tasty morsel.

The bleats took on a chilling sound, and Alex could hear the recognition in the cries that sounded half like a crow caw and half like a goat whine. It realized its father was dead, and the despair in the little creature's voice tore at Alex's heartstrings. He was a man and yet in tune with these sapient creatures. He was empathetic of what the little bearn was feeling, and it was acute and horrifying. The half-coherent thoughts of a young one unable to fully communicate reached his mind in jumbles.

Mama B landed a moment later between the perpetrator and her bearn, in a protective stance. However, if Alex didn't intercede, she'd be a dead trespasser, and he needed to question her.

Alex acted quickly and transported behind the girl, restraining her one arm, and twisting the other arm that wielded a knife. "Drop it."

She jumped in his arms, frightened, and futilely struggled against his hold. "Lemme go!" She wriggled, but he tightened his grip. "Where the hell did you come from?"

"I appear where I want, when I want," he said. "Now I'm going to let go of you. If you go for your blade or attempt to harm me in any way, Draca B here will torch you. If you run, I'll order her to eat you." He wondered if the girl was aware the fireproof of the draca was in their scales and in Alex's skin, and dragon's blood would not save her from flames. She'd only have his powers for an hour or so, depending on how much she'd drunk, but not his protections.

"How about option C?" Her tone was self-assured and unafraid. "Where I grab the knife and slit your throat, so you can't command the dragon?"

"I don't need my voice to command them, and if you even look at me the wrong way, she will kill you."

She froze in his grip and gasped. "You're the prince."

He did not see the need to correct her that he was king proxy now. She was uninformed of court events, which meant she was off the grid, most likely a criminal, a necromancer, or a rebel.

"And how would you know that? There are three Sapphirian males," he challenged. He was worried about Henry. Cobalt didn't trust him since his cousin deserted his post. Could he be in league with these people? Surely not. Henry could not kill a dragon.

"The king would never leave the castle, and Lord Henry has been reported fighting rebels out west, so you must be the prince." Again, her information wasn't current.

"Sapphirians transport, you know."

She yanked, trying to break his grasp on her, but he held her tighter. "Transporting a dragon? You're too strong to be anyone else. Everyone knows the queen has powerful blood magic, which would make the prince and princess stronger than other Sapphirians. Plus, Lord Emerald is virtually talentless, which means his son only has his mother Anne's powers, hence his Sapphirian blue eyes. Any simpleton could conclude Henry Sapphirian is much weaker than his cousins."

This was true. His cousins had blue eyes, not green like their father's. During training as kids, Alex had held his own against Henry, who was three years older, quite bigger at the time, and didn't have a curse weighing him down.

"I am the prince," he conceded. "Ready to comply, since you should be obeying my every order anyway?"

She nodded.

Alex let her go and spun her around. He froze as if someone dumped a bucket of ice over him. Her eyes were gray, a familiar, beautiful steel gray that made his stomach lurch in nervous flitters of unfounded desire. He let go of her, distracted by these conflicting feelings of seeing Toury in her and knowing this girl was an outlaw. Of course, she tried to run. He mentally pulled it together to command Draca B—who was begging to eat the girl—to stop her from leaving. Everywhere the girl tried to go, Draca B cut her off. The bearn tried to roar to help his mother out, but it sounded more like a hiss. Finally, the girl gave up, falling onto her rump and not getting up. Her hood had fallen down, revealing light brown hair in a messy braid, a gaunt face, and a protruding nose much like Lady Edwina's. Nothing close to his Toury, except those eyes. He was thankful for it, gaining his sanity back, although an ache in his heart for the real Toury remained.

"I do not need to ask who you are, Hematite, but I must ask why you are here and why you slew one of my dragons."

"I didn't."

"Oh, but you did."

"No, I bought some blood and drank it to enter their land."

"You knew I moved his body and that he wasn't killed here. How would you know that if you didn't do it? He was struck with white light magic—a Hematite power. The dame here agrees with my conclusions. Because you killed her lifemate, she really, really wants to slowly pull you to pieces and to eat you. Wait." Alex paused, picking up on the draca's very detailed description of wanted torture. "She says she'll start bit by bit and cauterize the flesh to stop the bleeding. That way, she could torture you for days, feed her bearn for ages. This little one is definitely game for that. He's just thinking 'kill it' and 'yum' over and over again."

The girl had been faking bravado, but now her bottom lip quivered with fright.

"Rise, slowly."

"I'll rise if I want to rise," she countered stubbornly. Tenacity seemed to be a familial trait for the Hematites.

"A rebel then," he pondered. He kept his tone neutral, but this did not bode well. His father, even his people, wouldn't accept Toury if anyone in her family was a rebel. He knew deep down that Toury knew nothing about this girl, but he was a little afraid of who she would choose if forced between family and him. She had always longed for a loving family, even if she wouldn't own up to it.

"Well, unless your aim is to stack up treasonous crimes, I suggest you stop with the insubordination and cooperate, or you will have to be burned at the stake. I really don't want to do that. But I could let Dame Draca B here have her fill."

She had the audacity to laugh at this. "Yeah, you do. All you Sapphirians want is to burn anything and anyone in your way."

"It's not nice to lump us all together with a false assumption. You're utterly wrong about me. So, what are you doing here?"

"Official rebel business." She opened her palm, and light magic formed into a ball.

"You use that, and my dragon will eat you," Alex warned her. He thought of the power Toury had behind her light when she was angry.

"You're worried the light will kill your dark magic?" She aimed her hand toward him.

"I don't have any dark magic in me anymore, but I know firsthand those lightballs smart a bit." He didn't actually remember when Toury's white magic had blasted him and killed the darkness in him, but he knew this girl's power wouldn't hurt him, since he'd lived after Toury blasted him with tons of light magic.

She appeared confused. She didn't know his curse was cured, meaning she either hadn't been on the sphere or had been somewhere so secluded, the news did not get to her. "Can she throw them?" the girl asked, bemused, dropping her hand.

"Who?" He feigned ignorance to get her talking.

"You know who. She's the reason I slew the dragon in the first place, to make this one go on a rampage, so you would come and arrest me."

"Ah, see? Admitting you did it wasn't so hard, was it?"

The girl scowled.

"Why would you want to be arrested?"

"To meet my sister."

He glared at her incredulously. "Couldn't you have just come to the castle and asked to see her?"

"And have you say no?" She laughed at him.

He did not like being misjudged—laughed at, even less.

"We were banished from court. Your father would have me killed."

"Toury is welcomed in court, along with your aunt, by the way, and a baseborn uncle you have, so you're off in that assumption. And I wouldn't have said no if Toury wanted to meet you. Now I know it would've been a mistake to say yes. Anyone who would kill a dragon without a second thought should be nowhere near Toury."

"Toury," she muttered. "My parents will *love* that little pet name you gave your prisoner."

"You're misinformed. She's no prisoner, and she gave herself that name. Speaking of my future parents-in-law, they're alive, then? In this realm, I take it? How many Hematites are there?"

"I said too much," she backpedaled.

"Ah, see? There we disagree. You haven't said enough, in my opinion. As much as I would love to torture you to get info out of you—it's only fair, you know, since you ruined the life of this draca, orphaned its bearn, and killed a protected godly creature—my suspicion is you were after her little one before we interrupted you, What were you going to do, kill a baby dragon?"

"Not kill it." Her lip jutted out stubbornly.

"Kidnap it then to send its mother on another rampage?" Alex shook his head. Why would the rebels do this? Merely to make him look weak, turn the people against the draca and, in turn, their rulers? He continued to list her crimes, "Not to mention all the collateral lives lost in this debacle—as I said, I would love to torture you, but Toury would not appreciate it. So get walking before you run out of stolen fire power. You'll get your wish to meet her, but it'll be in chains."

He prodded his prisoner to walk out of the Firelands. Dame Draca B wailed and roared of injustice in her thoughts and language. He tried to soothe her into understanding this girl would be punished. Although the dragon was angry, she stayed put and quieted down after a while, nuzzling her young. He saw other dragons approaching, most likely to use all their fire at once to incinerate their dead brother.

"Walk faster," he urged the Hematite girl, just in case there was a rogue draca who wouldn't obey him in the group. He had to keep this girl alive and get some real answers.

She hustled, her breathing quick and shallow. Good, she was afraid.

Once they were out of the Firelands, David and another soldier grabbed Toury's sister and cuffed her in chains. This appeared to placate the dragons, and their roars quieted down. He saw a huge fire in the distance, and they flew over it in circles in their unique way of mourning. He had only read about it, but seeing it in person...they seemed so human. Although he wished he could just transport the girl back so he could be done with this whole business, he needed answers. He needed to find all that missing draca blood.

13
A MISTAKE

Alex was asleep in his tent when David shook him awake. The image of Toury was dashed from his head. He had every detail of her memorized, but she was beginning to fade. Today of all days, he should be with her. He had been away from home for three weeks of wasted inquiries and pointless searches for the rebels and the draca blood.

"Sorry, Your Majesty. They still can't get anything out of her, and she insists she'll only talk to you."

Alex sighed, annoyed, but got up. He put his doublet back on and straightened up his appearance. They had tried to question her numerous times, but she was not forthcoming about the rebels. He was irritated that she somehow wrestled control from him. Because she was Toury's sister, and the practice was barbaric, he wouldn't allow them to torture her. Threats, he allowed. If she was anything like Toury, he knew they wouldn't have worked.

Their questions had only yielded her history and her name: Racine. She was only a year younger than Toury and had been left on another sphere like Toury had been, but on Lyft, the air sphere, not Earth. Her parents had returned for Racine two years ago. Recently, they'd made it to Earth, only to have trouble finding Toury because her Earth parents had separated and moved many times prior. When they found out Toury was a missing person, they gave up, thinking she was dead, and came to Fyr. That was when they found out Toury had been trapped into an engagement with Alex.

He neither liked, nor would he ever admit, that that last part was true. He had trapped her, and in turn, he assumed, her parents either joined the rebel cause or rejoined it; no wonder the rebels had the wrong idea. He had hoped that the rumors her friends spread of their compatibility would've resounded throughout the kingdom to show how it was a love match, but it hadn't worked, at least not enough. He hoped, quite desperately, that when he returned, things would be as they were. Was it foolish for him to hope Toury would be back to herself when he returned, to have missed him so much that she was no longer afraid of him?

Already in a foul mood, and noticing the sun wasn't quite cresting the horizon yet, which made him even crankier, he entered Racine's heavily guarded tent.

"Ready to talk now?" Alex demanded, annoyed she was keeping him from Toury, keeping him from sleep, from things that made him happy. He was afraid to take her back in case this was some rebel plan or she wanted to cause harm to Toury.

"Maybe," she singsonged. "If you loosen these chains."

"Do I look stupid?" he asked.

"Do you really want me to answer that?" she fired back with a grin. She was flirting with him, teasing him. She had the audacity to do so, and there was some kind of motive behind it. He would not call her out on it just yet, not until he figured out why.

He sat on the ground in front of her, since the prisoner tent did not have any luxuries set up, only the post and chains to keep her there.

"You think you're funny, huh?" He sighed, showing her his aggravation. "You are keeping me from my home, and my patience is wearing thin. Either talk, or I leave, and they can transport you across the land the slow way. Trust me; I'm probably the only thing keeping them kind. Soldiers, even mine, I'm loath to admit, aren't all exactly gentlemen."

Her eyes bulged at that thought. Good, she was unnerved. He would never leave her with some of these men, nor would they disobey his order if he demanded her safety, but it was an empty threat to get her talking.

"I have to meet my sister."

"Because...?" he prompted.

"Because our parents are alive, they're rebels, and they cannot have her marry you."

"Because they want me dead," he concluded. "I think you'll find your sister feels very differently on the subject." The things that scared him the most were true. Toury's family were rebels, probably hell-bent on destroying him and usurping his kingdom. Where would this leave Toury and him? Before the necromancer incident, she would've been loyal to him, but after what he had done, he couldn't blame her if she sided with her family. The thought of losing her forever to them was too much to bear, so he focused on the conversation at hand.

"So you say. I'm supposed to find out."

"And you think I believe your life is worth so little that you'd put it on the line for a conversation you'd have with your sister just to make sure she will be happy in her marriage? You do indeed think I'm stupid."

"No I don't, actually." She huffed, scooting a bit closer.

He kept an eye on her in case she had stowed away some kind of weapon. He did not trust her.

She sighed, seemingly letting her guard down. "If I tell you the truth, will you kill me anyway?"

"I don't have plans to kill you, but you will be punished for slaughtering my dragon and getting my people killed. And I doubt you'll be safe from the people's revenge. You killed more than a bearn's father, you know. I'm trying to see how many now parentless children I must find homes for."

She peered at the ground—he hoped in shame—thought for a moment, and bit her lip. Although her lips were thinner, it was very much a Toury expression. It made his heart pang thinking of how much he missed her.

"I'm supposed to break Toury out of the castle, set her free, and help her get back to our parents."

Alex laughed at this, which startled her. "Toury can leave the castle whenever she wants. She's not a prisoner, as you inaccurately called her before. Contrary to what you think, she wants to marry me. In fact, if you hadn't tied me up so long, we would've married today."

"Well then, I'll simply observe her and ask her to leave. If she stays, I'll know you're telling the truth."

"Again, this does not add up. You could've deduced all this by visiting her. She has visitors often, you know, friends. You could've even run into her by happenstance in Celestia. She goes there to shop and dine. You either don't think things through or are utterly misinformed about the situation."

"Well, that's the truth. In hindsight, I probably shouldn't have listened to the rebels. They seem to have been misinformed or purposely misconstrued it all to get me to the palace. Maybe you should let me go," she suggested. "I think I might be a pawn in all of this."

He smiled at this, and she smiled back. "What a Toury-type comment."

"Do we look alike?"

"No, not really. Just the eyes. You kind of look like your aunt."

She frowned at this. "Is Toury pretty?"

"I don't think there are enough words to express how beautiful your sister is."

At this, the girl frowned even more. "We don't look alike, but do we act alike?"

"Well, if I say I think stubbornness is a Hematite trait, what do you think?"

She laughed, leaning closer in toward him. He was still wary, but she didn't give off the impression she wanted to cause him harm. In fact, he caught on to what she was up to, but he wanted to see how far she'd take it, and he'd be careful to guard himself. She laughed heartily. He would never classify her as pretty, but when she laughed, those pretty gray eyes lit up. "I'd say she's exactly like all of us."

"In all honesty, I can see a little bit of Toury in you, your mannerisms and expressions, especially around the eyes. Toury's eyes are exceptionally expressive and beautiful." Alex realized too late he had inadvertently praised Racine's eyes as well.

Suddenly, those eyes were much too close to him, and fast breathing skirted across his lips as Racine made the move to kiss him. He froze, unmoving, and somewhere in the back of his mind, he knew this was very wrong, but those damn eyes made him weak. She pressed her lips against his, and for just a moment, he didn't react, thinking of Toury's beautiful eyes, her black shiny hair, her luscious full lips...but it was off, all wrong. The lips were not full, the kiss did nothing for him, and there was no energy flowing from her into him.

He transported and reappeared across the tent, watching Racine lean forward, mouth puckered, awkwardly kissing the air, with her arms stretched in the chains behind her, she had scooted that far to get to him. She realized he was gone and opened her eyes, giving him a feline smile.

What had he done? His stomach turned sour at the thought of kissing someone other than Toury. Well, he didn't kiss her back; she kissed him, but not stopping it was just as bad. He had only ever felt Toury's lips on his, and now...he was tainted. It was those damn eyes and how much he missed Toury. This Racine did nothing for him.

Not even lust.

He schooled his features. "Did you really think me that weak or foolish to allow myself to be taken in by you? What were you planning to do? Seduce me toward your freedom?" He forced himself to laugh at the situation, whereas inside, he was riddled with guilt.

The girl's face reddened, and then he knew she had been trying to seriously seduce him so he would free her. She was nothing like Toury then, no principles.

He said, "You could never be Toury. That was nothing, not even close."

The girl stared at the floor, and he thought she might begin to cry, so he sought to escape. "We head back to the castle immediately." Then he stormed out.

He went straight to Agate and ordered him to select two of his men to help oversee the search for draca blood. The three of them would go to the nearby forts with his directives, and the generals would supply the men to see the search through. Alex and the rest of his men would leave for the castle, and he would travel with his men instead of transporting. He was not in a rush to get back any longer. He had betrayed Toury when really he should be marrying her today had the dragon slayer not interrupted their wedding plans. Now he wasn't sure if it would take place any longer. He could not marry her without telling her what happened. He had hurt her again, betrayed her. She deserved so much better than this and everything he had done to her prior. He had prided himself on the fact he was virtuous and noble—unlike other lords his age who did what they pleased when it came to the fairer sex—but he was a fraud. The best thing he could do for Toury would be to tell her what he had done and to let her go if that was what she wanted. Toury had wanted autonomy—choices from him instead of orders—so he must at least keep that promise. Losing her would be better than lying to her, to himself, and becoming one of those monarchs who was false on the outside and depraved within.

And riding back home where he'd have to face the wrath of Toury was how he would spend his dismal eighteenth birthday.

14
A RUMOR

Alex and his men made great time across the land and were almost back to Celestia by supper the day after his birthday, much to Alex's dismay. Although he missed her more than anything and longed to see her, he did not want to face Toury. From the plucky and sulky tones Racine was giving everyone, he knew she probably would tell Toury the first moment she could. Alex had to tell Toury first, but he hardly knew how he could face her anger and disappointment.

Alex ordered a stop at an inn right outside of Celestia. The men were hungry, the horses tired, but most of all, he was happy to embrace any delay to wrap his mind around what he would say to Toury. He entered the little establishment with David at his heels. There were far too many of them to fit inside, so the prisoner and soldiers would dine outdoors. The innkeeper nervously flustered and then fawned all over him, which annoyed him. He ordered his men's food. Sure, he was cleaning out the inn's stock of food in one go, but he handed over an ample amount of coin to make this the most profitable day the little old inn ever had.

He sat in the corner. David insisted on standing watch, but at least he munched on the bread Alex made him take. They hadn't eaten since the morning and had traveled all day. It was so tedious a journey, the only thing that kept him from transporting home was his fear of facing his engagee. How had he let himself grow so spineless over a woman?

A man entered, drawing David's attention, but he went back to munching bread, realizing the man didn't seem to be a threat. The man greeted another man standing at the bar. They ordered drinks.

"Where you been?" one man asked the other.

"The palace," the second man answered.

This drew in Alex's attention. Maybe he could hear about how the necromancer trials were going or about rebel plans if he continued to eavesdrop.

"What business you got there?"

"Business by the way of Lettie, a cleaning maid. Adorable little thing."

"Speaking of fine beauties, they say that queen-to-be is a looker," the first man said. "You get to see her? My Penelope saw her in town, shopping.

Seems to think her the most beautiful girl in the realm—skin darkened as if kissed by the sun and hair like obsidian, she tells me."

"Naw, didn't get to see her. She's more than a looker from what I hear. Shares the goods as well. When the proxy is away, Cobalt comes out to play," the second responded. They laughed in unison at his last statement.

Alex froze, the potato he had speared with his fork hovering by his mouth. He had not heard that right. No, no, he'd definitely heard that wrong.

"Now, don't go saying things like that. A joke's one thing, but more than one pretty thing has been turned to cinders for lesser crimes. My Penelope said the king and queen proxy were thick as thieves, charmingly in love, and still able to marry. She could no more marry the proxy if she truly is sharing the goods."

"I'm not spinning lies. Lettie works in the palace. She saw them kissing, she did, Lord Cobalt and Lady Tourmaline, Queen Proxy-to-Be."

Alex dropped his fork with a clatter onto his plate, which drew the men's attention. The rumormonger paled and staggered back, almost falling over, while the other turned an odd red color like he forgot how to breathe. Alex wanted to hear the story, and yet he didn't. He sure wasn't going to ask these characters to relate it to him. That much he could not bear to hear.

"David," he said with restrained anger as he glared at the men, who stood there dumbly. He had to hold in the fire that begged to destroy these men. "Explain to these gentlemen what happens to people who spread false rumors about the royal family."

With an angry growl, he stormed outside, his food barely touched, the innkeeper at his heels, begging him to come back, while the innkeeper's lifemate was screaming at the men to leave their establishment. During this chaotic scene, David spoke to them in quiet tones, and from the expressions on their faces, they felt more than threatened.

Alex had to squash the rumor immediately, even if it was somehow true. He could not let his ill father hear about this. The king trusted Toury, forgave her for her unfortunate parents. If he caught wind that her parents were rebels or that Toury was unfaithful...it might just kill him.

Here Alex was, wallowing in his guilt for letting Racine kiss him ever so briefly, when Touring was seen lip-locked with Cobalt. His guilt instantly faded, and anger pulsed through his veins. He wanted to transport there, murder Cobalt, and banish Toury out of the castle—no, from Fyr completely. He'd send her back to Earth so he'd never have to see her again.

"Your Majesty," David pleaded, running to catch up with him. "Please, use caution. I don't think things are as they seem."

His face must have been thunderous, for David flinched as if Alex would actually attack him, and the soldiers shifted uncomfortably, slightly raising their shields to protect themselves from an upcoming wave of fire from him. Racine's eyes were round as saucers. Those gray eyes.

"Don't look at me with those damn eyes!" he shouted at her.

They grew rounder until she closed them and turned away.

"Your Majesty, let us continue the walk," David urged. "Cool yourself down before we arrive."

"Why? I should tear them apart limb by limb and make a bonfire of their parts."

"Because you are a just ruler. You're not a killer. You are a rational sovereign. Cool your temper, and go in there with a plan, maybe an inquisition and then a trial if it proves true?"

Alex scoffed, but one word got through to him: "killer." David was right. He wasn't a killer. Right now, he might be capable of murdering the woman he had loved without a curse making him do it. Regardless of her guilt, he would be racked with regret for the rest of his life if he laid a finger on her again. Deep down, he deserved this, but he still could not quench the jealous rage in his breast. One or both of them were going to pay.

He hesitated, taking in deep, ragged breaths, and told his men they had two minutes. They readied themselves and scarfed down their food, and their idle chitchat resumed. He listened to David, climbed on horseback, and when his men were ready, he rode toward the palace.

When he arrived home, there was no fanfare or even a greeting from anyone. In his guilt and then anger, he had forgotten that he should've sent word ahead to his mother that he was on his way back. As he climbed down and handed his reins to the stable boy, he told David to put the prisoner in the dungeon if there was room. He wondered whether, during their love affair, Toury and Cobalt had the time to actually do their duty and sentence the necromancers. Word had not reached him since he was on the move for a couple days, but if men in taverns had nothing better to do than talk about Toury's promiscuity rather than a mass of executions, most likely, his dungeons were still full.

David refused to go and delegated the duty to a captain. "You are not yourself, Your Majesty. I must stay with you."

"You won't interfere with this," Alex commanded, not that David was following orders at present, apparently.

"I am sworn to protect you at all costs. If I must save you from yourself, then so be it." David stepped in front of him.

Alex had gone from anger to pure unadulterated fury. And there was only one person in the way of him unleashing this rage on the two people who'd created it. David stared him down, his expression firm, and Alex's control over his emotions was slipping. He was worried he'd kill David if he didn't get out of his way, the fire demanding release, wanting to hurt something as much as he hurt right at this moment. He loved her more than anything, and he might've lost her forever. That thought killed him more than any of the jealous ones beating around inside his brain.

15

AMENDS

The morning following the mass execution and banishment, after a night of fitful sleep, Toury knew she had to repair this. There was still no word from Alex, but she had stopped expecting it. This had to be sorted out and quieted down before his return. She sought out Mary first thing, not daring to face Cobalt alone. She could not face the princess the day before, and like the coward she was, she hid in her room alone all night, even eating dinner there.

She stood outside Mary's chambers, pounding on the door. Mary would not let her in.

"Go away!" Mary finally shouted.

"I know why you're so mad."

"*Really?*" Mary screamed at her, but at least she had opened the door. "Wow, you are so clever!" Her eyes were red, puffy, and squinty, showing she had been crying—and most likely drinking—all night.

"You're not at all concerned about your brother's heart, but your own."

"That's, that's..." Mary flustered. "I have no idea what you're talking about."

"Cobalt is number five for the list. It's obvious. Please, just listen to me. I don't like him like that, not at all. And I think Cobalt actually has no genuine feelings for me. I've seen it before. He wants me because he knows he can't have me; it was some type of ridiculous manly conquest."

"So, you've come to apologize? I didn't hear an apology." Mary crossed her arms. She was going to be difficult.

"Mary, I honestly didn't think he could... I'm not secure, okay? I wasn't raised as a princess. I was raised by people who hated and resented me. I finally have a family. Please tell me we are still friends, sisters."

Mary's face softened a bit.

"I don't want your pity. I'm just explaining why I wasn't cautious. I didn't believe his silly flirty nature would result in yesterday's events."

Mary shifted uncomfortably.

"Look, I know you hate me right now, but I sought you out to make peace and to ask for your help. You see, I cannot hide things from Alex.

When he returns, I'll have to tell him what happened. Even though you're angry, I know you don't want to see Cobalt banished or worse."

Mary bit her lip, her expression full of sympathy. "You know he's to blame, Toury. I'm furious with him right now. I will go with you to talk to him. I want to give him a piece of my mind." Mary took up Toury's hand in hers. "He magnetized you."

"He what me?"

"The Cobalt family has stone power. They can elicit positive feelings out of people, cheer them up, relax them—"

"Attract them?" Toury covered her mouth. Oh, she was going to murder him if Alex didn't. Her confusion and desire for him to fill the hole Alex had left behind were Cobalt using his powers to pull her in.

"He does it all the time, which is one of the reasons he is so popular with the ladies."

"Mary, you better come with me. I might murder him without you there to intervene."

Cobalt entered the princess salon like a reprimanded puppy with his tail between his legs. He did not remove his eyes from the ground, and instead of bowing his head, he sank to his knees, showing his inferiority.

"Oh, get up, you fool," Toury barked at him. "Sit over there." She pointed to a settee. She sat on the settee across from him so there was a table between them.

Mary sat by her side. Madge stayed close by, taking a long time pouring the firespice tea.

"Lady Tourmaline, Queen Proxy," he began, dropping the "to-be" to assert she and Alex would still marry. "Let me say sorry for yesterday—"

"No."

He finally met her gaze, his eyes pained. He probably thought she was refusing his apology when she merely didn't want to hear the groveling.

"I don't think there's anything that you could say to make up for it, but that nasty black eye does the job quite well."

"Did you magnetize her?" Mary went straight into interrogation mode.

"I...I don't think—"

"Cobalt, own up to it. I know what you do. I hear the gossip," Mary pressed.

Cobalt blazed up red and avoided Mary's gaze. "What you must think of me," he mumbled, looking at Mary, his eyes sad.

This was interesting. He should have been apologizing to Toury, but he was concerned about Mary's opinion of him.

"What I think is of no importance," Mary said. The discomfiture was apparent on her face. She cared deeply for Cobalt, flaws and all.

"Will you tell him?" Cobalt asked Toury.

"Of course. There is no room for secrets between Alex and me."

Cobalt swallowed hard. "I know I deserve it. To be honest, I don't know what I was thinking. Not that I mean I don't find you—"

"Tread lightly." Toury sipped her tea.

"You know what I mean. I was not thinking anything through. I know I do deserve it, but Alex may banish me. This is the only place I've ever known. I spent more of my childhood here than at my home. Alex is my best friend, and assisting him is my life. I don't know what I will do."

She was beginning to feel bad for him, and yet if Alex was his best friend, why would he try to make a move on her?

"Banish you? He'll probably want to kill you, Cobalt. You tried to steal away the person he loves most in this world," Mary scolded him. "Oh, don't look so pale like a debutante having a fainting fit. I'll help you."

"Mary?" His head whipped up quickly at her comment. His eyes were wide, his mouth agape in bewilderment. "You want to help me? I thought...I thought the way you reacted yesterday... It has bothered me more than anything."

"And why is that?" Toury asked, hiding her smile behind her teacup as she took another sip.

Mary looked at her with eyes full of daggers.

"I've asked myself that a dozen times," he said in almost a whisper, his eyes burning intensely when they beheld Mary. "I don't want to hurt you, Mary, never," he said in earnest, leaning on the edge of his seat, bridging the distance between them despite the table. "And the way you reacted makes me think I've already done that. What I did was stupid and unforgivable, but it didn't warrant that reaction unless..."

Toury wanted to leave. Truly, this conversation should be private. As she moved to stand, Mary shook her head. Of course, she shouldn't leave her alone with Cobalt; who knew what he might try? Why would Mary still want him after all this? Toury hardly knew, but she was no good judge. After all that Alex had done, she still loved him. The heart was a ridiculous, steadfast thing.

"Unless what, Cobalt?" Mary pressed. They were dancing on the edge of a blade; one wrong word or move and things could get Cobalt into more trouble than he could live through.

"Nothing. I'm being an absurd, egotistical fool." Cobalt stood up, agitated, and turned his back on them. "I could never hope to attain... I'm undeserving." He turned to Mary, his expression appalled. "I'm a scoundrel. I'm tainted, impure. I've broken so many hearts, and there's one in this kingdom I never ever want to break."

He stared at Mary, his chest heaving with nervous breaths, and Mary stared at the floor, her face pale. For all her boldness, Mary was silent as a grave. She shot Toury an entreating look, but what kind of help did she want?

"I think that would be for her to decide, Lord Cobalt, don't you?" Toury said.

Mary smiled a little, so Toury knew she guessed her friend's desire correctly.

His eyes went wide when they met Toury's, and then his gaze darted to Mary, who finally peered up at him. "Mary?" his voice begged for her affirmation, and he swallowed hard. Then he went around the table and squatted down in front of her, taking her hands in his. "Is that true?"

Mary pulled her hands out of his and slipped out of his grasp, walking around him. "It won't be that easy, Cobalt. You are a scoundrel. You don't deserve me." She opened the drawer of the end table, pulled out the scroll, and made a motion for Lucy.

The maid went over to the desk in the corner and grabbed a quill and ink.

Cobalt stood, watching Mary, his brow scrunched in confusion. "Mary, I know. God and goddess, I know. Had I ever known you might even think of me in any other way than just a friend or a brother—"

"You would've behaved? Not likely," she scoffed. Toury could see it was a front. Mary was already madly in love with him. Mary took the items from her maid and handed them to the stunned Cobalt. "But you will behave from now on if you want it to come true."

Bemused, Cobalt glanced at the rolled-up scroll in his hands and asked, "For what to come true?"

Mary peered over her shoulder at him in a look that could only be described as coquettish. Cobalt's eyes drank her in as if he was beholding her as a potential lover for the first time.

Mary seated herself on the settee next to Toury again, becoming smugly regal. "What I've seen in the flames. Why else would you think I'd have been sweet on you?"

"Crush on me," Cobalt said, lost. Toury almost wanted to laugh at his shock and confusion. But what rang through his emotions was a regard that was real. Of course, the philanderer probably didn't know what to do with a relationship not built on his lust.

"You never had a clue?" Mary stared at him like he had three heads.

"Well, when you were little, yeah, but when I became interested in girls..." he was squirming and turning red.

"When you were caught having your fun with a chambermaid?" Mary challenged, her brows rising.

Toury was enjoying this way too much. She held back her smile.

Cobalt was lost for words but soon recovered. "That, yes. But even then, you started to ignore me."

"And you paid attention to my cousin."

"That wasn't... I don't think anyone knew what my relationship with Ruby was like."

Toury lost her mirth. "I heard you courted her and then put your name on my list weeks after her disappearance."

Cobalt ran his hand down his face in frustration. "I'm a scoundrel, and I know you both think ill of me, and I deserve that, but Ruby would not be upset by my forsaking her. Ruby had a secret that I caught onto. We decided to pretend to court to lead to a marriage of convenience. Aside from occasional heirs, we would not be in each other's way when it came to the women we wanted to dally with."

Toury had to muse over those words twice until she realized what Cobalt was telling them: Ruby loved women, and Fyr was a pretty backward place that didn't allow that kind of love. Mary was equally shocked and stared at Cobalt, who intensely met her gaze. No one said a word, and the silence became unbearable.

Finally, breaking the staring contest, Cobalt focused on the scroll in his hand, beat up and half torn due to Mary's lack of care. Toury didn't think he could be shocked any more than he was, but the length of the list floored him as he unfurled it. "How many men are on here?" His tone was already full of jealousy.

"I am the princess, Cobalt, so every man who is single?"

His lips pressed together into a firm line of displeasure. "I don't see you as a princess, not like they do. To them, you're just a step up in society, in power, a step closer to the king's ear."

"I know."

The tension in the room was almost palpable, and being on the outside of it was awkward enough for Toury. Despite the idiot's actions of late, she had to commend him for worrying about people using Mary and his jealousy of those who might want to wed her, rather than taking her unintentional compliment. She would never be satisfied with any of these men; none had she asked to sign her suitor list but him.

Cobalt tore his eyes away from Mary, sat down, dipped the quill in the ink, and signed his name on her list. He blew it dry carefully and handed it back to her, his finger brushing hers as he did so. Mary's breath hitched at his underhanded flirtation, most likely because he'd never dared to aspire to flirt with the princess. Cobalt's smirk seemed predatory to Toury, but Mary blushed and suppressed her smile. Awkward silence loomed.

"So, lovebirds," Toury teased. "What do we do about Alex?"

16

A CONFRONTATION

Alex was on a mission; only every single servant seemed to prevent him from finding out where Toury was. He had been gone so long that they were trying to catch him up, not realizing others were doing the same. They were inadvertently bombarding him, and he could hardly listen with the fiery anger pulsating in his ears. But when his mother cut him off with a hug, his rage began to slip away. "Never leave this long again, Alex." She touched his cheek. "Your father requested to see you the moment you returned."

"But I—"

"Immediately. He summoned you. Everything else can wait."

Pushing his anger down even more, he followed his mother to her tower.

His father was lying in his bed and appeared much worse than when Alex had left, if that were possible. He was so thin, his cheeks were chiseled, where they had been rounded by his love of food and drink. His hair was unkempt and sticking to him with sweat, which meant he was unable to regulate his temperature anymore. His skin was papery and gray, lips blue. If there was fire magic still inside him, it was very little. Alex wondered how he lived still.

"Well?" his father asked gruffly, his voice even sounding wounded and faint.

Alex told him of the dragons, the culprits, the rebels, but when asked the identity of the people, he gave him the alias: Cursebreaker. His prisoner was Racine Cursebreaker, and he wondered how long it could stay that way. Still, even now, betrayed by the woman he loved, he protected her. He was proxy, but his father was still king, and his commands could be followed. If he knew the Hematites were back and rebels to boot, he could override Alex and go as far as ordering Toury's execution. The thought to keep her safe and his father thinking well of Toury overrode his rage at her, so Alex also said nothing of what he had heard of Cobalt and Toury.

"Something else is wrong," his father mused.

"Nothing you need to worry about." Alex gave him a smile that was too grand and false.

"You seem mightily worried. What are you hiding?"

Alex wanted to smack himself. In public, he could keep a blank face and hide his emotions but not around those he loved. But what to tell his father?

"It's Toury," he said vaguely and shrugged.

"Women are always work, Son." His father chuckled, but it turned into a deep hacking cough.

His mother gave him a measured look, challenging and scolding him simultaneously. She didn't want him to distress his father. His mother turned her back on him and started placing stones on his father's chest, which alleviated the cough.

Once he caught his breath, he asked, "Well, what is it then?"

Alex decided to give him a truth. Maybe he'd have advice, although it was too late now. Nothing could repair this breach of trust on both their sides. "She hasn't been the same since the necromancer incident. What I did—"

"Was necessary for the good of the kingdom. She will see that in the end. She is no faint miss who would sulk."

"She's not sulking. She's a fraction of her former self. I've been wondering if letting her go would be the best kindness."

"And what happened to your whole tirade of 'there'll be no one else, she is it' nonsense?"

"There won't be." Alex met his mother's gaze, but she looked away.

She knew what had happened.

"Then, you will sort out whatever bothers you every time. You have a duty to your world. If you only want her, you're stuck with her, and she, with you. Marriage is tough. You'll argue, disagree, and go to bed in separate rooms in anger at times, but you have to make it work. Sapphirians must hold onto this sphere. We control the magic, balance it, and keep the dragons in the Firelands. You must make it work, Alex."

"Yes, Father," Alex said. He changed the subject and escaped as soon as it was polite enough.

Stuck with each other, huh? Not if Alex could help it. He, with David hot on his heels, demanded to see Toury. When he ran into the first servant outside the king's quarters, he was told she was with *him*. On hearing she was having a nightcap with Cobalt, in private no less, Alex's rage hit a fever pitch. He knew he should wait, not confront them while in this temper, but he couldn't. He wanted to catch them in the act so there would be no wheedling, no begging, no lies. Any guilt for what he had done vanished on hearing that Toury and his best friend were rumored lovers; only unquenchable wrath and piercing pain filled him now. He had thought distance would heal their relationship, but in the end, it had destroyed it.

He stormed at a brisk pace from the entryway, ignoring David's blabbering. Most likely, it was the voice of reason, but he did not want that right now. Anger at Toury and Cobalt kept him distracted from the self-hatred he felt. Maybe he never had to tell her of his betrayal at all, or maybe he should hurt her like she hurt him.

Impatient, he transported himself right outside the princess salon, David clasping onto his travel cloak at the last second so as to not be left behind. It annoyed him, for he was trying to go alone, but David knew best, much to his dismay. Alex had to admit he was not in the best mindset to face this. He might kill them...literally. David would stop that...hopefully...if he could.

Once there, he held David back so they could eavesdrop. He flattened himself against the wall, straining to hear. He could summon enough patience and suppress his fury to glean enough info to prove they were lovers.

"He'll never allow it," Cobalt said quietly. "After what I did—"

"You are not to talk of that again, ever. But Alex will be a problem." Toury cut him off.

"How do you think I should proceed?" Cobalt asked.

"Speak to my parents." Mary's voice instructed. Mary was there? Was she condoning this? No, no she couldn't be.

"But Alex has to approve."

Approve of what? Surely not of their affair. Or did they idiotically think he'd let Toury go so she could be with him? No. He calmed himself. She wouldn't need any permission from his parents to marry Cobalt, but she would need his to break their engagement. Nothing added up. Had it to do with the trials then? He was confused, but he wouldn't let it distract him.

"Alex will not approve. Let me be the one to talk to him about it. But it must be later, much later, for we do not know what he will do to either of us when he returns," Toury said.

Kill them, that's what he wanted to do. This was it; to walk in while they were talking about him was ideal for shock value. Let them know he was listening to their discussion.

He walked in quickly, Cobalt seeing him first, since Toury was seated on a settee facing away from the door. The blood drained from Cobalt's face. They were across from each other, much farther apart than Alex had imagined for an intimate scene, not next to each other, embracing, as his tortured mind had pictured. Mary was seated next to Toury. His mind was flitting back and forth between blood-thirsty rage and confusion.

Cobalt was up and bowing instantly.

"Sorry to interrupt." Alex's voice cut through the warm room like ice. It spoke of bitterness, regret, and a barely restrained anger.

Toury stood up, quickly spinning around to see him. Her face was not shocked, but full of joy at seeing him, making his heart shatter into a million pieces. The unaffected happiness in her expression could not be feigned. Toury was a horrid liar and could never hide anything, which was one of the things he loved most about her. She was different from the other women at court, real, without a smidgen of superficiality in her. He could see it written across her face and in the depths of those iron-gray eyes. She loved him, missed him, and his return meant everything to her. His resolve to stay angry faltered. He wanted to forget what he had heard, sweep her up in his arms, transport her to their rooms, and kiss her until he forgot his very name.

Then he noted Cobalt and Mary exchange some kind of coded look, snapping him out of the weak state Toury had induced. One way or another, he was about to strip that joy from Toury forever. Their relationship, their future marriage, and potential life together was over.

"Alex!" she exclaimed in breathless surprise.

Not having heard her voice say his name for weeks unfurled something in him. Alex's head spun in utter confusion as to what was going on. He could not lose focus on his need for answers.

Those steel-gray eyes locked onto his, triggering a pull in his gut, a wrenching sensation he wanted to sever. His attraction to her made him weak, and it perpetuated mistake after mistake. He had to end this, marry some idiotic debutant who would give him heirs, whom he didn't have to associate with on a daily basis. He had to be with someone who couldn't squeeze his heart into an incurable pulp like Toury did.

Toury rushed over toward him and hugged him. She smelled and felt so good. The god and goddess combined, she was heaven. Her body, so soft yet firm—just like her personality—pressed against him. The base part of him wanted to do something rash and inappropriate with Toury in front of Cobalt to claim what was his, make her his mistress instead of his queen. For god and goddess' sake, his sister was in the room. He cringed in Toury's arms at the horror of his thoughts. He was going insane over this, no better than an animal marking his territory with lines of piss.

Because he froze in her arms instead of embracing her, Toury pulled away and stared at him, bemused. She touched his cheek, and he allowed it for a moment, relishing in how good it made him feel to have her power flowing into him through her palm, but Cobalt had too, maybe even more. He stepped back, so her hand lost contact with his face, and tried to organize his thoughts into a coherent sentence.

"What's wrong?" she asked, perplexed.

Oh, he would enlighten her, all right.

17
BETRAYER

Alex stiffened in Toury's embrace as if she were a stranger forgetting her place by hugging him, so she pulled away in wonderment, her hand on his cheek, ready for the kiss she had waited ages for. She met his hard, cutting gaze but noted beneath some seething anger, there were exhaustion and pain in his eyes. He stepped away from her.

"What's wrong?" she asked, confused. There was no way yesterday's events could've reached him already.

"What's wrong! What do you think is wrong? I've been through hell, and I come home to this!" He threw his hand up and motioned between Cobalt and her.

So he had heard, but she would make him say it. His voice insinuated she had let Cobalt have more than a kiss. She could not fathom how he could think that of her.

"To what?" Toury asked.

"Your Majesty—" Cobalt began.

"Don't even say a word, Cobalt. I'm still contemplating what to do with you. Another word, and I think I might torch you. I am barely in control of my fire right now," Alex seethed.

Toury had known it would be bad, confronting Alex about this. In her head, though, she imagined telling him quietly and alone what happened, explaining herself. Never did she think he would've known in advance. This was truly problematic because it was obvious he had drawn up his own conclusions before hearing what they had to say for themselves. Her gaze darted between the two men, and Cobalt stared at the floor and went down on his knees in reverence to Alex. Cunning folk went down on bended knee, not nobles. His deference was a desperate begging of forgiveness.

"I put my life in your hands, Your Majesty."

Alex's eyes shot to her in challenge, expecting her deference and pleading or maybe for her to defend Cobalt. She did not balk, and she did not waver. She did not go down on her knees in submission like Cobalt. Although Alex's anger was a force to reckon with, she wouldn't grovel like Cobalt nor show such guilt. Yes, she had done wrong, but Alex and Cobalt were complicit in her mistake: the one forsaking her, the latter for taking advantage of her. She raised her brows in challenge, and Alex growled like an animal. She wondered what had happened to him and whether the dragons had an effect on his behavior.

"To what?" Toury repeated, crossing her arms. It had been a friendly nightcap, simply that. Mary and the servants were there with them. Mary stood behind Cobalt, looking at all of them anxiously, questioning whom to protect first from Alex's fiery wrath.

"Like you don't know," he scoffed.

Having had enough of this, Toury wanted to get him alone to talk. She met his gaze, and all she saw was pain. It took her breath away to know that he loved her so much that the very thought of her with someone else could hurt him so badly.

"Alex," she breathed and went to touch his face again.

He vanished in a ball of fire before she could graze his cheek. She dropped her hand with a sigh.

Then she started for the doorway but was stopped by Cobalt's voice: "Don't. He's angry. He's dangerous when he's angry. He can burn you to cinders with that temper, literally. Trust me. Let him blow off steam first."

Toury thought it over for a moment and then shook her head. "No. He doesn't get to hide from me."

"Toury, Cobalt's right," Mary interjected. "He'll hurt you, and then he'll be racked with guilt from it. We've seen that happen before. Please, Toury."

"He won't hurt me," she said with conviction. "He will hear me out."

"What will you say?" Cobalt asked, fleetingly meeting her gaze.

"The truth." Then she left the room, Madge tailing her.

With a deep breath, she opened the door to their quarters to find Alex, still in his dirty travel clothing, slouched in his armchair, drinking straight firewhiskey from the looks of it. She dismissed Madge, hoping Alex would not make her regret that. Deep down, she believed he would not hurt her, but if she provoked him—and she probably would—she might just have to remind him of his promise.

"We need to talk," she began after he said nothing and didn't acknowledge her.

Alex laughed sardonically and buried his face in his hands, rubbing his eyes roughly.

"What happened to you out there, Alex?" she asked softly as she crept closer to him. She weaved her hands in his hair, and he went rigid. She let her fingers dance across his scalp, and he shuddered, flinging his head back into her hands. His eyes were closed, head tipped back, and she leaned over to kiss those lips she had longed to for weeks now.

His hand shot up and curled into her hair, pulling her closer. She sighed, hoping all would be well, and she leaned around, resting on the arm of the chair, so they were side by side rather than kissing upside-down, but an edge and urgency came through his lips until it was almost vicious, and he bit her lip hard enough to cause her pain. She retracted with a gasp.

Alex stood up and spun around, his eyes alive with fire. Her flesh heated under his gaze, and she wondered if he would actually burn her. She wondered if she should have heeded Cobalt and Mary's warning. But he wouldn't break his promise, of that she was sure, not after what he had done before.

"What happened to you here, Toury?" he asked with spite.

"I'm sure you've been appraised with how the trials went and *other things*, since you're so bitter. Why did you vanish without hearing what I had to say?"

Alex's anger faltered a little, and he grimaced. "I didn't want to hear you defend him."

"Defend him? He's a scoundrel." Then she reached out to touch him, but he cringed, causing her hand to stop and hover awkwardly in the air. "You could at least let me explain."

"Explain what, Toury? That you were unfaithful to me with my best friend while I was gone a measly three weeks? Wow, how steadfast your love is, Toury. The only consolation I have is that they can test your virtue, and when they realize it's gone, we won't be able to marry."

"What? I don't know what you think you've heard or—"

"I heard 'When the proxy is away, Cobalt comes out to play,'" he said in a sick, singsong voice. "The kingdom mocks me and now calls you a whore."

Toury's fury built up at the accusation, and she slapped Alex across the face. The slap took him by surprise, sending him reeling. Bad move. He knocked over the chair that had been between them, barreling toward her. Toury backed up to get away from him until she was against the wall. His fire-hot hands gripped her upper arms. He glowered at her, face turning red, looking very much like his father. Toury wrenched her arms away and pushed him to create distance between them, knowing very well what happens when a red-faced Sapphirian lets loose his anger: fireballs.

"How dare you!" she screeched.

Alex froze, and his face shifted expressions instantly. He was hurt, but she didn't know what caused his mood swing. He backed up and turned away from her. She withdrew her hands from her throat, realizing she'd inadvertently gone to protect it, her subconscious remembering when he'd strangled her.

"Your doctors or healers—whatever you call them—will find out I'm still a virgin, *Your Majesty*. He kissed me, Alex, and I won't lie to you. I kissed him back, but it meant nothing. I was so lonely, depressed, and lost. The trials had me stressed out, and you barely even had written me—"

"You are blaming me for what you did?" Alex turned, aghast.

"I am responsible for my actions, but before you do something stupid like banish me or execute me, you are not wholly free of blame."

His eyes narrowed.

"You broke me, Alex, in more ways than one. You Sapphirians uprooted my life, forcing me here from Earth. You pushed and pushed and tricked me into an engagement. You chose your kingdom over me. You tried to kill me. You broke me, Alex, and then you left me. You barely wrote to me. I was completely alone, out of my depth, and I have no idea who I am anymore or who I want to be. You did this to me. Yes, I was weak, and I kissed Cobalt back, not because I like him, but because I was starved for kindness, attention, and a need to drive the loneliness away."

"If you don't have feelings for him, why did I interrupt a pretty cozy nightcap?" he countered.

"Cozy is not an apt description at all! It was awkward, but it had to be done. I had to tell him I was going to tell you about it, among other things. And Mary was there with us."

Alex appeared confused, as if he hadn't remembered his sister had been there. "What other things?" he demanded.

This was good. He was talking. Although she did not really want to stick Mary and Cobalt in it, she told herself she would hide nothing from him."I had Mary there with me for two reasons: security and because I think there's something between them."

"Mary and Cobalt?" Alex exploded.

"That is a whole other issue, and nothing warranted that reaction. I think she cares for him, and he might for her, but it doesn't matter. I want to talk about us."

"There is no more us." He said it with so much finality and defeat that she believed him.

Her heart lurched in worry. Would he throw away everything they had because of one weak moment? "I kissed someone. You wrapped your hands around my throat and tried to end my life. You've done much worse."

"I know that! But I can't get the picture of you two together out of my head."

"I can't forget your black eyes and your hands on me."

"Then it should be over, shouldn't it?" he said with apathy. "Months later, you cannot forgive me for what I did while cursed. I don't think I can forget this either."

Her hands began to tremble, and she recognized her faulty temper was raising up the light magic. She squeezed her fists shut, but Alex had noticed.

He backed away and grabbed his drink off the table, scrutinizing her. "Someone else kissed me too," he said quietly and downed the rest of his drink.

The news had more impact on her than the slap had had on him. Light magic burst from her hands, and Alex cast a ring of protective fire in time. He looked at her, shocked, but he wasn't angry, which was worse. He should lock her up for an attack on the king proxy, but the guilt on his face was worse.

Silence filled the room.

"Who?" she finally ventured.

"You don't want to know."

"I told you what happened. You must tell me."

Alex laughed uncomfortably and watched the fire. "Might as well tell you, end our engagement for good. I found the dragon slayer and held her prisoner. She thought she'd seduce me to escape." He stopped for a moment and glanced at Toury.

"And you let her?" Toury's heart sank.

"No, it didn't go that far. I knew what she was up to, and I let her kiss me, but I didn't kiss her back. I transported away from her."

"You let her kiss you?"

He crossed to her and took up her chin, his gaze softening. She thought for a moment he would kiss her. Toury had no idea how to feel or react if he tried. She had gone numb. "Something made me, Toury. I missed you so much, longed for you so much. Then there she was with the same damn gray eyes that make me weak. You make me weak, and I hate that."

"What are you talking about?"

"I let the dragon slayer kiss me, Toury, your sister, Racine. She's in the dungeons if you want to see her for yourself," Alex rambled.

"I don't have a sister."

"Apparently, you do, and she and Cobalt and the damn curse have ruined us."

It took Toury a moment to process what Alex had just said. Instead of demanding to see this unknown long-lost sister or to argue that their relationship wasn't over, she walked away and went into her bedchamber, closing the door. She could not react. Toury couldn't look at him.

"Toury?" Alex asked through the door. His voice was no longer angry but full of sorrow.

She understood now that his rage at her was not even about her. He was angry at her, yes, and he was angry at himself, but he was angrier at the fact they were beyond making this work. This she assumed because she was feeling the same. She rested against the door, knowing she could not let him in. For if he begged and pleaded, she'd forgive him, and he'd forgive her, but the wedges between them would always exist. Alex was right. Love was a weakness. He made her weak, and she hated that too.

She slipped down the door, sitting in a ball on the ground, and she fell to pieces.

Alex didn't bother to knock, come into her room, or try to soothe her. She had hated his dominance at times, but now she was wishing he would just barge in and tell her it wasn't over. The thought was hollow because she could see no way to come back from all of this.

Alex must've drawn the same conclusion. He never came.

18

A PHRASE

Alex woke up early; no, if he was honest, he hardly slept enough to even be able to say he woke. He also wanted to avoid Toury. Fortunately, that would be easy as he had a lot of work to do. He'd be overwhelmed if that cad Cobalt and Toury had not finished the trials. At least he didn't have to deal with an abundance of necromancers, but what was he going to do about the draca slayer? Punishing her would hurt Toury, and yet he couldn't set Racine free.

He was up so early, even the scribes and clerks weren't awaiting him in his father's—well, now his—study. He got some parchment out to write his list of decrees —laws he was going to overturn, things needing change. They had to come gradually. Changing the world of his ancestors' creation overnight would cause chaos. He had to do simple things, start with innocuous changes. Anything drastic might upset his father, who deserved a calm end.

As soon as the ink dried, the scribes showed up, along with the startled clerks, who raced around to bring him grievances, his correspondence, or disputes he had to settle or solve. It was work, his duty, but he welcomed the distraction, for it drove his guilt and anger from his mind. Toury wouldn't budge though; she was always in his thoughts, every moment of every day. And she always would be. He had to let her go, dislodge her from his heart, but he would never forget her. Like a draca only ever finds one partner, he had found his, and he had messed it up majorly—more than once—and now so had she. He didn't deserve to be forgiven for everything he put her through. And part of him, although he deserved it, could not forgive what she had done. When he closed his eyes, all he could see was Cobalt and her, tangled in each other's arms and lips. He would set her free, and he would wallow in regret for the rest of his days. It was what he deserved. Mary's line would rule after him. Ugh, he'd have to let her marry Cobalt so they'd have an heir to secure the throne. For he planned not to marry now, not ever, if it wasn't Toury. But the idea of Cobalt, the cad, marrying his sister rankled him. He could not sanction it. He pondered, in the lulls between signing documents that settled disputes and responding to grievances, on what would become of his kingdom.

His correspondence did not improve his mood. Agate reported that they still had not found the other Hematites, and only a fraction of the amount of dragon's blood had been found and seized. Agate believed the rebels had the blood, were in hiding, and planning to use it at some point. But the when and where weren't known to anyone. The only good news was, after all the Hollyhaven survivors were accounted for, they totaled almost seven hundred people. This meant three hundred had died, a lot but not as many as they had feared. That was another problem. Seven hundred people needed shelter and work. A good two hundred, Agate reported, were taken in by friends or relatives. Another hundred of them would fit in the Citrine estate—the orphans and perhaps those too feeble for hard labor, who could care for them. That left four hundred displaced people. He wished he and Toury were talking. She would have a million practical, kindhearted ideas.

His thoughts were disrupted by the door bursting open.

"Alex! What is this 'no one is permitted' nonsense." Mary tapped her foot, her arms crossed in annoyance.

"I'm busy, Mary, as you can well see. You didn't hurt my guards, did you?" Distracted, he signed a document with a flourish. It was a document that seized the Citrines' money and property, since they all died in the snuffing process, and allocated the property to be turned into a refugee orphanage. He handed it to a steward. He wasn't doing it to win over Toury; it was the right thing to do. Was it wrong he hoped she'd notice, though?

"Of course not. They're all terrified of me, so words work. Who knows why," she scoffed. "You can't solve all the kingdom's problems in a day, Brother. More importantly, you may be able to ignore your future bride, but you cannot ignore your sister."

Alex's jaw clenched. "What do you want, Mary?"

"To talk."

Alex sighed and flippantly tossed his hand in the air to dismiss his servants. All left, save their bodyguards.

"Why is Toury moving all her things into my quarters?"

Alex's stomach dropped, but he tried to mask his shock. She was moving out, but what could he expect? Part of him was relieved they wouldn't have to constantly pretend not to see each other's suffering. He stared at a document in front of him, although he couldn't focus on what it said, and shrugged. "Ask her. There are plenty of rooms in this place for her to live in, so I have no idea why she chose yours."

Of course, Mary could not be thwarted. "I meant, why isn't she living with you? Did you break it off over this Cobalt nonsense? He's an idiot when it comes to women, so he's more at fault than her. You know he magnetized her, right?"

Alex flinched at the accusation and leaned back in his chair, gazing at his sister. She would never lie about this. Cobalt could be arrested, tried for using his powers against a royal-to-be. Mary knew this. She was sacrificing Cobalt to defend Toury, and there was only one reason she would do that. She believed Toury was innocent. Mary should've warned her about Cobalt's powers; hell, Alex should've before he'd left. Great, more wrongdoings to pile on his already guilt-ridden shoulders.

He deflected onto Mary. "And now you want to marry that kind of man."

"I plan on making his life hell until he makes amends for all this."

"I will not let you marry him."

"You have no say. Just like father had no say about Toury."

"Toury is a moot point. We're not getting married, and I'm not accepting Cobalt as a brother. I could put him on trial," he challenged her. "It would restore the people's opinion of Toury. Would you like that, Mary? It might, of course, turn them against any marriage between you two."

Mary gave him a glare, but she did not appear at all worried. "Alex, did you ever wonder why I was sweet on him as a girl, why I fell in love with him despite his faults? His behavior has hurt me again and again, but it's like I never had a choice. From my earliest days, I saw him in the flames. I saw my future with him so many times, it's irrefutable to deny it. You say you won't let me, but I've seen it. It will happen."

Just like Toury and him; love is pain.

Alex sank back in his chair with a sigh, appraising his sister. She sat on the edge of his desk and played with a paperweight.

"You always had the best sight in the family," he allowed.

He remembered her always playing her silly little game of trying to find their mates in the flames when they were kids. He knew she had been sweet on Cobalt when they were kids. When he was fifteen, Cobalt was caught in a compromising situation with a maid, and the young spiteful Mary had given up on him. Since then, she never seemed to care. He wondered how she could handle the idea of him with other women repeatedly. How could she forgive such cavalier behavior?

"And you will marry Toury."

His fist clenched. He didn't want to ask, but he had to know. "You saw this?"

"I don't need flames to know what you'll do. You love her, and she loves you. I saw you two in that dress shop the day you met. It was instant. Anything, no matter how bad, can be overcome." At that moment, it felt far from the truth. How could it be overcome? He wished he had magic to erase the past.

"How?" Alex dropped his strong façade. He truly needed help with this. "I can't stop picturing him and her..."

Mary sighed. "It has a heavy weight on your soul. As you had been drowning in your curse, I have been drowning in heartbreak and jealousy."

"I'm not jealous!" As soon as it came out of his mouth, he realized he sounded very much so. And damn the god and goddess, he was. To even think anyone had a fraction of Toury's affection—whether magic was abused in gaining it or not—drove him mad with unadulterated envy and possessiveness.

Mary raised her eyebrows and smirked.

"Say what you will, Mary. There'll be no wedding."

That wiped the smirk right off her face.

"There *will* be a wedding," a matronly tone said from the doorway. His mother had entered.

Great, Alex should've known they would gang up on him. "You cannot make us marry."

"Alex, Cobalt only received a pardon from me because he owned up to what he had done and explained himself like a proper gentleman. He just left to hide out in his father's estate and already publicly announced what he has done. Why must you punish Toury? You should've seen how much she missed you. She was growing quite pathetic with you not corresponding much," his mother chided.

So Cobalt fled. At least he did the right thing and cleared Toury's image. But he did have to be punished. Alex didn't want to hurt his former friend. He also didn't want to appear weak to his people. Too much punishment, he'd be a ridiculous, jealous lover. Too little, and the people might think they could have their way with noblewomen and get away with it.

Alex ran his hand down his face in frustration. He had called her a whore. He was an imbecile. Things between Toury and him had to be mended. Without her, he could hardly function, and he couldn't take much more of this. His mother was adding onto his guilt, compiling it to an overwhelming agony. "With all due respect, Mother, Mary, this is none of your business. I want you to cancel the wedding, halt all plans. Don't make me order you as king."

His mother laughed lightly, finding his threat cute rather than offensive. "I will withhold the invitations...for now. I have different preparations in mind, but, Alex, all will work itself out."

Part of him hoped she was right, but he had no idea how to heal this rupture between Toury and himself.

His mother sighed. "As you know, Toury's birthday is in five months, and I'm planning a surprise party for her in style. Well, it's for you too, since you were dealing with draca and missed yours. That is what I came for. She's been so sad for so long that I want to see her happy. I know she'd object, so it must be secret. I think it would lift her spirits to have all her friends here. And it would solidify the court, now that its numbers have dwindled due to the trials. It would be a unifying party. And it would allow us to put off the wedding without too many questions."

The last thing he wanted to do was be on public display with Toury. They'd have to fake being the happy couple the entire night, but five months was a long time. Surely, their relationship would have some kind of resolution by then. The idea of that resolution being a permanent breakup made his stomach flop. Stress was building, and it had nothing to do with the problems in his kingdom.

He reluctantly agreed to get Toury down to the dinner party on the day and play along as if it were an engagement announcement party for Mary and that he would publicly forgive Cobalt, for there'd be no way to hide the preparations for one of his mother's parties. Apparently, his mother was telling him when and who to forgive as well. The life of a king; it never again would be his own; only his mother was apparently ruling—over his life.

When his mother headed toward the door, he saw Mary sneakily put a quill down and follow their mother. Mary stopped in the doorway. "Alex, she's living with me because she fears loneliness. She can't go to the guest wing because no one is there. She was so melancholy while you were gone. I had hoped she'd be herself again but she's..." Mary couldn't find the words, but Alex finished the thought for her: he had ruined her, broken her, and he didn't know how to fix her. Distance had not worked.

Mary gave him a sympathetic look and left. He picked up his quill that Mary had tossed aside so the ink wouldn't stain his documents. He noticed a piece of parchment with Mary's handwriting on it. He grabbed it, anticipating a joke or rude insult toward him in her silly way, but he stared down at a short phrase: *In the flames, I've seen ALL your children.*

His instincts wanted him to burn the evidence, but he couldn't. Mary would never lie to him, not about something like this. His heart began to race with the implications. He wanted it to be true. He knew visions changed. His changed so many times. Once, he had seen himself marry Toury on his birthday, and that obviously didn't happen. He'd also had a vision of her leaving to go back to Earth. He hoped beyond all other hopes that she didn't leave the realm. Even seeing her happy with someone else would be better than never seeing her again.

Children. He could not help but smile. He folded the slip of paper and slipped it into his desk as his men returned. Children. His line could go on and, more importantly, with the woman he loved. He let the thought spark some hope in his breast. He would figure it out. He would figure out what Toury needed, and just maybe he could win her back. At least he had some time to sort things out before this party. He only had to repair a shattered relationship and forgive a scoundrel. Rebels with draca blood seemed an easier problem to solve at the moment.

19
SISTERS

Toury wanted to avoid Alex, so she moved in with Mary. She stopped having her friends over because they were already seeing through her feigned cheerful demeanor since Toury was terrible at hiding her emotions. Alex had hurt her badly, Cobalt had destroyed her life, and she couldn't talk to her friends about it, not even Mary. Oh, the princess had tried to get Toury talking, but Toury was utterly numb. The fact someone tried to kiss Alex—and that this someone was her long-lost sister—was so distressing that it sucked up her every thought. A month had passed since Alex's return, and she hadn't dared to go see her imprisoned sister, but if she wanted to get over this and have any closure or to end her bitter disappointment and smidgen of jealousy, she would have to meet the issue itself head on. Toury was tired of feeling this way, suffering in silence. She would conquer it. She would get over it.

Toury went down to the dungeons, demanding to see the prisoner. The cells were almost empty now that the necromancers were gone. It was eerily quiet.

She approached the cell, and in the dim light, she saw a disheveled girl with mousy brown hair and a gangly thin figure. She stared at Racine as she approached the bars. That's when she recognized a bit of herself in her face. The eyes were exactly as Alex described them, but her nose was a bit bigger, cheeks sallower, and she wasn't as tan as Toury. There was a kind of resemblance in their lips, but Racine's were thinner—the lips that had kissed Alex's.

"My sister, the princess." Racine mocked her with a ridiculous over-the-top bow.

Toury wanted to correct her with the right title, but then again, she had been told her sister was a rebel and dragon slayer. It would be more prudent to not give away the king's condition if the girl was ignorant of it. She could not see her as a sister, could not quite believe it.

"My sister, the prisoner. You know, killing dragons is punishable by death."

The girl's eyes went wide for a moment, and then she tried to mask the weakness. She was surprised. Perhaps she'd thought Toury would jump for joy at meeting her and try to save her. Toury wasn't sure if she would yet, but she knew Alex wouldn't hurt her sister without warning her; if they had been on good terms, they would have decided what to do with her together.

"The prince won't kill the sister of his engagee, not when he can set me up as his mistress. We kissed, you know. His lips are utterly soft...and warm, but you knew that already didn't you?"

Toury kept her features still and did not even flinch, although the comment made her want to cry inside and lash out with white light. She took in a deep breath and called her sister's bluff. "The prince will not set you up as his mistress; that's far from his plans for you, and you know it. And as for your life, you ought to be kissing my boots and begging me for help. He's left it up to me to decide whether you live or die." This wasn't true, because she and Alex hadn't spoken about it at all.

Her sister's face contorted in rage, and she spat at Toury's feet. Her missile didn't reach her boots.

"Attractive," Toury said in the most arrogant tone she could muster in order to belittle her sister. "How the prince thought of me while you tried to kiss him is astounding. Oh yes, he told me all about your pathetic attempt to seduce him."

"Go away!" her sister shouted.

"You forget I make the orders. If I ask this guard to flog you, he will."

The guard turned and grabbed the whip and awaited orders. Racine eyed him warily.

"Or my bodyguard?"

Madge stepped forward, showing her saber.

"What do you want from me?" Racine asked, suddenly dropping her defiant mask.

"I hardly know, but when one was completely abandoned by her family, she ought to meet them when they come her way. I couldn't let them kill you without meeting you, but now I regret it. I thought I'd feel something, anything. But you're a stranger to me and a rude one at that."

"Don't try to guilt-trip me. I was abandoned too, you know. On Lyft, you know, the air sphere? Earth is paradise compared to there. Our deadbeat parents scooped me up two years ago. You know they kept him, though, the prized son," she said with derision.

"I have a brother? Our parents are alive?"

The girl's eyes darted around, realizing she revealed too much. Toury knew she would not be forthcoming with much more. "Much good it will do you. You're so far up the Sapphirians' asses, Mother and Father ought to leave you here to rot. Sapphirians are nothing but tyrants."

"They don't sound like the type of people I'd want to associate with, if they think that. And you know nothing. Alex is nothing like his father."

"You're the one who knows nothing."

"And yet I've heard it all," Toury shot back. "Our mother ran away with our father, breaking her engagement with the king's brother. Father supposedly cursed the Sapphirians."

"Dad didn't curse them, you nitwit. The king wanted him dead merely for his brother's wounded pride. Pathetic, all of them."

"'Supposedly' indicates I don't believe the rumors, so I'd avoid labeling me as the nitwit here. And you're one to chide me about rumors. You don't even know the Sapphirians. You only know what you've been told. I've lived with them for months. You're wrong about them all. Anyway, I tire of this conversation."

"Me too," her sister said.

Then Toury turned to leave.

"Mom and Dad are rebels, you know. How does your darling prince feel about that?"

Toury kept walking, not giving her sister the pleasure of seeing her shock and horror. What would Alex do? Dissolve the engagement? Capture and kill her family? As if Alex and Toury didn't have enough problems, they now had this thrown on top of it.

"Give Alex a kiss for me!" her sister called after her.

Toury wanted to lash out, but part of it was from her inability to give Alex a kiss, and her sister had deduced that. Toury refrained and left the dungeons, vowing not to see the girl again. Never had she met a girl so wholly unlike herself. Unable to process what was going on in her mind, Toury retreated to her bedroom at Mary's. She just couldn't face anyone with so many conflicting emotions. Lately, pain had won out. But today, Toury was proud of herself. By standing up to her sister, she got a boost of confidence. It was a simple fight, a battle of wits and snide remarks, and she held her own. Strange how after this confrontation, she felt better than she had in months, stronger, just as she had when she'd schooled the noblemen who'd challenged her.

She joined Mary in her sitting room. They sat in mutual silence, each enjoying the presence of each other's company, Mary embroidering and Toury pretending to read while she brooded over these developments.

The peaceful afternoon was disrupted. A knock at the door made her jump. So much for her being strong. She nodded to Madge, who opened the door. Alex stood there with a lost expression, his hands nervously fidgeting with his medallion. Toury glanced over to Mary, who tried to hide a smile. Mary concentrated on her embroidery, feigning disinterest. Toury was on her own to face him then.

"Lady Tourmaline." Alex bowed. Why was he being so formal and stiff and odd? "I was wondering if you would join me for dinner this evening?"

Weird. What did he want? "Join you?" Toury repeated stupidly, but she hadn't a clue what he meant, because they all dined together most of the time in the large dining hall.

It was awkward, to say the least, sitting next to Alex but not saying anything to each other, even when the queen tried to force them into conversation. In fact, the only thing she had said to him was to ask him to pass the salt and to thank him for it. He'd responded with a "welcome." He had practically ignored her for a month—except for the indiscernible stares he'd given her that were a cross between confusion and hurt. How pathetic they had become. Yet he was here talking to her in full sentences. Why?

"Yes," he said, his intense and anxious eyes boring into her. "I would very much like it if you and I could dine together tonight, alone."

Mary hid a laugh in a cough. Toury shot her a dirty look over her shoulder before turning back to Alex. He was asking her out. And the thought of being alone with him was equally terrifying and exciting. She had to be strong, not give in to whatever demands he was most likely going to throw her way. But here he humbly stood, a king asking her on a date and not commanding.

"Okay," Toury said to break the silence that had grown too long, making Alex wary. "Sure."

Alex's anxious expression was gone in a flash, replaced with a genuine smile. "Shall we say, at the sixth hour past noon? Meet me in our—I mean—my quarters?"

Toury didn't trust herself to say any more but gave him a small smile and a nod. She was going on a date, or what sounded like one, with her sort-of ex. This was more than weird.

"Great. See you then." Alex gave a stiff bow and left the doorway, Madge closing it behind him.

"That was interesting." Mary laughed.

Toury threw a pillow at her. Toury was in no laughing mood, her mind puzzling Alex's intentions out.

"You look so confused," Mary said. Again, there was mirth in her voice. She was enjoying this, much to Toury's expense.

"You care to explain what that was?" Toury challenged, pointing to the doorway.

"Don't look at me!" Mary protested. "You think I understand how my brother's mind works?"

"I just want to know what to expect, what he wants."

Mary shrugged. "You'll have to meet him later to find out, now won't you?"

"You're thoroughly enjoying this, aren't you?"

Mary sighed, her face serious for once. "It sounds like he wants to see you, talk to you. What do you have to lose when things are as bad as they have been these past weeks?"

Toury disagreed with her; she had a lot to lose. Her heart, herself, him forever—there were many things she could lose.

"Just give him a chance," Mary said in a chiding voice, making Toury feel immature. The fifteen-year-old wild child lecturing her about second chances was laughable.

"I will if you give no drinking a chance," Toury shot back. It was a low blow, but Mary was out of control, and Toury was spiteful that Mary was being condescending and laughing at her distress.

Mary's jaw set and her eyes grew colder than Toury had ever seen. Okay, maybe moving in with her was a bad idea. They had become like sisters, which was great, but sisters fight and torture each other.

"Not you too," Mary scoffed, getting up and walking away. "Mother and Lucy are both relentless enough. There's no need for you to join in."

"I worry about you."

"I'll be fine." Mary stared out the window. "The flames say so, but..." She turned with a triumphant smile. "If you give Alex a real chance, I'll quit drinking."

"Is that what you think this is? Alex asking for a second chance?" Her heart raced at the idea.

Mary shrugged. "Think about it. And if it's not, you will try to make it one as long as I'm good on my word." Forcing Toury to give Alex a chance, Mary picked up the firewhiskey bottle and handed it to Lucy. "And the one in my room, Lucy." Her maid followed her orders and left with the bottles.

Toury didn't like being told what to do, but Mary wanting them back together so much so that she was finally going to stop overindulging made her realize how important it was for them to become real sisters. She would hear Alex out tonight, whatever it might be. She longed for it to be a second chance, while fearing he was telling her he'd announce the end of their engagement.

20

A DATE

Alex was nervous. He paced the length of his sitting room for twenty minutes, David watching him warily. The servant most likely thought him mad. David would never understand what a hassle women were, how artfully one had to work to make them happy, but Alex wouldn't trade it in for what his servant would have to face in a land that chastised and made homoromantic relationships illegal. It was another law of the land he viewed as outdated. Another decree in the growing list of changes he wanted to make. That could take David away from him, though. Bodyguards were married to their jobs, not other people.

"Is she worth all this torture?" David asked.

Alex stopped walking and glared at his servant. How could he suggest she might not be? "Of course, she's worth it. Don't you dare suggest otherwise, David."

The man blushed. "Forgive me."

"You don't like her?"

"It's not that."

"You're jealous then?" Alex challenged.

Flabbergasted and red as a beet, David struggled to make a sentence but finally got out, "I don't like what she does to you, Your Majesty. It's hard to watch."

"I love you like a brother, David, so I can understand your concern, but I'm not..." Alex didn't know how to break a man's heart, although apparently, he did very well breaking a woman's. "She is the one, David. The only one I'll ever love."

David nodded, meeting Alex's gaze. David wasn't as hurt as Alex expected. Perhaps he always knew Alex would never look at him or any man that way. "Then you've got to win her over."

"Hence the pacing," Alex ground out. "Things are so messed up that I haven't a clue what to do."

A knock at the door froze him mid-step, and he straightened himself as David opened the door and let in Toury and Madge. Toury was beautiful, although dressed in a simple day dress she often wore around the castle. She thought they were staying here, but he couldn't tell her to change. No, there would be no commands from him when it came to her.

"Shall we?" He offered her his arm, and she surveyed the room, confused at not seeing a dinner spread out for them. He wanted to see the look of surprise on her face, so he didn't enlighten her. "David, Madge," he prompted.

David put his hand on Alex's shoulder, and Madge, catching on, did the same to Toury. He transported them to an empty dining room of a restaurant.

"Your Majesty." The owner went down on his knee as all cunning folk were expected to do. Another pointless law. Showing respect through a bow was enough. Why rub it in their faces that he was their better in powers? "The restaurant is yours for the evening, as requested."

Alex turned to Toury, who was still surprised as she took in where they'd arrived. The owner led them to a table and went into the back.

"You requested an entire restaurant?" Toury asked quietly in disbelief.

"It's safer, easier, more private. Would you want to be gawked at by everyone while we try to eat, overheard while we try to talk?" Alex asked her.

The servants loomed over them.

"You two, sit down, relax. No one is here but the chef and owner. I've got a dozen guards incognito outside. Please, enjoy a meal," he directed to Madge and David.

They awkwardly looked at each other and then sat down at a table that was close enough to rush to their aid, but far away enough to allow Alex and Toury some privacy.

"Is there a menu?" Toury asked, confused.

Alex smiled. "We're getting small portions of everything. I've never been here, but other nobles have said it's the best restaurant in all of Fyr." It certainly was the most expensive. "I've always been curious about foreign cuisine."

"Foreign cuisine? There are no countries on this sphere, just Fyr. What is this place?"

"Yes, but this restaurant specializes in foods from another sphere. It's called Eorthe, the old language for the Earth sphere."

Toury's confused state shifted into one of utter happiness. "I would kill for a slice of pizza."

"Good thing you won't have to take someone's life to get it," he teased.

"Alex," she took up his hand and squeezed it. "This is perfect."

Then they were smiling, staring at each other as if nothing had ever been wrong between them. The owner entered with the beverage selection, disrupting that blissful moment, and things shifted into an awkward yet pleasant conversation. He just had to get through this night without messing up.

After dinner, Alex transported them to the orchard, where Duric waited with a basket of dracaberries and wine as planned. He had kept things simple at dinner. He asked her about Earth, all the foods, and shifted subjects away from politics, necromancers, her sister, their relationship—anything that was a touchy subject for them. Toury seemed to want to talk things out, but he wanted to have one good night without the serious concerns pressing on them.

She chatted with little Duric Forager as he led them through a clearing by lanternlight to where the boy had put a blanket down near a pile of wood. He put the basket down, gave them a bow, and walked off, running at the last minute, like all boys who prefer speed to propriety often do.

"What is this, Alex?" Toury toed the blanket with her shoe.

Thank goodness she couldn't see his blush in the darkness. He lit the wood on fire, giving them some more light than just the star strewn-sky. "It's called a date on Earth, is it not?"

"Yes," Toury said quietly. She sat down, though, which meant he hadn't taken this too far. "Although, I would've been wary of boys, blankets, and star-filled skies on Earth."

"And you would also kill someone for that delicacy called pizza, so I should be the one who is wary." He heard David and Madge murmuring nearby, again keeping a discrete distance. "I can see why, though. So simple yet so delicious." He sat down next to her.

"What was your favorite?" she asked.

"I had never tried Earth food before. It was nice, similar to food here yet different. Here, things are a bit blander. Earth plays with flavors. I liked the food from your Asia. What he called Chinese and Indian."

"It's nice to know it's there. In case I get nostalgic."

"Do you miss Earth?"

She shrugged. "The food, the familiarity, but not really the people."

He didn't want her getting sad about her horrible, neglectful Earth parents. "Speaking of food," he pulled over the basket.

"I'm stuffed, Alex. I couldn't possibly."

He pulled out a dracaberry. "Freshly picked by your personal forager." Duric was the orphan boy who helped Toury on her first day in Fyr, and in return for his kindness, they gave him work and shelter.

"Well, I guess I've got to then. Keep Duric's job in demand." She laughed, picking up the fruit and taking a bite. It was an innocent action, but the fact he wanted to lick the juice from her lips made it seductive in itself. She met his gaze and looked away, surmising where his thoughts lay.

He picked up the bottle of wine and the glasses and began to pour. "Did you know I picked that job especially for him because it pays so well? Mushrooms were his trade, I believe you told me, but he's getting a handsome salary. Dracaberry pickers have to be especially trained." Alex glanced at the trees surrounding them. The fragrance of the fruit and its large white blossoms were deceiving.

"Your mother and I picked them, though," Toury said.

"Well, I don't like the idea of that. She didn't even warn you?"

"About what?"

"About the flowers?"

"They didn't look like this then. They were green and full of fruit, no flowers." When she said that, he relaxed.

"Ah. The trees go through many cycles annually. The flowers bloom before the fruit, but before they're pollinated, the flowers are poisonous. When crushed, the flowers have a poison that could knock a man into a deep sleep. A petal could keep him asleep for a day; a bouquet of them, a lifetime."

"Poor Duric!" Toury was appalled by the prospect of his endangerment.

"He doesn't pick them at those times, Toury. There's no fruit to pick those weeks. He's perfectly safe, just as you were."

He topped off their wine glasses. Toury glanced at hers a bit surprised that she had almost finished her glass.

"What are we doing, Alex?"

Well, that was random, and it hurt. He didn't speak but sighed, hoping she wouldn't break his heart in two. This had to work, a slow progress back to where they had been was what he was hoping for. He handed her the wine, stalling. "I'm doing things properly. You had no choice last time. This time, you do."

"So, I could say no if you show up at my door again?"

Alex's stomach sank. He nodded.

She touched his cheek, and they locked eyes. "Could, not would, Alex."

He wanted to kiss her, but images of Cobalt flickered through his mind. He pushed them away. He would not think about the scoundrel taking advantage of her right now.

"To choices." Alex held up his glass to drink to her. She held hers up, and they drank.

When the dracaberry and wine were gone, and Toury was trying to hide her yawns, he suggested they head back into the castle. He put the fire out with his mind, which made her cling onto him as they carefully trekked their way through the orchard and back inside. He should've lit their way with a fireball, but when she clung to him so tightly and they walked so slowly, he dismissed the thought to spend just a bit more time with her, this close to her. She didn't conjure any light, so she must've been thinking the same or utterly distracted.

When they arrived at her door, she hesitated before going inside. He kissed her hand and wished her goodnight. Before he could let go, her hand clamped on his. Her breath was quick, and she licked her lips, laced with dracaberry juice and wine. Toury wanted to be kissed, and he was happy to oblige. Alex kissed her gently, holding her in his arms for just a moment before he forced himself to let go and leave her standing there. He was going to be a gentleman, even if it killed him.

21
POLITICS

Alex did not come for a date the next day but sent a note about being busy. In it, he invited her to sit in on hearing grievances and reports—not a summons or a request but simply that she could come if she wished. It was a choice, as promised. Honestly, it all sounded pretty dull to her and hardly romantic. She never thought she was the romantic type, but last night had been amazing. Just to be in his presence again without worrying about anything—since he diverted her from topics that concerned their relationship or the kingdom—and to talk about their interests, silly inane topics they had never managed to cover.

Toury huffed. Mary huffed. The girl was in a right mood today, and Toury believed it was due to her avoiding her bad habits. Mary was good on her deal, so Toury should be good on hers. She should go and join Alex, who was showing he wanted her to be more of his partner, to learn the ropes, if that's what she wanted.

"Grievances and reports. He's too busy otherwise. He did invite me, though," Toury said.

"It shows he wants to see you, and he wants you involved. It depends if you want to be involved." Mary stared out the window, bored.

"Why don't you come too?"

"Don't use me as a buffer."

"I thought it might keep you busy. Did you ever think being idle is part of the problem? I can't imagine sitting around, never being allowed to do anything for myself or anything constructive."

Mary gave her a glare. "Are you calling me useless?"

"Inadvertently useless. C'mon, just do it for a day."

"Fine."

Toury and Mary entered the chamber to see Alex seated at a long thin table, talking to David. On seeing her, he stood up and crossed the room, all smiles.

"I'm glad you came." Then he directed his attention to his sister. "And you, Mary. Are you lost?"

Toury thought him cruel until both siblings laughed, and Mary retorted, "And let you two have all the fun?"

He led them, each arm-in-arm, to the table and pulled chairs out for them. He placed himself in the middle and motioned to David that they were ready. If Toury were to be queen one day, she'd have to learn the art of these commanding hand motions Alex made. He didn't even need words.

Despite Toury pressuring her to go and Alex mocking her, Mary thrived. During the grievances, a noble complained about his family name, Ruby, being besmirched due to one relative being a necromancer. Mary belittled him—before Alex could say a word—and insinuated Lord Ruby was a spoiled brat. Alex tried not to react, but his mouth quirked, and Toury guessed he was trying not to laugh. Toury slipped her hand into Alex's under the table and squeezed it. When she tried to pull away, he squeezed back and held it fast, telling her not to pull away. She let her hand rest in his.

"That's enough, Mary," he murmured. "But my sister is right, Lord Ruby. By association, you will struggle to find your influence again. I suggest making some moves to secure favor with other nobles and us."

"How do I go about doing that?" he spat.

"Your land is near Hollyhaven, no?" Alex inquired.

The man was thrown off, but Toury knew where he was headed instantly—or at least she hoped he would head there.

"Yes, but Your Majesty—"

"And you've not come to aid, to take any survivors in? Even after I asked any nobles who could to do so."

"I don't have a place to, the means—"

Mary snorted.

"Your cousin's estate lies empty. His assets are now yours. You are childless and feel you need two estates? Why is that?" Alex pressed.

The man looked to Toury, of all people, for help, the only person in the room who hadn't scolded him. Alex's eyes roved over her, and he squeezed her hand to prompt her to say whatever she wished. He would back her.

Toury stood up and walked away from Alex, who didn't seem to want to let go of her hand. "What His Majesty is saying, Lord Ruby, is that you ought to have bent over backward to help those in need, considering your precarious social position." She walked around the table, closing the

120

distance between the man and her, feeling much like a lawyer intimidating a courtroom witness. Not that they did that in Fyr. Here they stayed away from the suspect. She half leaned, half sat on the table. It unnerved the man.

"You find it in your heart to use your cousin's empty estate to temporarily house some of the victims of the dragon attack, I might find it in my heart to visit your sister," Toury said. If his family's image was suffering as much as he proclaimed, Toury could repair that easily through one visit. She had quickly learned how politics of the court worked on the female side.

The man's face went through shock, confusion, and stopped at jubilation.

"If I find myself at liberty, I'll join my sister-to-be," Mary added.

The man's smile became eerily greedy, but at least he'd do the right thing, even if it was for the wrong reason. If he helped others and Toury used her influence to help him, others would follow. Sure, they wouldn't do it out of the benevolence of their hearts, but it was the only way to manipulate spoiled nobles into doing what was right.

"Thank you Queen Proxy-to-Be. Thank you, Princess Mary. You dispel all my fears and worries. I will at once set up the place to house these poor souls until His Majesty decides where they shall remain."

"You're dismissed, Lord Ruby," Alex said, his eyes downcast, his voice quiet.

There was more flattery and brownnosing that Alex took uncomfortably before the man left. As soon as the man was out the door, Alex waved his hand, and the guards didn't let the next person in. Alex's voice jarred her when he said in an intense, clipped tone. "Toury, could I see you in private?"

"Ugh," Mary growled. "I came here for Toury's sake. I'm gone. Do all the talking you want. I'm leaving."

"No Mary, don't go," Alex said. "It is so much easier with people behind me. See the next person, if you will. We'll only be a moment." He stood up and offered Toury his hand and walked her around the table.

"I quite like this," Mary said with way too much enthusiasm.

He walked Toury to the wooden wall behind them, pressed on a corner where wood met wood, and it popped open. He pulled her a bit roughly into a stairwell and closed the door behind him, sealing them into a dark closet-sized hidden room, where only a few dots of light pierced through what looked like peepholes.

"Are you angry—"

She was cut off by a kiss, not just any kind of kiss, but one of intensity, of longing, of hope, love, lust, and his heart pouring from his lips. She was taken aback by how much emotion he transferred through that kiss. He pulled away with apologies, but she yanked him back to her, kissing him, trying to show him through her lips the equivocal emotions.

They only pulled away from each other when they heard Mary talking to a noble on the other side of the wall. Alex panted, his eyes alight like the fire he controlled. "Not angry. You're...amazing." He hesitated to say more, and Toury was afraid to let him say more. They were mending what was broken, and to force it might destroy it.

"We better save this poor soul from Mary's sober wrath."

"Sober?" Alex shook his head, probably trying to think straight, still lost in their kisses as half her mind was.

"It's a secret pact between her and me."

"You amaze me at every turn," he whispered. He pecked her lips one more time as if unable to resist. He pressed the catch to open the door and walked out, holding her hand to guide Toury back into the room.

Perhaps politics were more romantic than she believed they could be.

22

A BURDEN

Alex's life fell into a comfortable routine, and weeks began to shoot past, and those weeks turned into months. He had so much work to do but made time to take Toury on a date in the city once a week and have most of their meals together. She was always present for the grievances—where he almost always tried to steal a kiss—although she preferred him to update her on the reports. He couldn't blame her. A room full of men despising her presence, or that of any woman, was off-putting. He wanted her involved, though, and him needing to repeat the reports in the princess salon gave him more time with her. This involved his sister too, who suddenly appeared determinedly serious about her role as princess. Whatever Toury had done to convince her to stop drinking and take life seriously worked. Mary seemed to enjoy it, and he appreciated sharing the burden with them.

Alex and Toury's relationship was in a comfortable, stable place, but no talk of marriage was brought up by either of them, nor did they ever talk about Racine or Cobalt. It was stupid to ignore their issues, but Alex would not lose any ground with her. He was determined to marry Toury. To do so, they would have to face all of this, but not until she was ready. And she wasn't. Toury became distracted and a little melancholy as her birthday approached, especially when his mother announced she was prepping for an engagement party for Mary and Cobalt. Half of Alex wanted to spoil the surprise party to spare Toury any suffering, but as always, Mary surmised his thoughts and shut that down. Mary also brought him a reminder he loathed: he had to work things out privately with Cobalt before he publicly did. First, it was to hide this party from Toury—an excuse—but, second, he also missed his friend dearly. Before he could ruminate on it, he wrote Cobalt's summons to court and dispatched it, trying to figure out what he would even say to his friend or how he felt toward him. He had hated him for weeks, then spent a couple months pretending the man didn't exist. It had been four months since he had seen Cobalt.

Cobalt arrived that evening, which meant he rode out the moment he received the message, indicating he had been waiting every day for it. He also brought nothing but one saddlebag with him, which meant he expected only to be allowed to stay one night or, worse, he wouldn't leave or need any clothes, as if Alex could ever kill his friend. Oh, he thought of imprisonment or banishment, but it had been a fleeting impulse.

Cobalt arrived in time for dinner, which made things awkward, and yet it was a nice buffer for Alex, for he had time to wrap his mind around Cobalt's presence and what he wanted to say. Cobalt greeted Toury as propriety demanded but after that, never spoke to or looked at her, and even limited his comments to Mary. His mother, as always, played the perfect diplomat, urging conversation in various avenues to make everyone speak, though not necessarily to each other.

When dinner ended, Alex asked Cobalt to join him in the prince room.

"You still will not use the king's room?" Cobalt ventured once they were in Alex's room for entertaining.

Alex shook his head. "I think I'll rename this room eventually. I could never... I like it here."

"Your Majesty, let me say this before you decide my fate—"

"No," Alex stopped him. "No. I want this behind us. I want it gone."

"You cannot forgive me. What I did was reprehensible."

"Yes, it was. And I don't think I can quite forgive it." Alex huffed. He walked away and concentrated his anger into the fireplace, lighting the wood inside it. The release of his anger gave him momentary relief. The fire stayed controlled, despite his heightened emotions; good, he finally had a grip on the increased intensity of his power. Too bad his foresight didn't increase as well, because he would've known what Cobalt would say next.

"Then hit me."

"What?" Alex looked at him aghast, and yet when he let himself think about it, the idea was pleasant; the rage and jealousy bubbled in him.

"Hit me. It's the only way to get around this. You have to do something to punish me, so hit me."

"No." And yet his fists curled up on their own volition. The dragon-fueled temper of his wanted release.

"I deserve it." Cobalt began to list his crimes and with each one, Alex tried to quell the building fury. "I magnetized your engagee. I took advantage of her when she was weak. I asked her to run away with me to Earth. I even kept at it when she flatly said no. I threw away our life-long friendship for the idea of bedding a beautiful woman—"

Alex's fist made contact with Cobalt's jaw before his mind even registered the choice. The idea of Cobalt wanting to sleep with Toury had thrown him over the edge.

Cobalt dabbed his bloodied lip and smiled a little. "I would've magnetized her into my bed, and as always, my love would've died after I had her, and I would have jilted her. Who knows? Maybe she would've had to run back to Earth if my seed took root."

Alex saw red at the thought of Toury having Cobalt's child and rushed Cobalt, tackling him into a settee that skidded across the floor from his unfathomable power. Alex backed away, stunned and momentarily amazed at his own strength.

When Cobalt got up, he grinned leerily. "That's it! Fight me!"

Alex complied with another punch, this time to Cobalt's eye, and then he turned away, panting. David met his gaze and raised his brows in amusement, which brought Alex back to himself. He wasn't an animal but a gentleman, a king.

"That's all you got?"

"Stop," Alex ground out, pressing the fire magic down, quelling the dragon in him. "I don't beat men to a pulp who don't fight back. Sit down."

He kept his back turned on Cobalt, not trusting whether his temper had diffused, and ordered the servant who stood at the ready in the doorway to make them drinks and to get Cobalt ice. Cobalt denied it. Alex supposed the bruising would publicly show his due punishment, so he didn't press it.

Alex sat down. "The truth is, as sad as it sounds, I need my advisor, the one man I trust to help me."

"Trust?" Cobalt was taken aback.

"In everything but around the women in my life, yes. Sit down." The last statement had a bit of bark in it. Alex was annoyed by this situation completely.

Cobalt sank onto the couch so quickly that it was as if someone had kicked his legs out from under him. He looked foolish, and Alex knew that Cobalt was completely at his command now. There would be no objections about his decisions, but complete compliance. That's not what he wanted exactly, but it would do for a while. Alex could depend upon the women in his life to check his actions until Cobalt was truly forgiven in time.

"What do you want advisement on, Your Majesty?"

"One of the subjects that is sore between us," Alex warned.

"I'll be impartial. I swear it."

Alex took a deep breath, and it spilled out, what he had avoided, had been holding in, the real wedge between Toury and him: Racine. He told Cobalt about her, the rebels, Toury's parents being in on it, the failed seduction attempt—everything.

Cobalt whistled.

"What does the queen proxy-to-be say?"

"Nothing. We aren't on the best terms."

Cobalt's gaze darted away, ashamed.

"Things are better, but I don't want to bring it up and spoil the ground won. I know she visited her—only once—and the guard said it was mostly bitter words, but Cobalt—can I marry Toury if her parents could be planning to usurp my throne?"

He did his annoying whistle again. "Damn, Your Majesty. That's... You've been living with this for months?" He shook his head in disbelief. "I should've been here. I should've shouldered some of this for you. I can find out her thoughts if you like."

Alex gave him a glare, and Cobalt turned red. "I meant through Mary. I'd have Mary ask her. I shouldn't be seen anywhere with the queen proxy to-be, obviously."

Alex agreed and was glad he didn't have to command Cobalt to stay away from Toury like a jealous lover would. "No, I'll talk to her myself. You weren't here because you cannot control yourself. That reminds me. There will be no more indiscretions concerning you in the future with anyone in my court."

"No, Your Majesty," Cobalt choked out.

"If you are to marry my sister, you'll have to prove your worth. She stopped drinking, so the least you could do is stop womanizing."

"Marry Mary?" Cobalt's eyes darted up to Alex's, and they were full of so much sudden hope that it unnerved Alex.

"She has to do the asking, as is royal law, but she sees you in the flames, and I cannot stop her."

"I won't marry her without your blessing."

"A nice sentiment, but it all lies in her hands, not mine. And I think you'll find she might be more unforgiving than me."

Cobalt cringed. "I'm dedicated to changing my ways—in court and outside of it." So he was swearing off mistresses or brothels as well. Only time would tell if it stuck.

Alex then shifted subjects to spare his old friend and told him about the surprise party. Cobalt didn't seem to mind in the least that he was being used as a façade. In fact, Cobalt gave Alex the impression he knew he was lucky to be welcomed back at all.

Alex dismissed Cobalt and informed him he could take his room back. Alex wanted to punish him further, but his need to tell someone his burdens outweighed his spent anger. He needed Cobalt and trusted no one else regarding what to do about the Hematites.

***

Alex asked Toury to join him in his sitting room that night. He wanted to call it their room. He missed having her there. He hated having to walk down the hall to talk to her, but he never let himself transport there. He took every step as a penance for his wrongdoings.

At dinner, she said she would join him shortly after, since the family nightcap had dwindled. His father slept most evenings away, and his mother spent that time by his father's side, so there was no point in forcing the tradition. His uncle annoyingly tried to reinforce it, but Alex declined. The man was family, but he was sticking his nose into Alex's business all the time. He'd had to tell his uncle twice now he was overstretching his role and that he was not Alex's ealder advisor but only the advisor and tracker of the rebel insurgency. Alex also had to shut him up when it came to the insults he flung at Toury, thinking Alex would join in, due to the fight they had had. He'd banish a man from the castle for lesser words against Toury, but he was family, so Alex dealt with him and ordered him to stop talking regularly. This was yet another dynamic that had changed. His uncle had always talked down to him, probably thanks to how Alex's father treated his son, but now as sovereign, Alex demanded the respect his uncle wasn't giving him. Every time his uncle overstepped his bounds, Alex corrected him. After a while, his Uncle Humphrey began to not take the criticism well, nor did he like someone as young as Cobalt being named the ealder advisor, the top person to counsel Alex. He asked to go to his fort in Ludford. Alex had been happy to see him go.

After dinner and the official dismissal of his uncle, he went to his rooms. Toury was there moments later, knocking. She entered the sitting room, touched his chest— signaling she was about to kiss him—and stopped after seeing whatever emotion was exploited on his face. He could never hide from her. He couldn't kiss her because he'd lose the guts to do this.

"What is it?"

Alex jerked away, realizing from her reaction that his face must be expressing something uncharacteristic of him. Not wanting to make this worse than it was, he spat it out: "We've been avoiding a certain topic that cannot wait longer."

She paled and sat down. "My sister," she whispered.

"Tell me what to do, Toury, for I must do something to appease the people, yet I won't do anything to hurt you. No more. I've hurt you so much, and now things are back on a better path... I love you, Toury. Whatever it takes to keep you by my side, I'll do."

She breathed out heavily. "I can't make this decision."

"There's more," he forced out. "Forgive me for not telling you, but I had to affirm what your sister said through my uncle's intel, and then I didn't want to hurt you anymore. Your parents are rebels."

"I know. My so-called sister told me."

Alex sighed but was still not relieved she knew. She was staring at him expectantly, not putting the pieces together of what that truly meant.

"And so, you must see that leaves you and me in a precarious situation."

"Does it?" She appeared stunned, scared almost. She was making him say it, something that would hurt her again.

"Toury, I'll have to ask you before we can ever marry if you'd choose them or me. There's no in-between with this." He held up his hand, scared of her response. "I don't want an answer now. I want you to think this over. There's no going back."

"There could be a compromise, no? They could see that you are just, that you're a good person and that they have no reason to rebel."

He loved her positive mindset. He wished he had the luxury to believe it, but not taking the rebels seriously could result in his death, his family's, and the end of their rule. He shook his head. "In a perfect world, we wouldn't need to make hard choices. I want you to be ready to make that choice—whatever it may be—and we can hope your compromise can be possible."

"What do they want, the rebels? Reform?"

"My head after my father's."

Toury flinched and covered her mouth. He shouldn't be so brutally honest, but he didn't want her to have any illusions about her long-lost parents. Better to prepare her for the worst, and if they were rational people who wanted reform, that could be done.

"Then Mary's and my cousin's. They want to wipe out Sapphirians. To be honest, I do not blame them for wanting my predecessors dead. They've done horrible things."

Toury moved away from him and stared into the fire. He wondered if she knew how ruthless they had been, and he wondered if she knew more about it from her aunt and uncle than he did. But he trusted her. He would not ask or press. He would let her dictate the rest of this conversation.

"What will this do to you if it comes out?"

Alex shrugged. That was not what he was expecting her to ask. He had never thought about it and told her as much. "I only thought of you, honestly. It could completely destroy their movement or embolden it, depending on how the public takes to our wedding," Alex mused. "If we get married that is," he rushed out.

The overwhelmed expression on Toury's face told him he had said too much; he had just given her a burden that no human being should ever carry. Alex wondered if Toury still had enough love in her heart to choose him over her own blood, despite their abandonment and wish to kill him.

He steered the conversation to safer waters but could tell she was still overwhelmed with everything. When she said she was tired and had to go, he did not protest. He stole a kiss, hoping to impart his feelings on the subject and just in case it was the last time, in case she sided against him.

23

FALLING

Toury had many sleepless nights, not from nightmares—they were long gone—but because she had a life-altering choice to make. Alex didn't need a decision immediately, but she would have to make one soon. Only "soon" turned into a month. Despite the time passing, Alex didn't pressure her or even bring it up. He allowed things to keep going in their comfortable pattern. Like her, he probably was worried to disrupt the happy bubble they were in with reality. However, something was bothering her, holding her back from making a choice. She loved Alex, but he had forgotten an important day.

On that morning, she rose early and decided horseback riding would help her think. She needed to be alone and to clear her head, and riding in the fresh air usually helped. It was an extremely warm day, hot even, which wasn't the usual in the temperate climate of Celestia—rarely hot, rarely cold, since the sphere wasn't tilted on its axis like Earth. Not having seasons was weird, but it allowed people to travel to experience the cold of the north and the sweltering of the south.

She had to focus on what Alex had told her, what Racine had said. Her family were rebels, which meant they wanted Sapphirians—Alex—off the throne. Even if Alex was biased, usurping usually entailed hostile takeovers or assassinations. Alex might have to kill them to protect himself, much like with the necromancer's coup. Alex had so many plans to improve Fyr; if these rebels would just wait a couple years, one even, Alex would prove it to them.

Part of Toury fixated on the idea of no throne. Without a kingdom to rule, she would finally come first in Alex's life. She shook the selfish thought away. Choosing between Alex and her parents would be difficult, and finding a common ground or compromise was impossible. Not because Alex said so, but because she recognized that. One would try to kill the other. Not knowing them gave Alex an edge. She loved him and wanted to marry him. And yet, if she met her parents, would they change her mind? Or would she resent them, feel nothing for them, like with Racine?

Her thoughts grew a bit despondent, thinking of her awful parents and sister. And then she turned her thoughts to her new "family." She thought the world of the Sapphirians, but even they forgot her birthday was today. Alex not saying a word was the worst of all. She swore she had told him a while back, and that's something you don't forget about the person you're supposed to love. Fyr saw fifteen as the quintessential birthday, where a girl becomes a woman, but Toury still thought eighteen was huge; this was influenced by her entire childhood on Earth. Surely, the queen would be making her lengthy plans, getting a gown designed for her—all the over-the-top preparations she was known for—if she knew. The kind of parties the queen threw took months to orchestrate. Toury had too much pride to tell her since she was so excitedly busy with Mary's engagement party. The queen was dying for her children to settle down, so who could take this day away from her?

Still not proficient on a horse, Toury went off the main road in the palace grounds, taking an easy, smooth trail that went down to the lake, only to find people were there. From afar, she saw the form of Alex, knowing the slope of his bare broad shoulders, his wet dark hair plastered to his forehead, and those sculpted muscles that made her shiver when he turned. He was swimming. She had half a mind to go down to get a closer view of him in just his swimming trunks but saw he had company. It was Cobalt and a couple other young noblemen she couldn't recognize from that distance. Now would not be a good time. She had avoided Cobalt completely, except at dinner when she was forced into his company. Toury was glad Alex forgave him, for it gave him peace of mind and pleased Mary, but it would take Toury a while to forgive the scoundrel, for she could never trust him again.

She turned her horse around and took a path around the castle toward the orchard, despite Madge's concerns about roots. It was her job to protect Toury, but sometimes Madge was downright overbearing. She wanted to think, and Madge riding behind her and cautioning her every move like Toury was a queen made of glass was infuriating. For spite, she rode more quickly than she should into the orchard area. That's when the world upended, and by the time Toury realized she had been unseated, she was on the ground, the back of her head slamming into something hard.

Toury didn't remember the first few minutes after her fall. Her memories began again in snippets of being carried inside to her bedchamber—the one in Alex's quarters. The healers said she had mild brainshock, which she realized must be their word for concussion.

She was propped up in bed, drifting but fighting sleep, Madge prodding her and chatting about inane topics to get her to stay conscious. A healer constantly changed stones on a large necklace she had placed on Toury, and two other maids remained to make sure she ate the broth and bread they had brought in. Her mind became coherent, and her head ached a little less, so she knew, aside from the tender egg-sized bump on the back of her head, she'd feel better later. She wanted to be alone, but that wasn't bound to happen.

She hated being pampered and watched like this, and she realized the rest of her life as Queen Sapphirian would be this way. If she would be queen. She had to choose between her family and Alex. That's what got her into this head-aching predicament.

"Madge, I really need to know what these stones all do." Toury lifted the necklace to inspect them.

"I don't think now is the time for you to try a lot of brainwork, Queen Proxy-to-Be."

"Tomorrow then, you will teach me?"

"But what of blood magic? We've only gone through the basics."

"Both blood and stone magic, then. I'm sure I won't be able to do our combat training for a few days. I need it, Madge. Had I known, the whole Cobalt fiasco could've been prevented."

"Perhaps we should move onto stones then. But Queen Proxy-to-Be, please don't chide yourself too much. Had you been fully educated on his powers, you'd simply recognize what he was doing but not be able to stop him."

"But I was able to in the end. I pushed him away."

"It shows how strong you are to fight off stone magic." Madge sighed. "Stone magic is inherent in the stones, but people also exude the stones' powers. The last name is sometimes an indicator, as in how Lord Cobalt can exude the properties of that particular stone, but the Sapphirians do not exude the properties of a sapphire. Those sapphires around your neck, though, protect and heal."

"And blood magic transfers that person's power through their blood?"

"We only went over people. The draca blood His Majesty was trying to find would give the drinker dragon-like powers, most of the Sapphirian fire tricks. And there's the snuffers and folk like them. They can pull things from people by separating the power from the blood and removing it from the body."

"So, Tobias has...two powers?" Toury brought up the man who had helped them break the curse. He was a Sapphirian baseborn, according to Alex, so he could foresee in the flames, and he was knowledgeable about the old language and stone magic, but he had also snuffed the dark power from Justine.

"Yes. Like you were born with fused powers of your parents, Tobias was as well. And your aunt is a cursebreaker like your grandfather and father, but also a healer as I think your grandmother had been. All Hematites have the ability to use light to protect, but there are variations. She mainly uses it to detect ailments and then heal or purge curses, while your father—I have heard—was savvy with light projection and also cursebreaking, but not healing. The king's sister also has dual powers, blood and fire powers, just like Tobias. It happens sometimes, although the norm is the child taking on the father's powers, just as they do in eye color. There are exceptions of course, especially with female Sapphirians. Princess Anne's son, Henry, got his mother's eyes and powers, as will Princess Mary's children. The variations or merging of powers is seen more in families that are extraordinarily powerful."

Toury realized then that it was in their DNA—not that anyone on Fyr knew that term. The Sapphirian's DNA was stronger and overrode the spouse's. So Alex's children, all of them would have those iridescent blue eyes. Her children, if she married him. With those eyes, Toury would never be able to tell her children no. And they would burn up everything. Good God, she didn't even want to think about that.

The door burst open, cutting off her reveries. Alex stood in the doorway, his face pale, his breath ragged, and his eyes wide. When he met her gaze, he relaxed slightly. "Leave us," he said while catching his breath. He must have run up to her room from the lake. His hair was still damp.

Everyone started to leave, but Madge stayed seated by her bed.

"You too, Madge. I'll ring if she needs anything or if I leave."

If he left? Toury processed that comment as Madge bowed to them and hurried out.

Before she could figure out what he meant, he flew to her bedside and sat beside her, pulling her gently up and into his arms, cradling her. "I was riding and going for a swim when they told me about your accident. Are you all right?" He was genuinely distraught and anxious about her. He gingerly touched her face, examining her head.

She showed him where she was hurt because he wouldn't give up until he found it and saw it with his own eyes. "It's nothing," she brushed it off.

"It's everything," he said quietly, his eyes dancing across her face. "It's everything to me."

24

A MIRACLE

Alex's heart was beating uncontrollably in his chest. The only words that registered in his mind were "Toury," "accident," "head injury," and it was enough to get him flying to her room at Mary's, but Mary sent him to his own quarters. They had put her there—good. He had been afraid to transport while still wet, since it took more power and gave off a lot of steam. He ran there; only, when he meant to stop outside the door and slip in quietly, he was too anxious and burst in.

She was fine, only a bump, but even that was too much. He hated anything to happen to her or for her to feel any discomfort. He was to blame. She was riding in the orchard, most likely to avoid running into Cobalt, so as not to upset Alex. The main riding trails all passed the pond.

"What is everything?" she asked.

He had no idea he had spoken his thoughts aloud. "I'm so sorry, Toury. It's all my fault."

"I rode too fast, and I wasn't watching the uneven terrain. It was stupid of me to ride a horse in the orchard. With all the roots, I should've walked her in. Madge even warned me. It's not your fault at all."

"You were avoiding Cobalt and me. Don't deny it. But that was not why I was apologizing. Toury, I'm sorry. Can you forgive me for it all?"

"For what?" she mused.

"I'd say we could cancel out our mistakes, our idiocy, and start afresh, but I've still done more harm to you than you to me. I don't care about the Cobalt incident. I trust you, but I broke my promise. I said I would never hurt you again, and I broke that promise."

Her brow furrowed adorably. "How?"

"The first time it was physical, and this time, emotional. You were right. I shouldn't have left you. I should've brought you with me to Hollyhaven. And, more importantly, I shouldn't have let my wounded pride about that kiss get between us. I've tried to do things right, woo you properly, but I ignored the issues with Cobalt and your family. I brought them up, demanded you choose, and then ignored it because I was scared you wouldn't choose me. I should've faced those issues with you head on."

"Stop, Alex."

He grasped her in his arms, pulling her against him, their foreheads pressing together, his breath mixing with hers. "Toury, do you still love me?"

"Shut up, Alex, and kiss—"

He cut her off in a heat-seared kiss. The fire in him heated his core, pouring out to her through his lips.

"I choose you," Toury said.

His heart soared. It was a miracle. "Are you sure?"

She nodded. "I'm sure I'll want to meet my parents, talk some sense into them, but they left me, abandoned me. Instead of finding me, they hide and scheme of ways to hurt you. You are my family now. Mary is more of a sister to me than the one in that prison cell. Your mother is more of a mother to me than my biological or Earth ones. Even your father—"

He kissed her repeatedly until she pulled away, wincing. With great effort, he pulled his lips away from hers, only to realize, like a pathetically licentious animal, he had forgotten himself and was in her bed, pressing her injured head back into the pillows. Alex tried to pull away, but she hooked her arms around him and pulled him back to her.

"I'm hurting you," he protested.

"Then let me be on top."

Alex's stomach flopped, and his pulse quickened at her teasing comment. She laughed, smiling as she watched him. He knew his expression of shock and desire was probably amusing. Toury shoved him, so he rolled over, letting her out from under him, and he lay back, allowing her to lie atop him. Her weight on him was thrilling. His blood turned to fire. He wanted her so badly that reason was gone. He kissed her and pulled at her clothes until he felt he might go mad. "I want you. I need you. Move back in tonight, please."

"I will," she said. And when he saw the desire that matched his in her eyes, he almost came undone.

"Toury," he gasped between kisses. "You don't understand." He pulled her against him, trying to untie the back of her dress. "If you don't stop me, it's going to happen, and then we cannot marry."

She pulled away, sat up, and straddled him, making the situation much worse for him.

"You're torturing me."

"Ugh, chastity, such a double standard."

"Double standard?"

"Earth term, I guess. Different expectations for men and women."

"My champion of women." He ran his hands along her hips. "It's not gender, my love, but a royalty issue."

"If you say the word 'edicts,' I'll smack you." She referred to the ancient edicts the first King Sapphirian had laid down for royalty that were unchangeable.

"Well, I better not say it, but you're right. You still haven't read them? There's a copy of the book right there in our sitting room on the bookshelf. You probably should read that before we..." He was discussing them getting married like it was definitely going to happen. Sure, with her sitting on him and kissing him, it seemed like it would, but he was unsure how to make it more official without simply asking her if they were back on. "I mean, if we marry, you should know everything the role of queen will entail."

It was the wrong thing to say. Her smile faded, and she shifted her beautiful gaze off him. "Why don't you just tell me what ridiculous edict you're referring to."

"One I've told you about before," Alex said. He didn't want to be specific because it was embarrassing.

"The king proxy blushes." She smiled again at his expense, but it was worth it. God and goddess, she was beautiful. "My chastity? Then you should take the chastity test too." She was asking him to have the test where a stone was placed on the abdomen to determine the purity of women before marriage.

"I have never been with anyone. Do you not believe me?" He could easily talk of these things in front of Cobalt and some of the lords he was closer to, but with Toury, it was awkward.

"I do. I just don't like being measured for my virtue if you aren't."

"Okay, I'll do the test too."

"Really?" Toury was shocked, but it was such a simple request.

"Under one stipulation," he added. Toury huffed, annoyed, but he continued, "Marry me right after. I really can't handle another moment in your bed until we are married."

"Deal." She leaned down to kiss him, her body pressing against him in ways that threatened his virtuous heart. If he wasn't careful, it all might fall apart around them, but he had slyly gotten what he wanted. They were officially talking of marriage soon, but it wasn't enough. He thought back to the books he had been reading all those lonely nights by himself, and an idea sprang.

"Oh no!" Toury sat up suddenly. Her hand went to her head to steady her dizziness. "We've ruined Mary's engagement party!"

"Hardly."

"We have to go! It will look like we don't approve of her choice. That we haven't pardoned Cobalt."

"Have you pardoned Cobalt?" Had she even talked to him? And then a flicker of temperamental fire licked his insides because, if she had, Alex hadn't been there, and they could've been alone, and who knows what Cobalt might—

"No!" she cut off his ridiculous thoughts. "I might someday, if he ends up being a good husband to Mary, but not now."

He smoothed her springy hair down, simply drinking up the sight of her face. "We have to make an appearance, naturally, but not long if you feel ill." Truly, he wanted to stay here with her alone. He was on top of the world with her admitting she would choose him over her family. Things were almost back to the way they were before the necromancers, before the forced engagement.

"I can manage dinner, but no dancing. I'm sorry."

"Hardly. I only enjoy dancing because I can hold you too close and shock everyone. And publicly kiss you to shock an entire kingdom."

Then he kissed her again until they were interrupted by Madge's knock. She wanted to see if Toury was well enough to get ready and join the company.

They were arriving an hour late to their own party, but he was the king proxy, and she, a future queen, so they could do as they pleased. When they got to the great hall, the doors were closed. The footmen stood on each side.

"Why are the doors closed? And why is it so quiet?" she mused.

"Perhaps they didn't want to start without us." Alex shrugged, pulling her in for a kiss to distract her. As he kissed her, the footmen opened the doors. He quickly pulled away and took her hand in his, leading her inside.

"Surprise!" a massive roomful of people shouted in unison. She covered her mouth, her eyes wide. She took in the scene and the people there to see her and then turned to Alex, her eyes glistening with happy tears.

"Happy Birthday," he whispered to her. Despite all the people around them, he was so relieved—no, overjoyed—to see her happy again that he kissed her in front of everyone.

The crowd had fun with that, jeering at their expense. When he pulled away and led her to the high table toward his mother and sister, the happiness in their eyes made his good mood lift even higher. Everything was going to be okay with them now. Toury was going to be his lifemate. He had never been so sure of anything before.

25

FIRE

Maybe it was the fact she was overflowing with love and gratitude, or maybe it was the firewhiskey she allowed herself to indulge in, but she felt alive for the first time in her life since she'd arrived in Fyr. She had thought her new family had forgotten her birthday, but they'd far from forgotten.

Alex closed the door, finally shutting out Mary, who was babbling, and Cobalt, who was red faced from drinking too much firewhiskey. Alex moaned. "Six hours later, finally alone."

"Was it that bad?" she feigned insult.

He sauntered over to her, his eyes shining with a predatory gleam. "I'd celebrate the day you were born until I died of exhaustion."

She laughed at this. "Good thing a birthday is only one day then."

"I will celebrate you every day for the rest of our lives, Toury." He was suddenly so serious. He stared deeply into her eyes, and she thought he would kiss her, but instead, he shook his head slightly to gather himself. "One moment," he said as he vanished into a fireball.

She growled that he would abandon her after saying something so sweet.

Suddenly, he reappeared in front of her with an armful of presents. She smiled. Never had she had as many presents as she saw on the gift table downstairs. In fact, her parents on Earth never bothered with parties; they'd given her just one gift, and when she insisted on parties for a few rebellious middle school years, not enough people showed up to call it a party. My, how things had changed.

"I brought up the family gifts. I figured the rest could wait until tomorrow."

"There are far too many gifts down there."

"No such thing when it comes to you."

"Stop," she said, although her face beamed.

He kissed her and nodded to the settee. She sat, and he placed the presents on the table, handing her the first one. The king had given her a small framed painting of a woman.

Toury studied it for a moment and realized she recognized a bit of herself in the painting—the hair, dark skin tone, and nose. Her lips were the shape of Toury's but fuller. "My mother?"

"Yes. This was given to my uncle during their engagement. My father...I could not tell him your parents could be involved with the rebels. I didn't even tell him about your sister. He is dying, and I could not burden him with this. He finally sees you for who you really are. I couldn't set that back."

"I understand. Despite it all, I do love it. Just to know what she looked like...and the fact it means he's over his hatred enough to accept me as your choice."

Before she could become melancholy, he handed her another present. The queen had given her an amazing necklace of sapphires. It was a choker with dangling tendrils. It was magnificent but so expensive, she knew she could only wear it in the palace for special occasions. Next, Mary had given her a book called *Tame the Dragon: How to Control Men.*

Alex took the book and tossed it aside. "She always does these joke gifts."

"I want to read it," she teased. "I want to tame the dragon."

"Do you?" he asked huskily, and then they were kissing madly.

Only, he didn't stop. He unlaced part of her dress and kissed her lips, down her neck, and she was mimicking him. Despite his warnings, despite his insistence they stay chaste until they wed, she couldn't care less at that moment. There was a flame inside her, consuming her, wanting her to join the man who was fire, who set her alight with his touch.

When clothing started to come off, and Alex was breathing unsteadily, the magnitude of what lie ahead of them hit her. The gravity of her possible loss of virtue before the vows leveled her as if someone threw ice-cold water on the raging fire within. "Stop!" she squealed, her voice sounding distant and breathy.

Alex rolled off her, covering his face, murmuring thanks to the god and goddess. She heard Alex move about, and he kissed her head endearingly. She saw him retreat to his room, but he returned in his robe, carrying hers too. He kept his gaze steady on her eyes instead of her barely-clad body—always the gentleman—and he pulled her up into his arms, his hands lovingly framing her face as he gave her a chaste kiss. Then he slipped the robe around her with such control. Their ridiculous lust had them on the floor. She scrambled up onto the settee again.

"We got distracted. You need to open my present." He held up a medium-sized, thin rectangular box. Then he surprised her by going down on bended knee.

She was confused.

He smiled up at her and spoke as he untied the ribbon: "I've done some reading of my own about Earth and its customs. I know we do not wear marriage rings in this sphere, but when you marry me, you will wear something much grander."

He then opened the box, and she saw something shiny, something much too large to be a ring. Her hands went into the box, and she pushed the cloth away to see a round circlet. She lifted it to have a better look. It was a silver oval, rounded at the edges like Mary's, but the band itself was fancier with braided metal embellishment. The braided detail was like the queen's but not as extravagant, missing the sapphire studs at each braid's crossing that the queen's had. Toury had thought the queen's circlet beautiful but overly done. Even though the sapphires represented the queen's role, they weren't her; Toury had the inkling King Craig designed his queen's circlet to remind everyone whom she bowed down to—territorial, like ownership, to say the least. Toury liked the simplicity of her own, and when she examined the front, there was a huge sapphire and, next to it, two smaller purple stones: tourmaline. It was Alex and her together, a partnership; it was perfect. It was amazing and better than any engagement ring she'd ever seen.

"Alex," was all she could gasp.

"Will you marry me, Lady Tourmaline Hematite? Make me the happiest man in all of Fyr?"

"Yes, of course," she said after blinking back tears. The fact he'd researched what people did on Earth when it came to dating and marriage, and how he asked instead of demanding, made her finally feel equally in charge of their destiny.

He stood, placed the crown on her disheveled hair, and walked her over to the looking glass. When she saw how the circlet—the silver, the blue, and of course her color, the purple—contrasted against her dark hair and made her eyes vibrant, she looked regal, powerful, like a queen.

His eyes met hers in the mirror. "I didn't give you a choice the first time. I didn't ask you properly. I would never be satisfied until I remedied that."

"I think you did."

"Do you like it?" he whispered.

"'Like' is an understatement. I feel like a queen."

Alex's eyes lit up at this, wanting to resume where they had left off earlier, but he snatched up her hand and tugged her toward the door instead. "Come."

She grabbed her crown so it wouldn't fall to the ground and withdrew it from her head, clutching onto it tightly. "To where?" she asked after he pulled her into the hall.

"To mother's chambers. She will want to plan a wedding, and I want her to send out invitations right away."

"You can't. She could be sleeping."

"No." Alex laughed. "She won't be, and if she is, she'll want to be woken up for this. She's dying for us to set the date."

Alex had been right. The Queen was ecstatic after her grogginess wore off. She made major plans to have the wedding in one week. Toury thought that would be hard to pull off, but knowing the queen well, Toury was sure she had had everything prepared for the initial date of Alex's birthday.

For the first time, Toury didn't feel trapped. She was excited and ready. She marveled over how far she had come in this world and how it didn't seem odd to marry at eighteen in this sphere. She loved Alex, and that was all that mattered. They could do amazing things together.

And as they lay down together again that evening—too exhausted to even kiss or stay up talking the night away, he held her close. "I almost forgot. I have another present for you, but now it will have to wait till tomorrow."

Fighting off sleep, all she could muster was, "You spoil me."

He whispered, "Rightfully, and for the rest of our lives."

She fell into a deep sleep on the best birthday she'd had in her entire life.

26
A KEY

Alex decided to be mysterious about the present the next day. He left Toury an ornate key with a note since she slept in and he didn't want to wake her. It was the first night they had slept in each other's arms since he'd left to sort out the dragons. He wanted to lie about in bed all morning with her, but he had a kingdom to run. He had to figure out what to do with Racine. She had slain a draca and gotten a lot of people killed. Banishment would not work, since the Hematites apparently were ignoring that ruling by his father. He didn't want to kill her and hurt Toury, but the people wanted justice. He'd put off the decision so long that Cobalt was hearing rumors about Alex being spineless.

He was sure they said the same about his forgiveness of Cobalt, even though David had informed him Cobalt had been out to taverns sporting his black eye and split lip and regaling crowds with the tale of how the king proxy had beaten him to within an inch of his life. At first, Alex had been irate, until David explained that Cobalt—a great storyteller—painted himself as the blackguard and Alex as the ferocious and equally just and kind hero. Alex didn't have enough anger or hate in his heart to be militant and unyielding like his father to punish his friend publicly. He didn't want to be feared, but admired by his people.

All his correspondence did nothing to soothe his nerves. The other Hematites were well concealed; not all the draca blood was found yet, although Agate had located and destroyed what they estimated to be half of it. Alex had a bad feeling, yet if the rebels planned to use it, why hadn't they? Draca blood had a shelf life of about six months, and then the power faded from the blood over time, more and more needed to use fire power. After a year, it spoiled and became worthless. Still, if the Hematites were involved in some rebellion scheme, he'd have to kill them, and Toury would never forgive him. Or they would kill him, and she would never forgive them. Somehow, no matter how he played out the various scenarios or what snippets the flames showed him, Toury and he would be the losers in this mess. He had to think of a way to change that outcome. Flames told him nothing but gave him glimpses far into the future that he couldn't quite understand.

The morning became evening, and then it was too late to take Toury to see her present. She pried and begged to know what the key was for, but he would rather show her. Much to Toury's dismay, between wedding preparations and his work, they didn't get free time together, except hurried lunches, until four days later.

He still would not tell her where they were going in the carriage. Finally, when it stopped and she peered out, she asked, "Who lives here?"

"The Citrines, or at least, they used to."

Her head whipped around, her face completely shocked. "Why are we here?" He could tell it disturbed her. Then she regarded the key clutched in her palm. "I don't want to sound ungrateful, but why would I want this?" She tentatively observed him, frightened she'd angered him, but he burst out laughing. She didn't seem impressed by that either.

"Sorry, Toury. I'm cruel to tease you, I know. It is yours in a sense, for a very specific purpose. Come. When we are closer, you'll see the sign." He alighted from the carriage and assisted Toury out.

A few people were watching them from the streets, but the gilded gates to the estate prevented them from getting too close. They traipsed up the long drive, bodyguards shadowing them, until Toury espied the sign a man was painting letters onto. He had the words outlined and was now filling them in: *Queen Tourmaline's Home for Children.*

She fell back but was purposely falling into him for affection, and he obliged by wrapping her into a tight embrace. She reassessed the house and studied it with a new perspective. He had to admit, it was a grand estate, gaudy and extreme in expenses just as the Citrines had been in life. Their deaths revealed great debts, though, since they'd never lived within their means. Alex had the house stripped of all its belongings and finery, sold them at auction, and used the proceeds to pay the Citrines debts off and to buy basic supplies, outfitting the place to function as an orphanage. The number of tower beds they had needed—which slept three children in the space of one bed—was extreme, but this house that had only kept ten spoiled, traitorous nobles now could house a hundred children and the twenty-five staff it would take to run the place.

"Alex," she whispered. "This is...I have no words."

"This is how I atone for my wrongdoings. Only, it doesn't feel like any atonement. Seeing you happy is simply rewarding."

"I've forgiven you. You don't have to atone for anything anymore."

"I've got to until I forgive myself. You are much too easy on me. I'm still not up to scratch for those bruises I made on your neck." He referred to

144

how he had let himself go dark and almost strangled her. He would spend the rest of his life making up for it. "And then there is still everything else I must account for."

She refused to meet his gaze. "I won't listen to you disparage the man I love. Self-wallowing is beneath you," she said in such a regal voice that he could easily envision her commanding from the throne, the circlet atop her head. "Anyway, show me my orphanage."

As soon as they returned to their quarters and Madge and David set out their lunch, Toury dismissed them. Alex was undoing the buttons that kept his clothes too tight to his wrists and neck. He really should just dress how he wanted, and maybe the kingdom would follow. Maybe he should get Toury to make a prototype of this thing she missed called "jeans." He was so lost in these thoughts, he hadn't seen Toury approach him and grab the nape of his neck.

"Your generosity astounds me," she said, searching his eyes for something.

"It's nothing. I wanted to please you. I wanted to do what is right for the people. It just happens to be so fortunate that those two align."

"No, you saw me with Duric. That was when you saw a problem and sought out a solution as soon as it presented itself. It wasn't just to make me happy. You feel for those children. I saw your face when you saw them begging. There were orphans in Hollyhaven?"

Alex nodded and looked away. "You give me too much credit." He pried himself loose from her grasp. He would not have her paint him as some hero when he had let himself be oppressed for so long. "I've wanted to do something like this for years. It wasn't some problem I was ignorant of or thought myself superior to. My father ruled a certain way, and I was taught that his way was the only way."

She searched his face, trying to understand him with those gorgeous gray eyes. "What way?"

"Well, I told you before that he wouldn't let us give charity to beggars because he believed it rewarded laziness, and to not even look at them because they were too far beneath me. But it went deeper than that. He believed that since they don't contribute to society, they aren't even citizens and don't deserve rights."

Toury's mouth dropped.

"I do not want you to think ill of my father, but you've seen him only at his lowest, weakest, his kindest, and maybe even the most regretful I've ever seen him. Your parents are rebels for a reason. People are unhappy. In some ways, he was a tyrant as king and saw himself as being better than everyone else. The Sapphirian race, he proclaims, is better than the rest of you."

"Are we really so different?"

"No. Power sets people apart. I've got fire in the land of fire. It makes me the most powerful man in the land. At least, that's what my ancestors proclaimed thousands of years ago when they took over and brought peace to the land."

"And now the peace has been disturbed."

"My great-grandfather, Rowland IX, outlawed dark magic and slaughtered many necromancers. Dark, as you saw, can snuff out the fire, so it is a great threat to the throne. My grandfather, Rowland X, was a harsh and unjust man, so I've heard. Within thirty years, he had angered enough of the sphere to start a massive rebel uprising. There was a decade of war. The next Rowland, my father's older brother, died in that war without issue. My grandfather died a few years before I was born, and the rebels disbanded—or so I thought—accepting my father as a much better option than what the Rowland line had offered. Then, as you know, the curse occurred. My father became harsh, not overturning any of the cruel and limiting laws his ancestors enacted during the wars. He even added in some. We're balanced on the edge of a knife right now; one side is peace, the other, war breaking out again. Only this time, I have both necromancers and rebels to contend with as my enemies."

"My parents."

"Inherited enemies. I do not want to fight them, Toury. I will only do so to protect our future, you, my people. I hope to show them there is no reason to fight, that I will bring balance back to Fyr."

"You are. You will."

"Change has to come slowly, or I upset the content half." He was stressing himself out again, but he wanted to share his vision with her, share everything with her. "I'm planning massive reformations, but it'll take a decade to fully pull off."

She wound her arms around his neck again, and he let her pull him into a kiss. It was a kiss full of assurances, strength, and affirmation. She believed in him. God and goddess, he wanted her. The fire in his blood raged to be fulfilled. He pulled her against him with so much enthusiasm that Toury gasped and kissed him back with rigor.

The food was forgotten, a bedroom door kicked open, outer clothes strewn, and heated kisses ensued. He did not want to stop, and why should he? They would be married soon enough, a dark part of his brain, which he could not blame on the curse since it was gone, coaxed.

Alex was at a precipice. They would marry in two days' time, but he was so close to his prize, both of them more than willing to take this as far as it could go. But in the back of his mind, the good part of him stirred up. He knew they couldn't, shouldn't consummate. Even after the marriage, they should be careful, despite how hard it might be. Toury didn't even understand the half of it: the consequences.

"Toury," he panted. "We can't." He pushed himself away, relieving her of the burden of his weight and settling down next to her.

"They won't do that damn test again on our wedding day, will they?" She referred to the Royal Measure, the stone test they had given them that very morning. They had placed stones on both of them to measure certain attributes, virtue being one. Toury was so angry about him stopping their liaison, she growled.

"No, we're cleared, my love. And we signed our marriage license already, so no child could be seen as baseborn. All that remains is our vows. But I need to be honest with you. I don't want you to be surprised by anything. When we...consummate..." His face grew hot. "You will become a mother...pretty quickly."

"I know how this works, Alex. They explain this to us on Earth in school."

He laughed nervously for what he was about to impart, because there was no easy way to say it to her. He was terrified she might get cold feet even. "I'm not trying to patronize you. I know you understand procreation, yet it is different for Sapphirians."

She went rigid and would've pulled away if he didn't have her trapped in his arms. "What do you mean? You don't have anything weird going on down there, right? Or some freaky ritual or something?" She tried to sound lighthearted, but he heard the catch in her voice.

He pressed his entire body against hers with what was probably a display of overconfidence. "What do you think?"

"Really?" she chastised him, pushing him away and almost off the bed.

He grabbed her wrist to bring her with him if she persisted in knocking him out of bed. She stopped, and he loosened his grip. Then he combed her hair behind her ear three times until it behaved.

"What do you mean, you're different?"

Alex sighed. It was now or never. He would not have her surprised later on and act like it was simply fate. He would warn her now.

147

"Sapphirians descend from dragons, as you know. And to put it plainly, we are the embodiment of fire." She was lost, and he had no idea how to word this properly. "*Everything* about me is more potent than any other man."

Her mouth curled into an adorable O. "So, when you said I would become a mother, you meant right away." It wasn't a question but a statement. "I will get pregnant the first month?"

"It's not even a question, considering your fertility as well."

"How would you know how fertile..." Then her brow contracted. "The test didn't measure virtue, did it?"

"No, it does, but orange sapphire measures fertility, among other things."

"That stone shattered!"

"Exactly."

She mulled it over for a moment. "So, if we both are crazy fertile because your stone shattered as well...I will be a mother soon."

"Yes," he said in a strained voice. Afraid she'd rebuke him, he kissed her soundly until she pulled away and cradled his face.

"Thank you," she said, hugging him. "We will always do this, promise me."

"Do what?"

"Always tell the truth."

He nodded, feeling bad for all the things he had hidden from her in the past, not blatant lies, but omissions, which were just as bad. He wouldn't lie to her anymore.

She gazed upon him with nothing but love in her eyes, so much love, he could see it shine through, and he knew his eyes were the same. He could not wait to marry her. Two measly days until they officially belonged to each other.

27

WEDDING DAY

The castle gates were open; the crowds were loud with jollity and cheers. She could hear them calling to the king proxy with well wishes and love. This day was going to be the best day of her life, and the people were happy to make her their queen, for her and Alex to be together. Having the blessing of the people was as good as having a family's blessing. Uncle Gareth and Aunt Edwina helped her into the carriage and climbed in after her. Her aunt was still being snotty about "the baseborn" being recognized as family but agreed to give Toury away with him as her only welcomed family. Her other family's whereabouts were looming, a pressing concern, but she pushed it from her mind. Surely, if they wanted to get to her or Alex, they would attempt so at a time they only had to battle a dozen soldiers. The palace was swarming with a couple hundred guards—an army really—and very public.

They drove the carriage from behind the castle to the road that ran along the inside of the walls until they reached the gate to make a grand entrance down the drive. Children chased them with smiles and cheers; the adults waved and hurried to follow to see if they could get a closer view of the wedding. The majority of them were cunning folk, so Toury wondered who these supposed rebels could be. The most downtrodden were supporting their marriage before they even knew Alex's grand plans to help them.

The carriage stopped about halfway down the drive, and she was helped out. Gareth gave her hand a reassuring squeeze; her aunt reminded her to smile, but Toury was nervous—oh-so nervous. She trembled, and the pair steadied her.

"A simple walk down the cobblestone path home," Gareth said.

She nodded.

"Look like the queen you will be," her aunt commanded.

Toury steeled herself, held her head high, and the trembling transferred to her heart. Outside, she was calm, collected, happy. Inside, she was freaking out and needed to see him. If she could just see Alex, she could make it up there.

It wasn't a long walk to the front steps of the palace, but it felt miles away. There were so many people there watching. She passed by hundreds of cunning folk, the little ones on their fathers' shoulders to get a glimpse of her. A line of soldiers separated the cunning folk from the nobles. There were more nobles than she had met before, so it was impossible to find her neglected court friends in the crowd. She made a quick mental note to invite them back to the palace once things settled down. She was sure they'd hound her over the juicy details of her wedding night—the idea of it made her even more nervous—but she missed their free spirits.

A cacophony of elated voices reached her ears, drowning out any coherent thoughts. When she was about halfway there, she saw him on the steps in front of a wreathed arbor. Alex was dressed in fine clothes, much more elaborate than his plain style. They were cut and sculpted for him, and he had gotten a haircut since the morning. He was the picture of a king, regal and proud, and he would be hers for the rest of their lives. He was trying to keep a steady, sober expression, to remain his aloof self, but his mouth quirked up into a smirk when their gazes aligned, and he couldn't keep it contained anymore: the beaming smile came out. It was contagious. she smiled even broader.

Then she was there. The authority said something, and her aunt and uncle responded in unison. Toury wasn't sure what; she only had eyes for Alex. He took her hands in his, squeezing them gently, his inner fire warming her cool, nervous hands. This was home, here with her hands in his, staring into those sapphire eyes.

The authority greeted the people and began his speech about this day. Everyone quieted down to listen. She heard nothing but whispers, a baby crying, and the authority's booming voice.

"The Sapphirian rule ends now!" a shout sliced through the quiet. It was followed by sudden bursts of flames appearing all over. People darted out of these flames. They attacked soldiers.

Alex went rigid but then pulled Toury to him protectively. Men with knives rushed from the crowd to engage with the guards who swarmed around the arbor to protect them. Mary and the queen were stunned, mouths agape, to the side of the landing. Some of the cunning folk in the crowd and these people transporting in were apparently working together. Absolute pandemonium erupted. People were screaming, crying, fighting, running. Mary and her mother vanished in a ball of fire, Mary transporting them, hopefully to safety.

"Transport us, now," Toury commanded Alex, trying not to lose her cool.

"I can't," Alex said, strained.

She looked back to him to see his eyes frightened, his back rigid, and a gleaming knife at his throat.

Oh, God, no, not him. Not now.

A man's grubby face with a protruding nose peered at her over Alex's shoulder. "Back away, little Tourmaline, slowly, or your little prince gets it." He called him "prince," so these were the misinformed rebels.

Toury met Alex's gaze, which had gone from scared to resolved and steady. He must have a plan. She marveled at his calm. He let go of her, and she backed away slowly. That's when she noticed the man's eyes: steel gray, just like hers. Identical.

This man wound his arm under Alex's to trap his shoulder and keep him immobile. "What's wrong, girl? Don't you recognize your father?"

Toury gasped and faltered back into the arbor and had to steady herself. Her father. She couldn't think. Didn't want to know. All that mattered was the knife at Alex's throat.

"Damn it," Alex growled. "I can't kill you if you're to be my father as well, now can I?"

She marveled at his bravery and wit in such a situation, but her father retaliated by nicking Alex's neck.

"No!" Toury gasped. "No, please! No father of mine would hurt the man I love."

The man's eyes—she could not think of him as her father—darted to meet hers. He was surprised by her confession. He was utterly and genuinely shocked. "You'll be no son of mine. She won't be marrying you. The cursed line ends here."

"I broke the curse!" she shouted to stop him, for it looked like he was about to cut deeper. Blood ran down Alex's neck, pooling in his collar. His eyes boiled with rage, and his face went red. Toury met Alex's gaze, and she nodded for him to go ahead with his plan.

Alex suddenly was a ball of fire, and the rebel had to leap back and put out the flames on his clothes. Alex lunged for her, grabbing her wrist, while the man recovered and yanked something off his belt. Alex transported. Just as they vanished in the flames, something flew at them. At the last moment, as the world faded out of focus, Alex yanked her protectively behind him.

Toury opened her eyes, not realizing she had closed them, and saw they were in their sitting room.

"Bar the door, Toury," Alex commanded.

She followed the order, thinking nothing of it at first, but when she struggled with lifting the bar due to how heavy it was and how her arms couldn't move much in her dress, she wondered what he was doing that he couldn't help her. She heard him repressing a scream through clenched teeth that made her miss the slot, sending half the bar onto the floor with a thud. She yanked it back up—hearing a tear in her dress—and finally got the heavy wooden rail resting in its slots, securing the room.

It would've been simpler for him to do it himself, so something was wrong. She turned. "Alex?"

He simply stood there with his back to her. Then there was a rattle of some metal hitting the ground, and Alex turned, his face pale, eyes a bit distant, his hand on his abdomen. Red seeped around it, and he faltered.

"Alex!" She gasped and ran over, helping him to the ground.

He groaned. "Toury, the safeaway, remember, in the bathing quarters, go." He was telling her to go to the hiding place he'd once shown her.

"No, no, I'm not leaving you. Let me see. I can heal you."

"That's an order!"

"I don't take orders. You should know that by now." She was scared. Part of her fretted that this could be the last time it could happen, so she kissed him.

He weakly returned the kiss, and then his head fell back with a thud onto the stone floor. He laughed and winced. "Aye, I know it."

Toury wasted no more time. She pulled his hand off the wound, and he contorted in pain. Blood spread up his doublet. She yanked the material open and then tore his shirt.

"I imagined the wedding night much different than this," he tried to joke.

"There will be a wedding night, Alex. I swear it to you," she said, firmly placing her hands over his wound, using all the strength of her light magic to heal him.

He grimaced and cried out and then went still.

Toury panicked but tried to get a grip on herself. His chest was rising and falling. He'd just passed out from the pain and maybe blood loss. She poured in more healing light, but the wound was not closing. He wasn't healing.

Then a puff of fire revealed Mary, who gasped and ran to Alex's side. "Heal him!"

"I can't! It's not working!" Toury tried again, hoping it would somehow work, but the wound wouldn't close.

"I don't understand! He's bleeding out. Why won't your magic work?"

"It's not my magic that's the problem, I don't think." Again, Toury tried to heal him but the wound mockingly gaped at them. The blood was spreading down his clothes and onto the floor. She applied pressure to the wound, trying to staunch the blood.

"My brother will not die." Mary gave an angry growl, elbowed Toury out of the way, and lit a fireball into her palm, placing it on the wound. She withdrew screaming, her hand completely bloody, her skin somehow peeled off her palm.

Toury soothed her and healed it, and took a shaky, defeated breath. "You just showed me why. During tutoring, I learned that when magic backfires like that, it's poison."

Banging at the door made both girls jump. Toury covered Alex's wound again. Mary opened the door, despite Toury's protests. In rushed the queen, Madge, and David. David went to bar the door again.

"Wait," the queen commanded when she took in the scene. She kept her regal demeanor, although paling when her eyes met Toury's. "Lady Edwina was not far behind us."

Yes, her aunt would know what to do! She was renowned for her skill with antidotes for poison.

The queen moved to the ground and placed Alex's head in her lap, trying to talk to him. He wasn't responding.

Toury's eyes welled up once she saw her destroyed wedding gown. There was so much blood on it, way too much blood. "Poisoned," Toury said, instantly regretting the whiplash of shock that went through the queen. She continued her fruitless efforts of trying to rouse Alex.

Mary braced Toury's shoulders, trying to soothe her, but they both ended up crying. Aunt Edwina burst in, breathless, and rushed over. She sat down and pried Toury's hands off his wound, which made the blood flow afresh. David barred the door, which made Mary jump again.

"Poison," Toury told her. "The wound won't heal with my light magic or Mary's fire."

"An antidote?" the queen demanded.

"Without knowing what kind, administering one could be deadly. We have to know what kind of poison, or he'll bleed out." Her aunt didn't sound defeated, but stared at the wound pensively as she ran her hands over the wound, not touching but scanning it.

"It skinned my hand but did nothing to Toury. Does that limit it?" Mary asked.

"Yes. I know what family of poison we are dealing with. I'm going to pull the poison from him. Then, Toury, you can heal him, and if you have any energy left, see if you can heal me."

"No, wait." Toury said torn. "Will you die?"

"Possibly. I've had a full life. No more arguing, or our future king will die." Then Edwina placed her hands on his wound.

The color came back to Alex as it leeched from her aunt. Completely conflicted, Toury felt overwhelmingly guilty that she was happy Alex was improving.

Their attention was drawn by a burst of flame. Her father appeared in front of them, somehow able to transport right into her sitting room. He must've drunk dragon's blood. He had Alex's powers. "Dear sister, desist right now," her father said.

Edwina kept her focus on Alex. Toury was too shocked to move.

David engaged first in fighting him. Madge joined in, but before they could overpower him, four other people appeared through flames in the room. The queen splayed herself over Alex to protect him, Mary was throwing fireballs, and Edwina slumped over, her complexion ashen. Toury, torn, reached over to Alex's wound and threw all her healing power into it. Then she used her other hand and did the same to her aunt. All her energy was draining. Exhaustion set in quickly, like a dark, heavy blanket being thrown upon her. Her light was waning, and she had an inkling that it meant her life was leaving her.

"Stop it, Tourmaline!" the man shouted. "Stop! We came for you! I'll spare the prince if you come with us."

She let go, unable to heal anyone anymore.

"No, Toury. Alex wouldn't want you to," the queen said, her face conflicted. It was the truth, but the queen needed Alex to live; so did Toury, and so did the kingdom.

She stood up and turned toward this man. David and Madge were lying immobile on the ground. She prayed they weren't dead. "Do your worst," she spat at him.

Her father's expression was bemused. "I'm here to save you." The way he grabbed her arm and yanked her towards him belied that statement.

"Save him," Toury commanded with the most austere voice she could muster, as she used the last of her power to build up white light in her hand to try to blast a man who had the same power and Alex's fire combined. It was pointless, but she wanted to fight as long as she could. "And I will go quietly."

Her father smirked with some misled pride, no doubt. "Cyssan fram death."

The queen inhaled sharply and translated, "'The kiss from death,' dracaberry blossom." The way the queen gazed at her aunt's limp form, with sorrow and empathy—Toury knew the poison had no antidote. She remembered. Alex told her on their first reconciliation date how the dracaberry tree's pretty white blossoms were collected carefully and used as what Earth called sedatives. He had said one flower petal would put someone to sleep for a day, but in concentration, the person may never wake again.

Too late, Toury realized her father had lunged for her, and he grabbed a hold of her arms. He pulled her toward the window as three of the rebels cornered Mary, who stopped using fire and fell onto the floor in defeat next to her mother and the unconscious Alex and Edwina.

The last rebel had just secured a rope around the window's stone mullion and then started climbing down in haste. Her father ordered her to climb down a rope ladder. In her huge gown and slippers, she made slow work of it, to the rebels' dismay. They grumbled at her.

"Just transport me. This is hard in a wedding gown and slippers, I'll have you know."

Her father, who was closest to her, being right above her on the rope, responded, "Draca blood doesn't last forever. I'm afraid you must climb and do so faster, or I'll be forced to cut the rope and let us fall once we are at a safe distance from the ground."

Toury looked down and was queasy for a moment. The palace was four floors, but the towers were five, so they had a ways to go. She was no longer worried about her footwear but about her strength lasting until they got down the remaining four stories. She hurried as fast and as safely as she could.

Once she got to the bottom, she was relieved. Her arms felt like useless rubber. She had no strength to heal her chafed hands. Her father said he was sorry and brought down a cudgel on her before she could block it. Pain shot through her head, and then it faded away as blackness crept over her vision, and her body sank.

28
A WAKING

Alex felt pain. His last foggy memories were of Toury barricading the door. He opened his eyes and recognized the canopy bed coverings. He was in his bedroom. It was dusk. A servant was putting wood into the fireplace to start a fire—not that Alex needed it. Events suddenly came flickering back to him.

"Toury!" He sat up, but pain sliced through his abdomen, and he fell back onto the bed, unable to withhold a scream. Two steady hands pressed him down gently into the bed. A voice hushed him. He looked over to see his mother's strained and exhausted face. "Toury?"

His mother stared at her nervously wringing hands and blinked back tears.

"Mother!" He could not handle the suspense.

"She's... They took her, the rebels. They won't hurt her. It was her father."

"I have to get to her." He tried to sit up but writhed in pain.

"Stop, Alex. You're in no state to get her. Lie still. You were stabbed, the dagger laced with poison. Lady Edwina and Toury saved you. Don't let it be in vain. We have no idea if Lady Edwina will ever wake again. They say her healing magic is continuously fighting the poison, but they're not sure how that will end." His mother's voice faded away. He tried to cling onto the image of her face, her voice, but it was futile. The pain radiating throughout his body, the sharp, agonizing one in his side, was too much to bear, and he drifted into a relieving, numb unconsciousness.

When he woke again, Madge was by his bedside. It was dark; a fire in the grate was the only thing lighting the room.

"Where's David?"

Madge started at his voice. "He's alive. He's mending from injuries. He is fighting with the healers, wanting to get back to your side. I'm sorry. I failed her, as he failed you."

"No," he said. "No one failed anyone. Most of the kingdom was elated about the wedding. No one could foresee rebels storming. Madge, I need you to get Lord Cobalt."

"I will ring for him, but he may be a bit busy. He is helping Princess Mary, who is Lady of the Castle." Mary was ruling in his stead, good, but odd his mother would let her.

"Where's my mother? Finally resting?" Why was his mother not in command?

"No, Your Majesty. I believe she's with your father."

"How is he? Does he know of the attack?" The stress would be too much for his father to bear.

"Rest, Your Majesty. Cobalt can brief you. I don't know anything, being in the healers' chambers, then here. Please, rest."

He grumbled about being treated like a baby, but his eyes were heavy.

When he woke again, Cobalt was over him, shaking him gently awake. "Your Majesty, sorry to wake you, but time is of the essence."

"Please, brief me. They won't tell me anything," Alex moaned, pushing himself up on his elbows, ignoring the pain in his side.

Cobalt blew out a huff of nervous air. "Firewhiskey?" he suggested, walking over and pouring two ample amounts.

The sunrise lit up the room. How long had Alex slept?

"God and goddess, yes," Alex sighed. "But your behavior frightens me. Give me the worst first. No, tell it all to me at once."

"Get that down you first," Cobalt instructed. He raised his glass, and they downed them.

Alex grimaced but found comfort in the whiskey burning down his throat, reminding him of the fire magic that went through him. "Now, out with it."

Cobalt took a deep breath. "King Craig Sapphirian passed away last night. I had the Hematite baseborn try his blood magic to find his half-brother or the queen to-be, but they are cloaked. I have trackers on them and will join the search as soon as possible. Also, there was poison on the knife that stabbed you, and now Lady Edwina is unconscious from taking the poison's effects into herself. Oh, and Mary and I publicly announced our engagement this morning."

"Engagement!" Alex sat up too quickly and almost retched up the firewhiskey from the pain. He groaned and batted away Cobalt's assistance.

"Your father died, and you fixate on that?"

Then it hit Alex. His father was dead, Toury was missing, and now he was the king. He could not go looking for her and leave the kingdom in chaos after the attack. He could not go anywhere, not having any children and his successors being Mary, the missing Henry, and then no one. He saw

157

how very easy it would be right now for the rebels to end the Sapphirian line.

"I heard it all, Cobalt, but why did you even slip that in?"

"Mary thought it would strengthen your rule."

"I will get Toury back and marry her," Alex said firmly.

"You misunderstand. I meant, it's less likely to have another attack if you are married and Mary is on her way to be. You see, your cousin Henry is still missing. Your uncle is trying to wrestle control from your sister "due to her grief," so, Your Majesty, before I go to find your queen, you need to get out of bed and show the people you are alive and well—even if you must fake it."

"You didn't give it to me all at once," Alex scolded.

Cobalt swallowed hard. "I swear that is the whole of it. Mary and your mother have banded together and are handling your uncle quite well on their own. It amazes me, the power that Mary wields, and she is so strong through all of this..."

Alex raised his brows at his friend to challenge him about his subject content. Cobalt always talked about the ladies to Alex, but this was his sister.

Cobalt caught on, realizing how very different this would be and then diverting his discourse to safer waters: "...but I fear she and your mother need time to grieve. And you, King Alexander, you need time to grieve your father as well."

The title "King Alexander" hit him hard, but he pressed down his emotions. "I'll grieve once I have Toury here safe. Now help me up, and ring for David—I don't care how bad off he is. Then I need you to go find Toury. We've lost enough time." Alex threw the covers back and moved his legs to the floor. "I think. How much time did I lose?"

"Just a day." Cobalt cringed at whatever expression Alex had made, though Alex had no idea which of the array of emotions he was feeling came through on his face. "I had people searching for Toury the moment the castle was secured. You know I will find her," Cobalt said with determination. "I'm a damn good tracker, if I may say so."

"And when you do, you will behave. Mary may trust you now, but I do not."

"Yes, Your Majesty." Cobalt stared at the floor like a scolded child.

"Don't let me down."

Cobalt grabbed his wrist, and Alex grabbed his. It was an oath handshake.

"I won't," Cobalt promised and then yanked Alex up.

Alex felt as if someone filleted his entire body. His growl turned into a scream. This was not just a wound and blood loss—although he never had either in such severity—but the poison, even though it was gone, had exhausted his body. He took a deep breath. He could do this, because he had to. "What is the time?"

"It is two hours after the dawn."

"Good, I need a couple hours to be presentable. Get the town criers to announce that I will do a speech three hours after the noon." Alex took a few tentative steps and made it to his desk. He leaned on it. "Summon David, if you will, and take whomever and whatever you need to get Toury back. Ready them, and then come back to help me. I don't think I can do this speech without you. As soon as the speech is over, leave immediately."

Cobalt bowed and exited. The bell went off in the other room to summon David. Duty before worry over Toury. Duty before getting upset about his father. Duty came first, Alex told himself. He would wash, get dressed, schedule his father's pyre service and Alex's coronation, and let the people see him alive. The idea of not waiting for Toury bothered him, but he'd be king regardless of when she returned to him. Waiting would only look like weakness. Some had already mistaken his ability for forgiveness as weakness.

While he waited for David, his mind pondered on why the rebels, particularly Toury's father, would stop their wedding and take her away. The fact he was her father was the only thing that was keeping Alex sane. The man would not hurt his own daughter, but doubt crept over him. Would he hold her for ransom? Would he hurt his own daughter...for a kingdom? More importantly, would Alex give it over for Toury? The dragon in him told him he would, in a heartbeat. The man in him was more rational but only slightly. He'd already been forced to choose between his kingdom and Toury before. He had made the wrong choice last time, and it would forever haunt him. He could never do it again. And that would not bode well for Fyr's future.

29
HEMATITE

Toury's head ached. Her stomach roiled. She was moving, possibly in a wagon. Her heart picked up a rapid pace, remembering how this had happened not so long ago when the necromancers kidnapped her. She heard voices speaking, so she continued to feign sleep.

"Are you sure we lost the trackers?" a man asked.

"We've been driving for ages, zig-zagging all over Fyr. I'd hope so," a different man retorted. He seemed annoyed at the first man. "Are we going to talk about what happened back at the palace now that we've changed carts three times and trust everyone on this one?"

"How hard did you hit her?" a woman's voice fretted, changing the subject. A hand touched Toury's forehead gently, and she withheld her instinct to flinch. Her hair was smoothed off her forehead in a kind gesture. "She's been out for a day."

"I told you, I had to. She wouldn't leave him. She genuinely loves him and said as much." She recognized the voice as the rebel who said he was her father.

"I thought they took her from Earth? I thought she was being forced into the marriage against her will," the woman said, exasperated.

"I'm not sure that was all true," he countered.

"But the commander's intel said—" she pressed.

"Somehow, he must've been misformed," her father said.

"How's that possible? The commander is in the loop."

"I'm questioning that now."

"The commander tells us what we need to know. If you believe the lies of a little girl over our leader, I'm questioning your alliance. Why'd you let the whelp live?" another man asked, annoyed. "I saw you throw a poisoned dagger at him. Your aim never misses, and your magic can charm the dagger through the dragon's trapdoor, as we both saw. He was there dying, and then you go and tell them the poison so they can save him!"

"There is no antidote! I had to, to get her out of there. You don't understand. Toury was healing him toward her own death. We went in there to save my daughters. I never agreed to an assassination. It was a bonus for the rebel agenda, true, but our goal was to make ourselves known and to get my daughters out. I bought us a hell of a lot of time. I doubt the prince will be well enough for at least several sunrises to chase after us, if he lives at all."

He was severely underestimating her and her aunt's abilities, but that was a fact Toury would withhold. She believed her aunt had gotten all the poison out, because the contrary would ruin Toury. The wound had closed, and Alex was strong. Alex would come for her, and if he couldn't, he'd send an army to get her. She knew Alex would never let her go; just as the dragons would never find another mate, neither would he. Nor would she.

"But the Sapphirian line must end!"

"We never said that," her father continued. "We agreed we wanted reform. A peaceful reform would be best. We have the future queen in our possession. We can demand what we want and get it. We can explain things to her, show her the truth of what is going on, have her make the much-needed reform."

"She is not the one in power," another man said.

"Do you not know how easy it is to influence a man?" the woman said.

"He's easy enough to persuade." Toury recognized Racine's voice.

"Yeah, then how'd you end up in prison?" the other man chided.

"Because I'm not her," Racine spat out. The annoyance and jealousy she tried to hide still came through. It made Toury happy to know that. "She could persuade him to do anything."

"Yeah, but to give up his throne?" the man challenged.

The carriage was silent. Toury's stomach sank. She didn't know the answer to that, although a small voice in her head reminded her he'd already sacrificed her to save his kingdom once. With the roles reversed, would he give up his kingdom to save her? Toury didn't want to think of the answer, for whatever choice he could make, it would be wrong. He would be forfeiting her life or the fate of all his subjects. Who knew what the rebels' plans were and what chaos would follow if they usurped the throne?

"Regardless, the fewer deaths, the better for our cause and our necks," her father said. "I'm not looking to abandon my children on other spheres again or to spend decades away from Fyr. I'm finally home, reuniting my family. I'm staying here."

The carriage stopped, and Toury heard people climb out.

"You spared a Sapphirian? What were you thinking?" the woman asked. The return to the subject meant the two people—her father and the woman—had to be alone now.

"I was weak. You should have seen her face. She loves him, and he loves her. It was clear. I shouldn't have been able to get ahold of him, and he took too long to transport because he wouldn't leave her behind. He went to her so he could transport her to safety instead of saving himself. And the dagger..." He hesitated, his voice shaky. "I almost hit her. My aim was off because he burned my arm, and he shoved her behind himself at the last moment so he'd be hit by my dagger instead. Those are not the actions of a selfish man. Imagine what his father would've done. He would've used the queen as a shield."

Toury doubted that, although she agreed the king was half the man Alex already was. Toury wondered how her father had burned, since he had been drinking dragon's blood, but maybe it didn't give a person all the Sapphirian powers.

"I saw our baby girl and how what I was doing was hurting her, and I couldn't do it. So help me, sweetling, I couldn't break her heart, even if it was what was best."

Sweetling? Our baby girl? This was her mother. Toury was afraid to pretend to wake up, but she wanted to see her mother. When her bound wrists were suddenly tugged upward, she didn't have to feign surprise and was able to "wake up."

The captors refused to speak to her or answer her questions. They wordlessly dragged her into a small rundown building that had a lot of doors close together—townhouses they called them on Earth. It was a poverty-ridden area that she didn't know actually existed in Fyr. She had seen poor Duric begging and other orphans and the elderly; she and Alex had discussed her charity reforms as well as her orphanage. But this, this was something new. She didn't know there were slums. Did Alex, who hardly left Celestia, know how bad it had gotten in some areas? These would be the areas his father would've completely ignored.

She was tossed onto a worn settee, where she finally could have a good look at the people in front of her. There was the gray-eyed man, apparently her father, and then she saw her mother, the woman in the painting the king had gifted her—although aged. Toury just knew when she saw the same untamed black hair, darker complexion, and the same button nose she saw in the mirror every day, that the woman was her mother. The eyes and mouth were different, dark-eyed and full-lipped. These were her long-lost parents. She should've felt complete, happy, or ecstatic. But just like meeting her sister, she was angry, so full of rage. She hated them. The only person who had ever given her love and affection was Alex—and the Sapphirians. They were her true family.

"What do you want from me?" Toury demanded.

"Tourmaline," the woman said with tears in her eyes as she reached forward to touch her. Toury shrank back, making the woman hesitate. "I'm your mother."

"I figured that much out for myself, considering he said he's my father, and I look like you." Toury paused for effect, trying to stay in control and be the powerful person she would have to be in this world if she were lucky enough to live to be queen. "What. Do. You. Want?"

Her parents looked at each other, unsure for a moment.

Then her father spoke: "I know you may be upset right now, but if you hear us out—"

"You interrupted my wedding! Kidnapped me, tried to kill my engagee! Why would I ever hear you out? Not to mention, you are criminals who broke numerous laws of the land and got hundreds of people killed. And you abandoned me!"

"This is a mess," the other man muttered. "You should've let the prince die."

"You have no clue what you've done." Toury laughed bitterly. "You mean the king proxy," she corrected them.

They were taken aback.

Then she laughed. "You didn't even know? Well then, you attacked the castle on old information." She shook her head at them, like a mother scolding her child. "If you had eyes in your head, you would've noticed the king wasn't at the wedding, not even on the balcony to watch. The king is dying. I was keeping him well for a while, but he wanted me to stop. If you wanted his blood, your fight is pointless. Alex is already ruling. Any day now, the king will pass. And I would've been queen if you hadn't stopped it all."

"You actually want to marry him?" her mother asked incredulously.

"I love him. As much as you cannot understand my propensity to love, I cannot fathom your propensity to hate a young man you don't even know," she spat out.

"Told you, lost cause." Her sister picked dirt out of her nails without a care.

Draca

Toury hadn't noticed her there in the doorway. Things were looking down at the moment if rebels were able to spring Racine from prison and attack Alex. Was he safe? Was the castle secure?

"He loves her," Racine said, "She pathetically loves him. But she's no savior."

"That's enough!" her father barked.

Toury laughed. "You guys are so behind. I was the savior. I cured Alex's curse and disbanded the necromancers. I just held trials and condemned most of the necromancers while he was chasing you for killing a dragon to get its blood in order to abduct me it seems."

"Lemme guess, you slaughtered them all? The dungeons were almost empty when I was there," Racine spat. "Tell me, Sister, did you like watching them all burn?"

"Burn?" Toury scoffed. "I, and Alex, abhor the practice. I wouldn't be surprised if he outlaws it after the king passes. We snuffed them. We learned something in defeating necromancers: they cannot exist without the darkness. Once you snuff the darkness out of them, they die. The few who lived through the process were powerless and transported to other spheres in servitude."

They all looked at each other uncomfortably, and a few men shifted their postures. She was getting to them. One left the room quickly, and she knew he'd try to glean info from somewhere to corroborate her claims. At least none of their eyes were black. Even when her sister was furious with her during the one conversation they'd had, Racine's eyes remained gray.

"The court has been completely cleansed of hypocrisy," Toury added.

"Oh yeah, so who's in charge of the Sorcerers' and Magicians' Guilds?" another man asked, assuming the answer would reveal her ignorance.

"Lord Cobalt and Tobias Firebrand."

The man didn't mask his surprise well, and they all exchanged more uncomfortable, shifting glances. They were starting to second-guess their cause, she hoped.

"Lord Citrine?"

"Dead, the entire family. His daughter tried to kill me three times." They were quiet, so she added more for shock value, "Alex gifted me their estate as an orphanage. He brought the Hollyhaven elderly and those orphaned by you to stay there."

Racine glowered at her. "Aww, isn't he so sweet." The sarcasm dripped from her voice, thick like honey.

Her mother found interest staring at the dirty floor; her father's mouth was grim, and he avoided her gaze. Their shifty looks reeked of shame. Good. Hundreds of people had died because of their idiocy. Why hadn't they sent someone to talk to her? Sought her out? Why this over-the-top, unwanted, and unnecessary rescue mission?

"And the curse is definitely broken?" Her mother conveniently changed the subject from their murderous behavior.

"Yes, I destroyed it myself. However, the king will die from his. It was different, permanent, and in every inch of his body, whereas Alex's...it's hard to describe...it had a place it hid, or he pushed it into so it couldn't rule him."

"But how can we tell?" Another man flung his hands up, annoyed.

"I didn't see it. I thought he was just good at hiding it," her father said. "Can you see the darkness, Tourmaline?"

"Yes. In their eyes."

"Me too," her father said with a small smile on his face and some pride shining in his eyes. It unnerved her.

Racine made a snorting noise from the corner, a scoff of jealousy. Her reaction meant she couldn't.

"Look, Tourmaline, you are not just the savior to banish the dark. You will do more than that," her father said, animated.

"I will," she said, glaring at her sister. "Once I get out of here, I'll be queen, and I will make many changes."

Her sister laughed. "He won't let you do squat. You're arm candy."

"I promise you. I can and will do as I please as queen. Alex is nothing like his father. Had you not kidnapped me, he might've even listened to your grievances, being family. But now..." Toury laughed for effect. "Now, if one hair is out of place on my head, he will burn you all with just a look. And see," she raised her arms to show her chaffed hands and wrists from the rope. "I have wounds already." She could easily heal herself, but she wanted them to squirm.

She counted seven people in the room, including her family, who shifted uncomfortably. She realized then that she had the upper hand. They were acting on assumptions and had no clue who Alex really was, what he was capable of—his power or his kindness.

"I would like to be alone," Toury challenged when the silence grew uncomfortable.

Racine snorted. "She thinks she's a queen already."

"I would be the queen had you not meddled where you weren't wanted," Toury shot back.

Racine's scowl faltered into a mope.

"We wanted what was best for you," her mother said with hurt in her voice.

Toury could no longer take the woman's pleading eyes and turned so she wouldn't be persuaded by her emotion. "Tell me, *Mother*, how would you know what is best for me when you don't even know me?"

Her mother gasped, and Toury regretted hurting the woman instantly. Racine giggled until she was elbowed by one of the men to stop.

"Take her upstairs," her father said, some defeat seeping out in his tone.

Her mother took her arm and prodded her toward a steep worn staircase. "Honestly, all we've done from day one was try to protect you."

There was no room for both of them to fit up the stairs, so Toury was pushed ahead of her mother. "So 'protecting' me entailed abandoning me on another planet, where I was miserable, and then when I come back home and I finally learn what it's like to be loved, to learn what family is, you tear that from me too?"

On the landing, her mother yanked her arm, making her spin around to face her. "We had to! My god and goddess, we didn't want to! We had to hide you and Racine somewhere safe. Back then, we weren't sure which one of you was the savior. There were the necromancers growing in power, who would kill you and anyone with strong light powers, and the corrupt Sapphirians, who wanted our heads and could see parts of the future on Fyr but not other spheres unless they were directly involved in the vision. It was the only way. And please, don't refer to the Sapphirians as family. They've brainwashed you."

"You don't know what kept me safe. My aunt and my uncle are alive. I have real family too."

"Uncle?" Her mother didn't know she had a brother-in-law.

"A baseborn I legitimized. He's not the point—"

"Your father and I were discovered and evaded death twice. We had to split up. We would all be dead, including you and Racine, had we not split up. Two toddlers slow one down, you know."

"How practical of you," Toury scoffed.

Her mother's face set in anger. "It was the worst thing I ever had to do in my entire life, giving up my children, and I've committed murder and other heinous crimes. Nothing can compare to the loss of a child—even if it's giving the child a better life—it cuts as deep."

"We have different definitions of a better life."

"Do you realize if we never left you on Earth, the Sapphirians would have never found you and brought you back? Everything happens for a reason. It's fate," her mother insisted.

Despite wanting to disagree, Alex had said the same thing. Toury was almost glad she had been abandoned, rather than being raised by these people, and she was definitely glad for Ruby bringing her back home and instilling in her power and knowledge.

Instead of being petulantly combative, Toury simply turned away from her mother and walked down the hall where she was directed. Part of her felt bad for the woman, but she was too bitter at the moment to admit it.

They entered a small bedroom. Her mother made small talk, pointing out the chamber pot, wash rags, water basin, and two tankards of water, and handed her some clothes.

"Racine said I have a brother, and yet you kept him?"

Her mother's face showed pity for Toury, and she didn't like being weak and vulnerable. "He is...so much younger than you two. Things had quieted down, your father and I were reunited on the water sphere, and it was safe."

"How young is he?" She looked at her mother dubiously, for she was maybe just hitting middle age, but she was sure Racine was only a year or two younger than Toury herself.

"He's eight."

"And you involved him in all this?"

"We needed to come home, for you. We thought you were kidnapped from Earth, forced into an engagement, but it appears our source was mistaken."

Toury thought about her mother's words. She'd left Earth against her will, technically. Ruby had orchestrated this and made her the savior. It was true she was forced into an engagement by Alex, only because she was stubborn and in denial of her feelings. Had Alex waited just a week or two, she would've gone willingly. Regardless, she had no regrets nor ill will towards any Sapphirian.

Then suddenly, something came to Toury. She might be able to maneuver herself out of this if she played her cards right. "What do you guys want, besides killing my engagee?"

"We didn't want to kill him. We wanted to free you from that Sapphirian prison. We would rather have him step down, give up the throne. Allow Guilds to rule. On Earth, they call it a republic, no? Democracy?"

Toury wanted to correct her use of Sapphirian prison, but that would be a lie. She had seen the castle as a gilded cage, but it had been months since she had stopped believing that. It had become...home. She had embraced the idea of spending her life with Alex and helping him change the world for the better.

Instead, she said, "The guilds fight, and the sorcerer's numbers have dwindled. There is no stable government, aside from Alex, who is holding together fragile pieces. You'll start chaos. You'll tear the country in two and restart the rebel wars."

"Come." Her mother motioned her to the window.

Toury saw it had bars on the outside, so no escape that way was in her future. They had broken her from one "prison" and thrown her in another—a strange thing for parents to do.

"Look." Her mother pointed outside.

Toury gazed past the iron bars to the people out on the street. There were quite a few people bustling, dressed in dirty rags, some begging with cups, some women catcalling men, trying to sell their bodies. A few children were running through the streets barefoot.

"What do you see?"

Toury saw loss, pain, suffering, and starvation. This was a horrible place, and these people were poor creatures. But that was what her mother wanted her to say so that she could admit it was all Alex's fault. It wasn't. How could she blame a man who was only a boy months ago without any control over what his father did? "What do you think I see? A bunch of poor people. What does this have to do with your agenda?"

"We want reform. Less taxes for the poor, for royalty and court to answer for their crimes."

"Alex and Mary are innocent of any crime," Toury shot out before her mother could say more. "And Alex and I just did that! The necromancers were mostly nobles. We cleaned it out."

Her mother gave her a wide-eyed once over as if to say she was brainwashed. Instead of chastising or arguing with her, her mother pointed. "That woman there is Irene. She was the king's mistress, and when he tired of her, he passed her on to Lord Citrine, who passed her down and so on. Now she can't even work in a brothel. She's got five kids from three different men and no way to feed them. The eldest has fire power, just so you know."

Toury was sure the king had indiscretions, but Alex had never. The stone test showed he was virtuous, just like her.

"Over there"—her mother pointed—"is little Davy. His mother was burned at the stake for stealing bread for him to eat. His father was a rebel, butchered by Lord Tiffany for wanting exactly what we want, economic spread, the ability to live off working wages."

Toury shook her head.

"You disagree? Well, over there is Misty, a powerful seer just like Irene. As it so happens, they're sisters, but not even Misty's sight could save herself from shame."

As if Misty knew they spoke of her, the woman's eyes shot up to the window, staring at them.

"She befell one of the worst fates. The king's brother took her innocence without her consent, a fate I well know."

"What?" Toury squeaked out.

"I loved your father. I was forced into an engagement because the king's brother wanted me. Prince Alfred was a sick and perverse boy, and everyone knew it, even King Rowland X, who had altered the succession so Anne could rule before Alfred. When I would not marry him, I decided to make sure he couldn't by—"

"Creating me." Toury hoped to avoid a description of her parents' relationship. Having been through the chastity test, Toury knew exactly how one would fail it.

Her mother laughed softly, but it was forced. "We married in secret, and after finding out he couldn't marry me, Alfred Sapphirian took me anyway to make me his mistress, to torture me and scar me physically and mentally, most likely in hopes your father wouldn't want me after that, but he did. Your father and I were in love, so we fled once I started showing. For all nine months, we didn't know who your father was. Then you were born with those beautiful gray eyes instead of those horrid blues, and I knew I was free. We named you after both sides of the family so no one would even think to question your parentage. But the king seemed to hide his brother's sins, and Alfred was dead by then anyway."

"Because you cursed him."

"No," her mother said. "We didn't. The king pinned that on us, making us criminals. I think he knew what his brother had done and thought we should be the culprits. I was angry for years, but I realized that he must've seen our actions as justification for his brother's actions. No, his anger was because he thought we cursed him and his newborn child."

"The king did speak kindly of you, actually. I got the impression he liked you and hated my father for taking you from court."

Her mother allowed a little smile. "King Craig was kind to all women, of course, but he was two-sided, and I've heard the bad side came out more after the curse. He had an unmatched temper, an arrogance, and was an elitist."

"I agree." Toury allowed.

"And Alfred." Her mother cringed. "He was the worst you could ever imagine. Selfish, arrogant, sadistic, temperamental, ornery. Every terrible trait you could imagine, the man possessed. He would physically and mentally torture people to make himself happy."

Toury couldn't help but think how very different Alex was from his deceased uncle. Sure, he could be a tad arrogant or selfish, but he was getting better at thinking of others before himself. He had been the one slowing their physical relationship down, the very opposite of her mother's story. He wanted Toury as his lifemate, not a mistress.

"I wasn't disagreeing with you at all, and I'm sorry that happened to you, but you have no clue who Alex is. He sure is not his uncle nor his father. As soon as he took over for his father, he's been talking about job stimulus projects and wants me to head my own charities, on top of my orphanage. We've spoken of orphanages and disability centers, migrating people expense-free to areas where work is seasonal. He's constantly going through old bills and undoing them. He dotingly calls me his world's champion for women. He has been shifting laws that hindered women and is overturning them. It will all start going into effect when he is crowned. He said it'll take a decade, as he has to do things slowly to keep the nobles from revolting, but he has it all mapped out. He always asks my opinion on state matters. You have no idea what progress you just disrupted."

Toury tried not to think about the possibility of never discussing those plans with Alex again. She had to believe he was alive still, that her healing and her aunt's leeching of the poison had been enough. There had been so much blood, though.

"Sometimes men say things they don't mean in order to—"

"Don't," Toury snapped. Not this excuse again. Alex wasn't saying these things to get her in bed. He was the one trying to stop her from taking things too far. "No. He was marrying me, not trying to seduce me. You ruined what was supposed to be the best day of my life, and I hate you for it. I can't even wrap my mind around the resentment I bear toward you for abandoning me with people who didn't care at all about me."

Her mother's lips pursed in disapproval, and then she wordlessly left the room, locking the door behind her.

Toury wasn't sure which idea cast her mother from the room, mentioning a Sapphirian in a good light or accusing her of being a terrible mother. Toury thought the former took precedence over everything. No wonder the king thought her father had cursed him. That hatred was so strong, it might have unhinged the woman.

30
A SPEECH

Alex had another firewhiskey. His mother said nothing, numb in her grief, but even Mary—the wild one who had been known to drink too much and before she was allowed to—gave him a look of censure. She was still sober in the face of all this horror, which was great, but he didn't need her disapproval when he was trying to hold himself—mind and body—together. He glowered at her. She sighed, looking to Cobalt, entreating him to do something about it.

"I think Alex knows his limits, Mary. He's in a lot of pain."

Alex was smug that his friend chose his side. Mary glared at Cobalt.

"What? Mary, come now. You'd light him on fire if he did the same to you. I recall you actually doing that just last year when he criticized your drinking habits."

"I think it's best you shut your mouth now, dear," Mary told Cobalt.

"Absolutely not." Cobalt stood up, annoyed. "You think you can order me around because you're the princess, and sure, you can. But I won't be your lifemate if this is how you expect it to be."

"And I won't be yours if you always side with him!"

"My king? I can't...not side with the king!"

Mary stood up in a huff, crossed her arms, and went to the other side of the room, staring out the window at the masses of people they heard on the grounds. They were mad for opening the gates, but Alex would not hide and cower behind his walls.

"They're chanting your name, Alex, and their flowers and gifts are piled up out front. This is good," Mary shifted her tone.

"It's still dangerous," his mother fretted. "One arrow, Alex, is all it would take."

"They will not attack me. They want change, but they don't realize yet that I'm going to deliver it," Alex said quietly. Everyone watched him, making him suddenly self-conscious. "Cobalt, mind helping me up?"

As Cobalt helped him up, Mary demanded, "What changes?"

"Reform," he said and left it at that.

"For whom?"

"The orphaned, the disabled, the mentally ill, the unemployed, the sick—you name it, I'm going to fix it. I will tell you all about it, Mary, but for now, let's get this over with."

Mary stared at him in a new light, with awe and appreciation, he thought. She took his other arm, looping it through hers, supporting him, but making it appear to be a loving, relaxed gesture.

"Alex," his mother's voice cracked. They stopped, and with pain, he turned, noting she was already dressed in her black mourning clothes. "You have the best heart I have ever known."

"I get that from you, Mother."

Then they were outside on the third story's balcony. When the crowd saw him, they roared with delight. It gave him enough energy to let go of Cobalt and Mary. He walked to the wall and waved. His other hand leaned on the wall, for he was limited in energy.

"Alex," Cobalt whispered, his voice full of trepidation.

He waved Cobalt off and motioned for the crowd to quiet down. Cobalt and Mary were scanning the crowd, awaiting another attack. Alex himself was hypervigilant, but he had a feeling the rebels were gone or wouldn't dare attack again now that the soldiers were on high alert and Alex's archers were on the roof at the ready. The rebels had taken what they wanted and gotten out. What they intended to do with Toury was another problem he didn't dare let himself worry about. Racine, on the other hand, he was glad to be rid of. Now he didn't have to decide what to do with her.

The crowd quieted down, and a few shouts resonated out about how they loved him, and long live King Alexander. Then silence rang.

He took a deep breath and used his diaphragm to project his voice, despite his side's protest. "My people! I stand here to prove to you that I am alive and well, despite the unforgivable actions of the rebels, who disrupted and ruined what was to be the best day of my life and halted our steps toward a brighter future. The black flags fly, as you see, not for me but for my father, who has passed during all this turmoil. He passed peacefully, believing his son was being married and that his line would continue on.

"The rebels will be caught. They will be punished. They have attacked me and my intended, stabbed me with a poisoned dagger, but I tell you now, it will take much more than that to kill the *draca*!"

The people screamed in accordance. He was winning them over while reminding them of the ancient language of the first people of Fyr, that his rule extended all the way back to those times. He was the legitimate heir, the draca, or dragon, born of their fire. He wanted to remind them he was more than just a man.

When they quieted down, he continued, "They will be caught by you, all of you, who must be my eyes and ears, who must help me in any way to find information, turn in these villains, and bring our queen back to us so she can officially rule by my side, as my partner."

He paused to take in the now quiet and shocked people. "You heard me right. You see, these foolish rebels are trying to destroy the monarchy, but that will only create chaos and allow tyrants to rise. As a kingdom, we have our cracks, and these rebels seek to exploit those and break us entirely. I offer more. My queen and I have plans of reform, of changing the very structure of our kingdom to seek equality and help where needed. The weak and unable will no longer suffer to the confines of fate. We will lift them up.

"I have recently—in battling the necromancers—learned that noble blood does not always mean noble intentions. Now, this is not to say nobles will be under attack. I want no turmoil, no war, but for all people to be judged for their character, their actions, not by their social status or by the strength of their power. We will defeat the last of the necromancers. We will eradicate the rebels. And we will prevail into a golden age where everyone can prosper, and all that our children will know is peace and happiness. This I promise you, my people, who are the blood force of our kingdom, the power that pulsates life and fire in this world.

"And for the rebels, who I know are out there." He was sure he was only talking to a couple of their spies. If they wanted to kill him, they would 've stopped Lady Edwina saving him, or would have seen his death through. "You have no cause, for tyranny and greed are not in my vocabulary. You now fight for your own greed and thirst for power. You do not have my people's best interest at heart. And if my queen is hurt in any way, you will die by the stake. You will be the last to burn to death, because my first decree as king is to cease execution by fire. No one will ever burn to death again for a crime in my kingdom, except any person who attacks a royal or a royal-to-be.

"So please, my people. I thank you heartily for coming to hear me on this day of grief and woe. We will get our queen back with your help, and we will forge a brighter future for all of us. Go home in peace. Dream and plan for a future of your making. The palace will be closed for mourning, with the exception of my father's pyre and my coronation. But I urge you in our mourning period to write your grievances. No one will be ignored. This I vow."

The crowd erupted in applause and cheers. He waved to them, noting the shouts had turned into a rhythmic chant. They were saying the same word over and over again, the ancient word for dragon: "draca." At that moment, he knew he had won them over, and the moniker would be how he'd always be remembered. He would be the Draca King to them, the same name that had been given to the first King of Fyr.

No longer being able to handle the pain, Alex turned and rushed inside, grabbing Cobalt just as they entered the doors and throwing all of his weight onto him. Cobalt caught him and helped him sit down. Cobalt shook his head, and Mary stared at him in awe.

"What, was it bad?" Alex grimaced. "I kind of made it up as I went, but they seemed to love it."

"It was...incredible. Oh, Alex," Mary threw her arms around him, hugging him. "You will be the best and most loved monarch this sphere has ever seen."

He met his mother's proud gaze, who wiped tears from her eyes. Then he took in Cobalt's expressionless face. "You're not pleased."

"The nobles will not take this lightly. After wiping a fifth of them out for being necromancers, this is going to look like you're usurping any power they have. They will resent you."

"Nay." Mary gaped at Cobalt as if he were crazy. "If they are judged on their character, they will grovel and simper over Alex to keep what they have, be more charitable. If Alex has the poor, the cunning folk, and the Magicians' Guild, he has the majority of the kingdom. Nobility is a minority. The masses are what matter. Plus, he just undermined the rebel cause. Ingenious, really."

"You two need to cool the arguing. You're not even married yet, and you bicker like an old couple," Alex murmured, rubbing his temples.

Cobalt blushed, and Mary giggled.

Alex sighed and then explained further. "Don't fret. We'll see in the correspondence whether they are irate or groveling. And there are always other ways to make them happy." He met Mary's gaze and smirked. "Say, Cobalt, you liked the look of Crystal gardens, no?"

"You know, I have a green thumb, and those are the most illustrious gardens in the kingdom, aside from the palace's."

"Well, they belonged to a necromancer and traitor, and they can be yours if you bring my bride home."

"Really?" Cobalt smiled broadly and stood up immediately, ready to leave that moment. Then his brow wrinkled. "Hey, I see what you just did there. So, you'll bribe them?"

"Oh, no. Only you. I'll reward them after they do good on their own accord. It will be yours. Please, get going. Toury needs to come home."

Cobalt rushed over to Mary, mumbled a few whispers, and kissed her cheek before he fled. Mary sighed and flopped down on the settee. She took up Alex's hand in hers.

"No protests about putting your man in danger?"

"Nope." She shrugged. She was too relaxed.

"Mary?" he prompted. "Do you know... You saw it in the flames! Why didn't you tell me?"

"And miss a speech like that?" She scoffed. "Yes, I saw it last night but didn't want to get your hopes up. Toury hardly needs Cobalt to save her. Didn't see how, but I think all will be well."

"Of course. I never would suspect anything less from Toury." Then he smiled happily. She was coming home. She would be okay. "So, you let him go just to make sure that thread of the future would happen?"

Mary's brow wrinkled. "No, I really like those gardens. They're so close to the castle, I was thinking we could extend the wall."

"Might look a bit greedy to the nobles," he murmured, closing his eyes and laying his head back. The speech had taken a lot out of him.

"Not if we can eventually invite the court back—a very selective court, of course, for our safety."

"You would make a good queen, Mary."

"No thanks." She laughed. "You can bear that burden, Brother."

He drifted asleep, feeling someone move him to a lying position on the settee before sleep overtook him completely.

31

RANSOM

Toury woke up on the pallet stiff and sore. The pallet hadn't been that bad, like an Earth mattress but on the floor. She had been overly spoiled in the palace. It was easy to forget what normal was when she was surrounded by luxurious sheets, delicious foods, gilded furniture, and more money than she ever knew what to do with. She was famished, having not eaten since the wedding, which was now two mornings ago by her guess; due to nerves, she had hardly eaten before the wedding either. She had drunk the water that was intended for the water basin but was growing parched.

As she stood up, stretching out her weary limbs, her head spun either from a lack of food, the blow to her head, or both. She went to the window to observe the bustling street. She amended that comment about having too much money; she knew exactly how to spend the Sapphirian riches: helping those who were downtrodden by no fault of their own—like Misty, who was still standing on her corner in the wee hours of the morning, hoping to snag a client.

Misty's soothsaying eyes shot up to Toury again, staring through the grimy window at her, as if she knew Toury was thinking about her. Toury waved. It felt childish and silly, but she didn't want to bang on the window, screaming for help, and draw the attention of her captors. Misty nodded to her, so Toury tried to think of a way to signal that she needed help—even if the woman was in with her rebel parents, it couldn't hurt. Toury tried to open the window, which she knew was pointless, but she hoped it would make the woman realize she was trapped. Misty simply looked away.

Toury ran her finger down the dusty glass to reveal a line. She formed the word "Help" backward and then waited patiently for the woman to look back. She could bang on the glass, and Misty would hear, for she was that close. That would bring attention to her from those downstairs, and from the early dawn light and lack of sound below, they likely were still fast asleep.

Toury waited. Misty gave up on snagging more clients and went to enter the ramshackle house across the street. She suddenly stopped and peered up to the window. Misty read the word, and Toury tried to give her the most desperate and imploring look she could muster. The woman fingered her neck, touching a necklace that was not there. Then it clicked. Toury touched her own bejeweled neck, feeling the nearly priceless gift from the queen that wound around her neck, which had half disappeared under the dull, scratchy nondescript dress they had given her.

It was a gift from the queen, the necklace Toury had worn on her wedding day and was going to hand it down to her first daughter when she came of age. Yet it was the ticket out of here toward safety and a liability the rebels had overlooked. If they noticed it and took it from her...it might be enough money to fund a huge campaign against the royals, against her family.

Toury met the woman's gaze and nodded. She unclasped it and held it out to symbolize she would give it to her.

The woman's mouth dropped, and then she scanned the street. Not seeing anyone about watching her, the woman nodded and entered her house.

Toury took the necklace and, not knowing what else to do with it, slipped it down into her cleavage, tucking the jewels snug in the corset under her breasts, where they uncomfortably poked into her breastbone, but it was the only way to keep them safe. She smeared the word "help" off the window and was glad she had, because the door unlocked, and her father entered with a board serving as a tray of sorts with food and a napkin. Strange to bother with a napkin when you serve food on a piece of scrap wood.

"I've brought you breakfast," he told her with a grin as if this were a normal situation and this was him showering her with affection. He placed the board down and gave her a once over. "That dress suits you. All that finery is ludicrous on a person." He snorted at the pile of white and brown material in a pile in the corner, the brown being Alex's dried blood. She had prayed all night that he was still alive.

"It was a wedding dress. They're supposed to be fine," she said coldly.

Her father's mood darkened.

"This dress," she added, "is okay, but the material is coarse against the skin. I never dress in ridiculous finery on a daily basis, but the fabric is softer. In fact, I sometimes wear a shirttail and breeches."

Her father laughed hard at this. When he calmed down, he pointed to the food. "Breakfast."

She scrutinized the hunk of cheese and bread. Hardly appetizing. "I might like dressing down, but I do not like eating down. Is this cheese moldy?"

"It's supposed to be," he said defensively. "You need to eat. You've been through a lot."

"Thanks to you," she added.

Her father rubbed the back of his neck uncomfortably. "I need you to write a letter."

"To whom?" She grabbed the bread and started to devour it.

"The king."

Toury's stomach lurched. Why the king and not proxy? Why not Alex? She looked imploringly at her father.

"Because he's your betrothed and should know you're alive and well."

It took a second for it to click, but Toury understood this was her father's way of telling her she was right. The king had passed away, Alex had the throne, and now the rebels believed they had something to work with. Alex was alive. She suppressed any celebratory expression from her face, although inside, she was more than relieved.

Toury noted that what she had thought was a napkin was actually paper. "What do you want?"

"What do you mean?"

"This is a ransom letter, no?"

"You're my daughter." His voice was incredulous.

"You took me from Alex. He'll want my return, so my guess is you'll ask for something in exchange for my return. Is that not ransom?"

"I won't threaten to harm you, so no. It's a trade."

"Trading with someone you stole. This is ridiculous. Let me go."

"The cause needs you. We need you, especially after yesterday."

"What happened?" She was afraid to ask, but it had to be good news for Alex, for her father seemed a bit put out and more on edge. He sat down, playing with a rumpled quill.

"Your darling king gave a speech of empty promises that pulled the cause right out from under us and put us into the fire. He's a smoother politician than I had believed."

"Probably not empty promises, and you put yourselves into the fire. What did you think would happen if you took me? That he would kindly ask you to let me go? He is a good man, but like all good men, he has his flaws. His infamous Sapphirian temper is directed at you."

"I am not going to offer you to him. I'm not letting you suffer the fate of an unhappy marriage to him."

"You have no idea what would make me happy. Plus, you admitted you could tell he loved me. He could've died saving me."

"You were awake," her father accused. Toury had forgotten she'd overheard that part in the wagon when she was pretending to be unconscious. "A life with a Sapphirian will be suffering, one way or another."

"He's not like his father, and the complete opposite of his uncle."

"All Sapphirians show their true colors eventually. He's calling himself the Draca." Her father said it with scorn, trying to make out that Alex was full of excessive pride.

"Or are the people calling him that? If they are, you're screwed."

"Screwed? Earth term, my little one? I understand your meaning, though. They brainwashed you, those Sapphirians."

"Maybe they did," Toury allowed, "with kindness, a sense of belonging, and acceptance for who I am. If that is brainwashing, then I embrace it."

"He used you. You're the savior, and he used you to save his own neck. The only reason I don't hate him, the only reason I saved him in the end was because I realized there was more to it. After using you for his own needs, he was making amends by marrying you. That's what I thought until I saw both your faces when he took my ill-thrown knife. No man who uses someone would take a dagger for her unless—"

"He loves her. Let me go," Toury pleaded. She gave her father sad eyes and a feigned pout, the kind of puppy-dog expression she imagined a little girl should give her father when wanting something.

The look clearly wounded him. He stood up quickly and put an inkpot down on the board next to the paper. He offered her the quill, avoiding her gaze. "I cannot," he murmured. "Write what you will to the king, but keep in mind, we will read it. You will tell him you are safe and well and give him our terms." Her father paced. "You will be let go if he publicly decrees Fyr a republic. And if he pardons all rebels, I will tell him the person who created the curse."

"You know who?"

Her father nodded. "Did you think I was hiding all these years from King Craig?" Her father laughed at the thought. "No, the cursemaker knows I know. My life is in danger, has been ever since the day I..."

"You what?"

"I've said too much."

"You want me to like you. You want me on your side. I suggest you tell me anything to paint yourself in a better light than what I know of you:

a man who abandoned me to save his own neck, who uses his children as pawns in some deadly feud."

When he turned away from Toury, she knew her barb had hit home. Then he paced. Thinking he was done with the subject, she penned the opening to the letter.

Then he turned with energy and a huff of breath, announcing he was going against his better instincts to tell her something. "I caught a person cursing the baby prince and ran them off. Did you notice the difference in the curses, little Tourmaline? How the king's was so much stronger than his son's? I was unable to banish King Alex's, but I was able to shrink it into that place you said it liked to hide: his heart." He sighed.

That was how her father had gotten into Alex's sitting room! Alex had said when he transported, he had to envision the place, and her father had been there before.

"It was a weakness of mine. I should've let the curse take him, but you were already growing inside of your mother, and I could not live with myself if I didn't help a poor, helpless newborn prince. Had I not limited the curse into that place, Alex might not be here today."

Toury could say nothing. She didn't want to stop listening to the story. She wanted more. Even though she wanted to hate him and her mother, she was wavering, wanting him to keep explaining how he was the hero of this past, not a villain, some compromise of her mind and heart so she could have two families. But she knew it was futile. She had chosen Alex. She'd told him so and didn't regret it, and her parents were against the throne.

"I don't regret it, you know, even though I was caught in the prince's tower and had to flee and abandon my children. I did what was right. I limited it to his heart, inadvertently making the only person capable of breaking the curse a woman who had light and healing magic, who could claim that very part of him. I just never wanted it to be you."

Toury refused to be taken in by the story. "You admit he loves me, so why are you refusing me this marriage?"

"He loves you enough for the curse to be lifted, but if he truly loves you more than his kingdom, he will take off the medallion."

Toury's heart sank. Her father knew her weakness. He somehow knew she struggled with being second in Alex's life. Despite not raising her, her father knew her. Out of both her parents, from what she had seen, she was more like him. "As you said before, he didn't choose me last time. What makes you think he won't do the same again?"

"If the curse is truly gone as you profess, there is no dark side to him. Even though I'm loath to defend the boy, he will be clear-headed now. King Craig Sapphirian was a poor king to start with. He wasn't raised to rule, but the spare, second in line after his brother Rowland. His life was full of dissipation, greed, and taking everything he wanted. After his father and brother died and he had to suddenly rule, those faults didn't leave him, but once he was cursed, his decisions, his moods, his personality were tainted even more. He was inherently evil, although he must've been strong enough to stop the necromancers from overtaking him. Little did the necromancers know of the savior, and little did they know, I helped limit the curse in his son."

"If you object to the curse, not Alex, you can stop all this rebellion."

"No, we object to a monarch completely, Tourmaline. I've been to every sphere, and they all have it wrong, but Earth has the closest solution to equality and democracy."

"Full of wars, disputes, annoyingly fake politicians, and inequality as well."

"We will not allow a monarch to continue in Fyr. Make your king understand that."

"And will you go so far as to kill him, despite your daughter's wishes?"

"I do not command the rebels. I'm merely a cog on one gear of many in a large machine. I'm not the commander. I believe the one who does command wants nothing better than to see Alex lose the throne and his head. And before you even try to ask, few know who the commander is, and I don't have this privilege."

"So, you blindly follow some man, and for what? You don't know his loyalties, his goals, his real intentions."

"We fight together for the same purpose, to see an end of the monarchy."

Toury huffed. How could they be so blind, so trustingly stupid? "Or simply to see another person put on a throne. You can't trust someone you can't see or know. How do you know this commander won't take the throne once he's wiped out the Sapphirians?" She cringed after saying it aloud but pushed the thought from her mind. Alex wouldn't die. He couldn't.

"There is trust in the cause."

"Your only cause is revenge!"

"And why not?" he shouted at her, taking Toury aback. "What one of those Sapphirians put your mother through, put us through, until you were born—you cannot know how long that affects you. For life, Tourmaline, for life." His tone was defeated, and she could see a paralyzing type of despair in her father's eyes. He was a broken man, half-mad from what a terrible dead man had done to her mother.

"And he is dead. The curse got him."

"I wanted to do it with my own two hands, but there was you to think about."

"Killing every last Sapphirian won't be the same."

He laughed dryly. "I used to think it would, but when I hurt the prince I had saved, I realized how wrong I had been."

"Then let him live," she begged.

"It's his choice whether he keeps his head or not. He must forfeit the sphere. And you must write to convince him to do so."

She wouldn't convince her father any further today, but she wanted to sway him. She wanted this impossible compromise where a world could exist with Alex on a throne and her parents in her life. "I would like to write this alone," Toury said, stalling.

Her father sighed and stood, gripping her shoulder in a soft squeeze before he left.

As soon as she was alone, she paced the room, sat down, stood up, paced again. What could she say to Alex? How could she ask him for what they wanted while imparting a message to him to not do it?

Then an idea struck, not from the Ruby knowledge bank, but from her own creative mind.

32
A MESSAGE

Alex peered down at the missive a second time. It had been brought by a messenger from Celestia, who only could tell him that a man had appeared in a ball of fire and handed over triple the fee to deliver the letter to the palace. His temper wanted to burn the letter to cinders, but he withheld the urge. This was Toury's terrible penmanship scrawled across the page; the words were hers, but the sentiment was not. He knew the subject wasn't hers.

"What does it say?" Mary said, exasperated.

He had opened it and left his mother and Mary in suspense long enough, not purposely, but because it was hard to grasp. "It's the demands, written in Toury's hand." His eyes scanned it again. *Come on, Toury!* The sassy, strong girl he knew would do something, impart something. He scrutinized every word chosen but found no clues.

"And they ask for?" His mother clutched her handkerchief, twisting it in her fingers, as she was oft to do since his father's death.

"Pardons in exchange for the culprit who cursed us, my throne for Toury's safe return."

His mother swooned. Mary gasped. His chest tightened. As usual, Mary went off, most likely saying what she would do to the Hematites and rebels in colorful words, but he had no ears for her. He was absorbed in examining the letter. It had smudges, which broke his heart. Her handwriting with the quill had improved drastically, so it showed she was under duress while writing it. He pored over the letter, noticing the randomized smudges, not from her pinky moving across the paper but...intentional.

He grabbed up a quill and started writing on a separate scrap of parchment, ignoring his sister's rambles and his mother's questions until he got her coded message down, each smudge being under a letter: *Never give in.*

He sat back, covering his face. It had been terrible enough believing she would ask him to give up his birthright—his only purpose—and hand the lives of his people to these rebels. It was worse that he wanted to. He'd give it up for her, which was utterly selfish; to choose her over his people was not the action of a king. Duty first, he had been taught. There should be no room for a heart, for love, but he didn't believe that anymore. When he had said he was his mother's son, he had meant it. He didn't want to live by the Sapphirian way anymore.

"What is it?" Mary demanded.

"She coded a message: 'Never give in.'"

Mary smiled. "She'll get out of this, Alex, or Cobalt will get her. I saw it."

"What will you do about them?" His mother inquired.

"Who? The rebels or the Hematites particularly?" Alex mused.

"The Hematites."

"I'll give them their pardon for the cursemaker's identity."

"No." Mary shook her head. "Her father attempted to kill you."

"And what do you think killing him will do to Toury?"

"What will it do to our kingdom? You must fight fire with fire." Mary stomped her foot like the little brat she used to be.

"Mary, that person could still curse you, my children, and yours. He must be stopped."

"Point taken," she growled.

"I need time to think," he said as a dismissal. Once alone with David, he slipped the King Medallion off his head and held it in his hand. He stared at the worn silver disc that was a couple generations old. It was the original metal the first Sapphirian king had forged but had been melted down and remolded every few hundred years due to wear and tear. It was more than just metal, a symbol of who he was, what his role would be, and his duty. He wanted to cast it aside to save the woman he loved. It seemed like a simple decision. Toury was more important.

The tiny sapphire in the medallion caught his eye. The blue stone was embedded in the metal as the dragon's eye. The dragon was carved in the metal in intricate detail. Its wings curled in slightly around its frame, with its regal profile and tail both curving to make the image circular. Although its wings were in a more relaxed pose, its claws were drawn ready for attack—like Alex himself, the dragon in him warring with the man—full of both calm logic and a fiery temper and will. At the top, it read, "Se Draca," and at the bottom, "sciele riscian moncynne." Translated to modern English, it read, "The Dragon shall rule mankind." This reminded Alex that he was in charge of every Fyrian on *his* sphere. They depended on him. To hand over this medallion would be forsaking all his people to an unknown and possibly horrific fate.

As a child, he would look at the medallion on his father's chest with pride and couldn't wait for the day to wear it. And now his father was gone. Never did he think that would happen when Alex was eighteen. The King Medallion, they called it, and yet a few Queen Sapphirians had worn it, the first being two hundred years ago when a king only sired daughters and changed the patriarchal law to allow first-born females to rule after the males. Prior, when there were many Sapphirians still around, the crown was given to the closest male relative, an agnatic monarchy that ignored female lines. Allowing queens to rule was a move toward treating women better. How Toury, his champion of women, would love to hear that piece of history. If he ever saw her again. This was not a decision he could possibly make.

"Your Majesty?" David interrupted his reverie.

"I'm fine, David." Alex slipped the medallion back on, refusing to think it was an inadvertent choice. "What is next on my agenda?"

"Sleep. It is late, Your Majesty."

He could not sleep that night. First was his realization that Toury's scent had left her bed. It had been three days since she'd graced her bed, but her scent was already gone. He could not sleep, worrying about her and concerned over his father's funeral pyre the next morning. The castle had to be open again to allow mourners in. It was tradition for the people to wish the former king on, while the new king used his own fire to send his predecessor to the next realm. He had seen his father's cold, immobile body, but to light his father on fire... He cringed at the prospect.

Soon he rose from bed, not having slept. Exhausted beyond belief, the effects of the stabbing still lingering in his system—fatigue and a minute ache in his side—he dressed and met his equally exhausted sister and mother. The latter couldn't speak, and the former simply stated, "I will drink today, Alex, to Father, but not tomorrow."

"I will drink to him too, Mary. Moderation and control."

"Can you do this?" she asked quietly.

"I must."

Then he held his head up high and feigned strength by pulling on all the energy he had left in his reserves. He walked out to absolute silence. The blinding light of the sun obscured his vision for a moment, but then his eyes fixated on the massive pyre of wood and the shrouded body, only his father's head visible, the sun glistening off the King Medallion that rested on top of the shroud. He had already worn it but switched back to his Prince Medallion for the ceremony. Behind the pyre was a line of soldiers, and behind them, a silent crowd, paying their respects. No shouts, no anger, just some quiet weeping and sniffles. The rebels weren't making an appearance. What were they waiting for? He wanted them here so he could channel his anger and grief at something, someone, burn them.

Alex kissed his mother's cheek and then his sister's. He gave Mary a look to do what ceremony wouldn't allow him to do: help their mother. Mary nodded and took their mother's hand in hers, squeezing it. He removed the Prince Medallion and placed it over Mary's head, marking her next in line.

"Only until your son is conceived," she said firmly and loudly enough for the front of the crowd to hear. "The flames tell me so."

The crowd murmured, and he heard them spread the word back like a rippling tide of hope. His uncle Humphrey, who stood on Mary's other side, appeared surprised by her comment. Alex was glad he was there to help his mother and sister while he was busy with the ceremony, but he was also wary. His uncle had come back for the wedding and stayed for this, but Alex hoped he'd leave soon. He knew his uncle would try to influence him as he had tried with his father. His father never let him, and neither would Alex, but it hadn't stopped him from trying to assert control over the castle already.

Alex looked away from his uncle's stern gaze and back to Mary. He gave her a small smile, took a deep breath, and turned to the crowd. He climbed up the steps of the pyre bed and removed the King Medallion from his father's chest and handed it to Lord Cobalt, Duke of Edington, his friend's father, and Tobias Firebrand. They held up the medallion together as heads of the guilds and placed it over his head.

"The Sorcerers' Guild passes on the flame to King Alexander Rowland Sapphirian, the first of his name." The duke smiled upon him as a father would his son.

"And the Magicians' Guild likewise passes on the flame to King Alexander Rowland Sapphirian."

"Long live the king!" They shouted in unison. The crowd boomed it afterward. They started to descend, but waited for Alex to follow; he nodded them on. The Duke looked confused, but the firebrander smirked before he urged Cobalt's father along.

Alex was going to do nothing by halves. He was starting a new reign, and he needed them to know he was the true ruler of the land, a message to these rebels that he would fight fire with fire. He was the flame. Burning his father from afar was too impersonal, so he lit the fire around them both and watched as the flames ate away at his father's flesh. Having no life in him, no blood flowing, nor magic inside him, he was penetrable, a mortal after all. According to his ancestors, Alex was a part of the dragon gods. Immortal in the flames. When the smell of burning flesh started to make him nauseated, Alex walked down the pyre steps, his inflammable clothes merely steaming. Alex quietly watched from below as his father was taken to the other realm.

He ignored the whispering of the awed crowds and their cries to his health, happiness, and long reign, and joined his mother and sister, taking them both into his arms and hiding their faces into his shoulders. It was to protect them, shield them, allow them to feel something. It was also a message, an honest one of what his reign would be. Now coronated, he was king, and he would rule with equal love, respect, and intimidation. He would get Toury back and forge a future no one expected. He would stop these rebels, just as he stopped the necromancers, with Toury by his side.

33
SAPPHIRIANS

After Toury had finished her letter to Alex, she had been left to her own devices. When the light started dimming outside, announcing the arrival of dusk, the door unlocked. She looked over, eager, famished, hoping whoever it was had more food. It wasn't her father, but a man with some bread and a glass of water; he placed it on the floor as if she were an animal. She asked a bunch of questions—mixed with shouted demands about whether Alex had received her letter—but he turned a deaf ear and didn't say a word. Having not been given a lunch, she inhaled the bread.

Her breakfast was large the next morning—at least in comparison. She had nothing to do all night and morning but think. Overall, she had to admit, if her parents were to be believed, the Sapphirians had a terrible history. If she believed in Alex and all his promises, that corruption would be gone now. She wanted so badly to believe him, but his track record of promises wasn't so great when it came to her, though he had been trying to make up for it. That's why, in her letter, she warned him not to give up his throne for her. She didn't want to be hurt by disappointment again, by not coming first. Worse, she dreaded the guilt she'd feel if he did choose her. If he lost everything because of her, she could never forgive herself.

There was some fruit, bread, and butter sent up for her lunch. Man, things were so bad in these slums that lunch seemed like a bonus until she looked at the fare. The fruit was beyond the point of ripe to almost rotten—of course, no dracaberry since her favorite was an expense—and the bread was stale and hard. She wondered if it was this bad, or if they saved the worst for her to prove their point.

They were right, though. Smoke from factories billowed on the horizon; the closer ones had lighter smoke—steam perhaps—but both were choking out the view of the sun. So there was electricity for the "important" parts of the area, most likely these lord-run businesses. Down below her, the sewers steamed, making her thankful the window protected her from the likely stench. She watched the people in the street below. They were downtrodden, weary, overworked, and underfed. Children were begging, some trading off items of value for coin—most likely pickpockets. The people of Fyr were suffering. Alex would have to make drastic changes to correct this level of misery.

She understood them now—her parents. She could not resent them for abandoning her, for thinking they were saving her from a horrible fate. She saw them for what they were: weak people, hurt beyond reparation. She was the same as them. They had hurt her, Alex too, but she could change. She could forge a path, not of revenge but of forgiveness. She would not hold a grudge like her parents and let it fester inside until it was all she cared about. They were flawed, unchangeable. Alex was changing. She had made her choice and was sticking with it, but they didn't know that yet.

When her stomach growled again, she knew it must be time for dinner. Time could be measured by the sun, but her stomach was more accurate. She was surprised when her mother arrived and motioned her out of the room. "You may join us for supper below."

Toury swallowed a nasty retort. Had she gotten so used to commanding already that people telling her what she was allowed to do bothered her? That rankled her. And yet, the power she could have to help those people outside was almost intoxicating.

When she entered a back room, a large old table almost filled the room with a dozen people crowded around it on mismatched chairs and stools. They all stared at her, making her feel on display. It brought back images of her disastrous wedding, all the people watching, the screams, Alex bleeding out... She swallowed a lump that was trying to form in her throat. She would be strong. He was alive. That was what mattered most.

Her father stood and pulled a chair out for her, his noble upbringing still there under his gruff surface. None of the other men rose, though. Strange how these customs had seemed so new not quite a year ago, and now she anticipated them, expected them. She was no longer an Earthling but a Fyrian—another sign to her that this was her kingdom and Alex was her future path.

She sat down, ignoring how the men ogled or glowered at her and rolled their eyes at her aristocratic demeanor.

"Hi," said a small boy next to her with Hematite-gray eyes. Whereas she looked like her mother and Racine like their father, this boy was a perfect blend—her brother.

"This is Aschen," his father said with pride. Named after him, of course.

Here was the one sibling her aunt had longed for to continue the Hematite name—if he survived his parents' rebel nonsense, which was a shame. He was so innocent and curious; how could they mix a boy up in all this?

Toury gave him a smile, and he returned it, showing a gap in the top of his teeth. He didn't even have his adult teeth in yet. Anger rose up in her, an innate protectiveness. She wanted to separate them from this boy. Every sensation she had dreamed about when finding her long-lost family hadn't happened until now, no connection, no feelings but regret and resentment, but now—most likely because he was so young—she found that familial affection she had always longed for. This was something stronger than what she felt for Mary or the queen. She could see herself in Aschen, and she desperately wanted to prevent him from experiencing the pain her parents inflicted on her.

The men and women around the table watched her warily, and no one spoke, passing around a basket of rolls, a platter of pinkish meat—like pork but a bit too vibrant in color—and that moldy cheese she had refused to eat.

"What news from the capital?" her father asked a man with sandy-colored hair.

The man eyed Toury suspiciously and said nothing.

"You can speak in front of her, but no names," her father gritted out. It had to bother him that the others didn't trust her, but they shouldn't.

"The king proxy became the king this morning. Both guilds supported it. He has a flair for dramatics. Nothing like the Sapphirian cold stoicism."

"What do you mean?" her mother asked.

"He showed affection for his mother and sister *publicly*. And instead of lighting the pyre after being coronated, he started burning it, himself included, by his father's side. And he made a show of giving the head of the Magicians' Guild equal speech to the Sorcerers'."

"What does he mean by it?" her mother spat out. Apparently, she didn't like a Sapphirian acting human.

"Well the pyre is obvious, my sweetling," her father said. "He's reminding us what he is, who he is, who he descends from."

"He can think he's a god all he wants," a woman muttered. "It doesn't make him one."

"The problem is if the people believe it or buy into him being the *Draca*," a guy said the word with disdain, "it could be enough to divide the kingdom. The cause will be lost."

"The cause is already lost," Toury couldn't help but mutter. Then she realized the entire table was glaring at her. "He's pushing for reform, a solidarity of the people, so as much as you want to work against him, you're working for him."

One man spit on the ground in disagreement. The rest of the table began arguing with each other. Racine glared at Toury.

Their father quieted everyone down. "Forgive my daughter. They've brainwashed her."

"You ought to cut her loose, then."

"Even better, get rid of her. That would hit the king hardest."

"He'll just marry another." Several people nonchalantly spoke of her demise.

Racine smiled at the thought; her mother bowed her head in refusal to comment.

"That's my daughter!" her father shouted, slamming his hands down on the table. The light glowing under his palms shut them up. He closed his fists to pull the light back in. "No one will hurt her," he said softly.

Her mother still stared at the table.

"I just meant we need to make a move, a big move, before all this momentum is lost," a man amended.

"The commander has plans, but I'm not talking about them here," a woman muttered, her dark eyes—brown, thankfully—roving over Toury. "She is a threat to us. You should've never saved her. The commander will want her silenced."

"She knows nothing," her father defended. "She will stay with us, learn what is right. We've only begun to tell her the hypocrisy of the Sapphirians. She will move to our cause, see the true future is not paved by a Sapphirian, no matter how many silver-tongued lies he's spun."

Toury wanted to defend Alex, to tell them she would never give up on him, never see any good in a future that would hurt him, but she knew better and decided to keep her mouth shut. Her father was trying to stop a room full of people from killing her. Egging them on would be idiotic.

"We've sent the ransom letter. Let us wait before anyone does anything," her mother finally said.

"Do you think he'll even respond?" one man asked.

"That's putting a lot of stock in a cruel king's heart. What makes you think he'll even care whether she lives or dies?"

"You didn't see them," her father seethed. "I thought I was saving a daughter from the likes of Craig or Alfred..."

Gross, the spitting man did it again at their names.

"But she loves him, and he, her. He took a dagger for her. I think that proves he's willing to give up his life to save hers. How hard would it be then to give up his throne?"

Toury could hear no more. The way her own father talked freely about Alex's death, the fact these cold, heartless, scheming people were calling Alex's family the same without noticing their own hypocrisy, grated on her already frazzled nerves. She got up. A bunch of them stood, some holding weapons. Her mother grabbed her by her wrist to keep her from fleeing.

"You will sit," she hissed.

Toury used just enough light magic to blast her mother's hand off her. Her mother winced and used her own power to heal it.

"I will not," Toury said in her queenly voice, faking her strength and authority. "I'd rather rot in my prison than listen to you all scheme with my life and denigrate people you claim are heartless and cruel. All I see are heartless and cruel people scheming with people's lives, treating them as pawns in some game, not living, breathing, human beings. You say the Sapphirians are the problem, but they aren't."

Her father, his face bitter and resigned, got up from the table and pulled her arm with restrained anger. He shoved her up the stairs, making her almost trip and fall. "You better hope your king comes through, or the commander will kill you."

"And you'd let him. You speak of Alex using me to break the curse with scorn, even though he was saving the entire world from darkness, while you use me just the same but simply for power. Tell me, is your daughter's life worth so little?"

They were at the door, face to face. She was tall, almost the same height as her father.

His expression went blank, and he met her gaze. "You're no daughter of mine. You're a Sapphirian through and through." Then he shoved her into the room, knocking her off balance, and she hit the floor hard, barely catching herself in time to protect her face. The door slammed and locked behind her.

Toury sat up and blinked back bitter tears. This was her family. Her father had been the only one protecting her, and now because she'd called him out—on a truth he couldn't bear to acknowledge—he snapped.

The arguing lasted for an hour, the people left, and no one came to see her. She wondered if they would give her over to the dark-eyed lady or the spitting man when Alex refused to bend to their demands. The house quieted down; people were asleep, but Toury remained up, vigilant, waiting for that seer—yet again—to help her somehow.

Outside was in complete darkness; she guessed it was past 10 PM in Earth terms. There weren't any streetlamps, no moon visible on Fyr, no light at all. This sector was so poor, there wasn't much in the way of electricity. She could not bear much more of this, waiting for her family to disappoint and betray her again, abandon her. That's what her parents would do. They would simply leave her, unable to break their zealous desire for revenge but refusing to protect her. They would wash their hands of her, as they already had years ago.

A ball of fiery light illuminated the room, blinding and scaring her. She covered her own mouth, as to not shriek from fright. Alex had found her! When her eyes adjusted a second later, she realized it wasn't Alex, but someone much smaller. Her brother. He was holding a large vial of what looked like wine, and held his finger to his lips, telling her not to make a sound. Then he held up the little flask to her. He motioned for her to drink. Not sure why he was sneaking in and somehow using Sapphirian powers, she took it from him. What was inside sloshed around, and it was too thick to be wine. Dragon's blood. He was giving her the means of escape. She thought maybe her father... No, her father had made it quite clear whose side he was on.

The idea of drinking blood turned her insides, but it was her ticket to freedom. She uncorked it and gulped some down without hesitation. Then she almost wretched it up from the metallic taste. She took a deep breath, willing it to stay in her system.

"Misty's," her brother whispered.

Alex and Madge had told her about transporting. She just had to envision the place and let the magic seep out. She thought of the seer's front steps as she closed her eyes and let the magic out slowly. She felt a tickling across her skin, like dozens of fingers gliding across it, reminding her of Alex's touch.

Something tugged her hand, but she didn't let it distract her.

When she opened her eyes, she stood in front of the seer's door, who opened it and pulled her inside, along with her brother, who was still clutching her hand to follow.

"The necklace?" Misty asked greedily.

"Get me out of here first," Toury instructed. She was free from her prison but only across the street.

Misty huffed, "Come." She led Toury through the small shack, past sleeping children huddled on the floor, and out a back door into an alley.

Toury didn't trust this woman. Her mother had said the king's brother had raped her. "Why are you helping me?" she asked once they were outside.

"I want that necklace."

"Even though the Sapphirians harmed you?"

"I see the future, not through fire but light."

Irene appeared out of the shadows and moved to her side. Toury saw the similarities between the sisters now. "Get in here." Irene instructed and lifted up a flap of a covered cart.

There was a man in the front, a few years older than Toury herself, who looked strikingly like someone she knew, from what she could see in the shadows. But when he turned, taking the lantern from Irene, the light spilled upon his face, showing a profile much like the one she missed dearly. It was not Alex. The man's hair was too light, and his eyes weren't the right blue; they were a startlingly pale blue that matched Irene and Misty's eerie gaze. Misty pushed her hurriedly into the cart. Aschen climbed up to get in.

"No, you must go back," Toury whispered.

"I'm going with you," the boy said with a pout and continued to climb in.

"There's no time for this," Irene hissed.

"They will know that I helped you, that I talked to Misty, who told me where the blood was and what to do with it," Aschen said quietly. "You think they'll protect me from those people when they throw you to the wolves? You want Misty and Irene to then suffer after the information is tortured out of me?"

He was so wise, hardened for a boy his age. Toury nodded, unable to say anything. He could be playing a double agent here, but the dismal thought of him being left behind with their parents outweighed the danger.

"The necklace?" Misty pressed.

Toury reached into her cleavage and pulled out the jewels as promised. Misty clutched it in her hand, her eyes vibrant.

"Take care of my boy," Irene said, nodding to the young man.

He was going with them back to Celestia? Toury had legitimized a baseborn when she made Uncle Gareth family. Irene was making that part of the deal. Toury nodded. She would see what Alex said about it. This was technically his half-brother with that unmistakable face—and he had firepower, according to her mother—to prove it. The least she could do was make sure Alex did not take him out as a threat.

She grabbed Misty's hand and squeezed it. "Come find me with that necklace, and I will make sure you want for nothing. It is dear to me, but not more than my life."

"I know. You will," the seer said.

Then the young man flicked the reins, and the wagon lurched. Misty tucked the tarp over Aschen and her. They lay still and quiet, hoping nothing would stop their escape. Her brother clutched her hands for reassurance, and she squeezed them back for the same.

34

A Transport

Alex was still mad with worry over Toury, but his frantic anxiety staved off the grief from his father's death and pyre, and the pressures of being king of a torn kingdom. Every thought of his fixated on her. He prayed to the god and goddess for her safety, even if it meant the end of him and his reign. There would be no hesitation. He'd give up the kingdom for her, but his mother and Mary interceded in his moment of madness and tore the letter from him. They would answer it for him. After the ceremony was over, and he was king, he started to lose grip on rationality. It meant nothing without her. He couldn't care less about the medallion around his neck and the control he had over others. He wanted Toury. He would destroy the monarchy to have her.

The women in his life spoke sense into him. It wasn't in Alex's power to abolish the throne. Mary said she would take the throne if he abdicated, then Henry after her if he was found alive, which now seemed slim. The old edicts of royalty were unchangeable, carved in stone, literally, in the Draca Temple by the first king. It wasn't in Alex's power to bow to the rebels' demands for Toury.

"It is done," Mary said.

"What?" Alex's sight was blurring.

"You must sleep, Alex," his mother said.

"Oh, you answered the letter. I hope you didn't threaten them." A new worry ran through his mind. He should've pulled himself together and answered their demands. If they hurt Toury in any way...if she died...he'd torch the world and watch it burn. Mary had said all would be well but didn't see any more from the flames, nor could he, and neither knew how Toury would free herself.

"I simply reminded them of the edicts, that it is out of our power to get rid of the throne, and that I would rule if you stepped down—which I made sure they knew you wouldn't."

"You've made yourself a target."

"I've always been a target for these types. I was simply hiding safely in your shadow, and now I'm not." She shrugged, and he envied her ease in a situation like this, or her ability to feign it. "I've a letter from Cobalt."

"Why didn't he write me?" Alex demanded as he snatched the letter from her hand.

"He wrote to you, addressed to me. I think he fears interception. He wrote in code."

"What code?" Alex perused the letter, and his question answered itself. It was a code he and Cobalt had used as boys when they slipped notes unnoticed by the tutors during lectures. Cobalt had been one of the few kids allowed to learn alongside him when it came to non-magical subjects. He smiled softly as he remembered Ruby burning up the notes to try to save them from themselves and prevent them from getting in trouble. Ruby had always been trying to save Alex and Cobalt, and her final act of making Toury a savior proved that.

"Do you know the code?"

"No—yes. I created it. I just can't remember it all right now." He knew what several of the symbols stood for, but this would take time without the key. He transported to his room, ransacked his nightstand's drawer of mementos, and pulled out the little square of parchment that coincided the letters of the alphabet to their symbols. Then he transported back to his study.

Mary was waiting, cross-armed and foot-tappingly impatient. When he reappeared, she sat down across the desk from him.

He painstakingly decoded word after word, the code coming back to him from the recesses of his mind, making it easier as he transcribed along. Then he peered up at Mary.

"Well?" She pressed.

Alex read the letter aloud to her:

Your Majesty, King Sapphirian,

Found Toury, or she found us through some seer's help right outside of Mineria. Our scouts reported back that there are small bands of rebels on the horizon in most directions. I'm going to try to outmaneuver them, but fear the worst. Apart, they are fightable. Together will crush us. Making our way north, pushing back the smallest group of them, but I know the others are closing in on us. Send Mary to Dragon Rock as soon as you get this. It will give us one side of cover to keep them at bay. Mary can get Toury out of there to safety. No matter what you do, do not come yourself. This is what they are waiting for. This is no time to be rash, my king, stay put.

Your friend,
Cobalt

Alex sighed. His friend didn't want him there because it was an impossible battle. Cobalt would die in this battle, as he would never abandon his men, but if Alex went, would he die as well? Or could he turn the tide? Mineria. The fastest steed, even if the messenger changed horses, would've taken a couple hours to deliver this letter. It could be too late.

"I must go." Mary stood up. "Lucy, let's gear up. We have no clue what kind of battle we might be entering." Mary crossed the room. "Stay put, Alex. I mean it, and I'll bring her to your quarters. I'll be back with her, and then...I'm going back to fight with Cobalt." She was resigned.

Alex knew she wouldn't be stupid. She'd get Cobalt out of there and save his life, force him to abandon his men. He'd never forgive her for it, but selfishly, Alex wanted him alive as well.

He nodded, crumpling up the note. He would go back too. Once Toury was safe, he'd go back for his men. "David?"

"I already know, Your Majesty. Suit up for battle."

Despite himself, Alex smiled. David knew his mind as well as he knew his own. Alex would see Toury in moments.

"Your Majesty." Madge bowed. He had quite forgotten she trailed David, not having a role these past few days.

"To our quarters, and ready the queen-to-be's chamber for her return." He transported to his bathing quarter's closet, leaving David to go ready himself. Alex changed into scale mail and waited for David to arrive to help him into the rest of his armor. He spent the time pacing the length of their sitting room, anxiously waiting for Toury.

Had they hurt her? He'd kill them. Even if it was her father, he was a dead man if he harmed Toury in any way. How'd she gotten away? She was smart, crafty, but an entire army extracted her; they would not have let her go so easily. What had she gone through? He didn't want to know. Any mild discomfort would be paid back with his fiery wrath.

His pacing became frantic. He needed to see her. He had to see she was okay. He had convinced himself that she would be saved, and now, the moment she was free and so close to coming home, coming to him safely, he feared the worst could happen. She might've been safer with her father, sadly, under his protection, than out there in the unknown. With an army surrounding them. His heart thumped wildly. What was taking David so long? Where was Mary? Had she run into trouble? He had half a mind to transport without David. "Stay put," they had told him. Such a simple phrase that was so hard to follow when his heart, mind, and soul were determined to reunite with his other half. She had to make it back to him. He was dead without her.

He almost transported, his power funneling around him, flames licking his fireproof clothes. But he pulled it back in, thinking of how angry Toury would be with him if he risked everything and everyone, just to make sure she got safely back. In fact, she might see it as undermining her power and freedom. And she was more powerful than she'd ever know. She ruled his heart; ergo, she owned Fyr.

A flash of fire appeared, and Mary vanished into flames again, leaving Toury behind. He pulled her into his arms, searching her for injuries or anything amiss. Aside from some grubby plain clothing and a worn look to her appearance, she seemed fine, not a scratch, although she could heal that herself. Concern flooded over him, and he worried there was something wrong he couldn't see plaguing her. It was surreal; she was there in front of him—the joy of her return hadn't quite hit him yet.

"Did they hurt you?" He would torch them if they had laid a finger on her.

"Not really," she answered. "You're okay," she marveled. Her hands ran over his shoulders, down his chest, and onto his stomach, assuring herself he was real. They hadn't been parted for as long as his dragon-slayer chase, but it sure felt that way.

Instead of answering, he kissed her. He had no words, none would do anyway to explain his emotions at the moment. He was overjoyed she was here in front of him, alive, kissing him, and yet he was exhausted from lack of sleep and emotionally spent, having just burned his father that morning in front of an audience.

"You're going to the battle?" She took in his scale mail.

"Is it bad?" he asked.

"It's two to one, so yeah, not so good. I'm going with you."

"No. Mary just got you out of there. You'll stay here. I need you safe." Alex couldn't fathom her near danger again. There was no way she was going. He'd stay put if she proved that obstinate. Yet what if Mary and Cobalt's lives hung in the balance?

"Well, I need you safe too!" she protested, pushing him gently away.

"I just got you back. There's no way I'm marching you back in there!" She had to stay. He couldn't afford distractions.

"Alex, I love you. I missed you, but you're commanding me again. What of your promises about giving me choices? You said we would be partners in everything. Were those lies?"

He turned from her, growling. She was right, and he didn't want her to be. He wanted to be a tyrant, if only to keep her safe, but it would drive a wedge between them again. They had only repaired everything that had gone wrong in the past, and he was about to repeat it. He wanted to marry her. He had to give her that equality she wanted. If he went, he had to let her go, and he could not abandon his sister and best friend. "We stick together then."

She smiled. "I've got your back."

"And I, yours. I mean it. Neither of us can afford distraction for each other's welfare, so we literally stick together."

She nodded. "No more than a foot apart."

They waited only a moment for David and Madge to come, the latter suited up for battle as well. Madge had anticipated Toury would be fighting. Uncharacteristically, Madge shrugged off Alex's surprise and hugged Toury. "My lady, I—"

"No time for apologies you don't need to give, Madge. We need to go."

Madge had some plate armor and scale mail in hand. Alex allowed her to get it over Toury's head and attach the plates before he said, "Hold on."

He transported the four of them to where Toury told him to, a clifftop of Dragon Rock above the main skirmish. He examined the scene. Mary fought right below him at the base of the cliff, which split up the rebels into two groups: one fighting Cobalt's soldiers, another trying to get to Mary. His sister held her own, turning anyone who got near her into a fleeing torch, but flames were also coming from the east side; they licked around like someone was flicking a flaming whip, which he had never seen or heard of. He followed the flame back to a man who was wielding it on the defensive, his other arm pushing a boy back down into a cart. Who was he to have such powers?

"Who?" Alex asked Toury.

"No time. Take us to that cart, Alex," Toury said. The fright in her voice made him comply. When he appeared behind the man, startling him, the man's eyes met his, and Alex's stomach dropped. It was almost like looking at his reflection. A strong baseborn, of his father's most likely, who could throw fire around easily meant he was a threat. The man's glare when he recognized Alex increased his unease. When he noticed the steel-gray eyes of a Hematite boy, he wondered if Toury had led him into a trap. He pulled out his sword quickly and stepped back, creating distance between himself and this baseborn.

Toury huffed and stepped between the cart and him. "No time, Alex. My brother. Possibly yours. Both helped me escape. Same side."

"For how long?" Alex tried to impart to her that at any moment, one of these two might put a dagger into his back when he wasn't looking.

"For as long as you don't try to kill me, I won't try to kill you," the Sapphirian baseborn said.

"Deal," Alex said, still not wanting to trust him.

"This is your forte, Your Majesty, no? War."

"Yes, it is." Alex turned the intended insult into a compliment by not rising to the bait. "Divide and conquer. Mary has the north. You circle around west, and aim that power of yours at them there."

"And what will you do?" the man asked.

"Extract my men from here on the east."

The Sapphirian ran off. He could not transport, and the thought made Alex smile, wanting to one-up the man who was most likely his older brother, according to Toury's information. This was not good. He was worried the man was planted, a spy. The rebels could use him to usurp the crown, put their puppet on the throne in his place with that unmistakable face and him being older. Baseborns were never given positions of power or their father's name—until his future queen changed everything by making her uncle a Hematite in name.

He pushed rebel agendas from his mind and closed his eyes, pulling the power from underground into himself. He could conjure enough fire on his own to slaughter this enemy, but then he'd risk not being able to do transports.

"What are you doing?" Toury asked him. "Praying?"

He opened his eyes and gave her a hard look. "Pulling in more power. Ready?"

Toury nodded.

"I'll be busy separating friend from foe. I need you to blast anyone who comes near me with your light."

"I've got your back," she said again.

Then he got to work, tracing a line of fire in front of the rebel soldiers, separating them from his surrounded men. He could see the firelasher, whom he refused to think of as family, do the same. Mary caught on and separated more soldiers away from theirs. His men turned their attention to the west side—sandwiching a cluster of the rebels between their swords and the firelasher's power. Enemy soldiers came running at them, noticing his presence or because they had been cut off from their quarry. Toury blasted with light, then David bashed them with his energy, knocking rebels down. Madge, who rarely used her azurite power, read the minds of what each foe's next move would be in order to strike them down with her blade first. They worked as a team in tandem. Alex kept pulling up energy as he was expending it.

He needed to do more. He pulled up and in, drawing the fire into himself until he felt he might explode from the amount, and then unleashed it to the crowd of rebels in front of him. A series of strange things happened. The ground quaked; cracks formed where he stood and snaked through the ground. His fire was too powerful. The rebels weren't on fire, but had turned to ash, like how the draca's intense flames made ash sculptures of their victims. He couldn't stop and feared the ground would swallow his men whole if he couldn't control it. He tried pulling back, but it was now its own force of nature.

The ash sculptures of his enemies crumbled due to the earthquake, clearing his view to his men. If he couldn't stop it, he hoped to control it. Fire licked out of the cracks in the ground, and magma oozed. He pushed his power away from himself. The magma was thicker and harder to move than fire. He had never heard of anyone being able to do anything like this, manipulate earth matter on the Fyr sphere, but the heat and light were enough for him to control it just as if it were fire. He outlined his men, which was an easy task, for all soldiers had stopped fighting and were staring at him or the ground under them. Soldiers of both sides were stepping away from the chasm separating them. Mary snapped out of it first and threw fire at the northern band of the rebel army, and the firelasher to the west repeated her actions. Some of the rebel army fled south.

"Are we letting them go?" David asked.

"Alex, you're shaking," Toury quietly murmured by his side.

A rebel ran toward them, sword wielded, in a last desperate attempt to attack him. Toury blasted him with her light power. The rebel flew back from the power of it with a gaping hole in his abdomen. The momentary distraction let his control slip, and magma was bursting forth from the ground, pushing his men into each other onto an island in a molten sea.

Not knowing what else to do, he transported into the thick of his men. "Grab on!"

A dozen men reached out and touched him. He grabbed Cobalt's hand in his own and transported them back to Toury. Some of his men who weren't trapped rushed to join them. He transported back and fetched another dozen or so. This time, he fell to the ground. Toury rushed to his side and pulled him up. He transported again, the effort taking almost all the strength he had left. He transported another round of his men back. He fell to the ground, screaming from the pain of his body, feeling as if it would split into a million pieces. He saw Mary transport and bring over the last few men he could not, including the firelasher.

Toury was kneeling by his side again, her hands on his chest. "One more, Alex, one more transport."

"I can't take everyone. I'm used up."

"You're not," Toury said, shaking her head.

Then that pleasant flow of her energy surged into him. It wasn't burning away the dark as it had when he was cursed, but melding light and fire, like when they kissed, into a white-hot fire full of intense heat and power. He leaned up and wrapped his arm around her, kissing her.

"All right, lovebirds," Mary said. "I reckon I can transport more than you."

"Oh really? Doubt that," Alex quipped, getting up and helping Toury to her feet.

To show off, he mentally drew a ring of fire around them. The remaining rebels were running away or standing frozen and confused.

"Chain formation!" He commanded.

All men looped an arm through another's. He drew Toury into one arm and looped his other arm through Cobalt's. Toury grabbed onto her brother's shoulder, who held onto the firelasher. Mary was the link from Cobalt to the rest of his men.

"Thanks for coming. You shouldn't have, but I'm glad you did, all the same," Cobalt said.

"I came back first!" Mary barked incredulously.

"That you did, my dear, and I thank you for it, but I never expected less from you, Mary," Cobalt placated her.

Despite his effort, she still glared daggers at him.

Then, before Mary could even try to take the lead, Alex transported to the front grounds of the castle, just within the gates, the only place big enough for fifty soldiers that was safe. When they reappeared, they looked around bewildered, and Cobalt and Toury had to support Alex as his legs gave out.

"Show off," Mary said, but her barb was full of wonder. "You transported an entire army, Alex."

"And he started an earthquake, brought lava up from the ground..." Toury continued.

He couldn't even fathom the things he had done.

"No one, not even in the exaggerated tales of our ancestors, could do the things you have done," Mary rattled on, making him embarrassed and freaked out.

"Yeah, I know, so I leave you all to Cobalt's care and Princess Mary's hospitality. I'm going to lie down."

That got a few hearty laughs, but as he walked through his men—he could transport no more—they touched his armor as he passed, revering him. He was certainly having a trying rule as king, since this was still his first day, but he was damn well onto making a name for himself.

35

AWAKE

Toury gave her own commands about her brother's and Alex's half-brother's situation, knowing well that no risks should be taken, and yet they should not be treated as prisoners. Heavily guarded rooms in the guest quarters, where Cobalt and a few generals were rooming on the other end of the castle, seemed best. Then Toury got Alex to bed and collapsed next to him. Aside from a couple murmurs of missing each other and of love, he fell asleep instantly. Worried for him and how much energy and magic he'd expended to save all his men, she used her last energy to heal him a bit more before she was almost drained too. Sleep beckoned.

When she woke, Alex still slept, so she showered, called Madge, and got ready for the day. She went straight to see how her brother was doing. He was playing outside in the orchard with Duric. Alex's half-brother was watching over them, lounging in the grass, eating some dragon fruit. She wondered what Alex would do with him and how the queen would react when she found out Toury brought the product of her lifemate's moral indiscretion into her own home. Toury wasn't sure she could trust him, yet he'd helped her escape and fought valiantly with them in battle. Now, in the sunlight, she didn't see as much of Alex in him, despite some similar facial features. He had his mother's coloring but had that proud profile and the broad shoulders of King Craig. Irene's son and Alex were obviously related, but there was enough of their respective mothers in both brothers to differ their overall appearance.

"Will he kill me?" the man asked.

"What is your name?" she asked, instead of trying to give him answers she was unsure of.

"Tired of thinking of me as the baseborn brother?" He laughed and sat up.

"Well, yeah."

"Craig."

"Of course it is." Naming children after their fathers appeared to be the only way wronged women could out their seducers. "Well, Craig, His Majesty is still sleeping and has not spoken of you yet. I don't think he's the type of man to kill another merely for his parentage."

206

Craig laughed. "No, he doesn't." He gave her a pointed look in reference to herself. Then his tone changed. "I used to think of him as this spoiled little brat, but what he did on that battlefield, how he came himself to get us out of there, saved his men...he's not a bad guy."

Toury smiled at that. "What do you want from him?"

"Aside from keeping my head?" Craig asked. Then he let a breath out, thinking. "To have that last name, given some small position, a little coin, would all be a dream come true." Despite his rough upbringing in the slums, he seemed cultured, educated, and refined, not noble and innately powerful like Alex, but like your average Earth boy—except for the whole fire whip magic thing.

"I'll talk to him when things calm down, but you won't be cast out."

"But I must be guarded?" He raised his brows toward the big hulking soldier watching from the doorway.

"You know why," Toury said quietly. "You lived near rebels. You could possibly, although illegitimately, challenge the throne. You're someone rebels would back."

"I'd have to be mad to do that." He stared off, his face a bit worried. "He opened the ground and could've swallowed people up whole. He transported an entire army. I've never heard of nor seen such things. If the rebels continue, they'll fail."

Toury hoped he was right. She collected her brother, which was her intention for going out there in the first place, and sought out her aunt. It was time to try to heal her and wake her from her coma.

Toury knelt over the sleeping form of her aunt, who was much more at peace without the scowl she usually sent Toury's way for some infraction of her propriety. Toury knew, though, that when the woman would open her eyes, there would be pride in them. The words were few in praise from her aunt, but her gaze always gave her away.

Toury focused on those happy thoughts, the ones of her aunt that made her feel accepted, happy, part of a family, unlike her parents or sister. She grabbed her brother's hand in hers and gave it a squeeze, finding that warm sensation of connection she'd had with him before; his light power and the innocence of it called to her for comfort. She pulled that comfort to her and tried to amplify happy feelings. No healer, not even her Uncle Gareth, who thankfully survived the wedding attack, could wake her. If Toury could not, no one could, for she was the most powerful healer known in the land for being able to break Alex's curse. She wanted to believe what they said only so she could wake her aunt from this, but she feared the only reason she could save Alex had been the power of their love. She loved her aunt but not like the multifaceted kind of love she had for Alex. He had become her family, friend, lover, and her entire future. She let her feelings for him swirl inside her, hoping she could use love for anyone as magic.

When it felt like she'd burst from the power of light inside her, she let go of her brother's hand, put her other hand on her aunt's chest, and pushed everything she had into her at once. The blast acted like a defibrillator—not that anyone on Fyr would know what that was—the way her body bounced on the bed.

Nothing happened, so Toury tried to gather up some more strength and maybe ease it into her instead, but then her aunt suddenly sat upright, scaring them all. Her brother screeched, Toury fell back onto the ground, and her aunt gasped at their frightened faces.

Toury was stunned and speechless. Her aunt stared at Toury's brother, confused. "Aschen?" Then she met Toury's gaze. "Toury? I'm alive?"

"Yes, aunt, yes," Toury said, scrambling up to hug her. "I woke you. It's been days; a lot has happened, but how do you know my brother?"

"Brother?" Her aunt examined Aschen. "He's...he's your brother? He looks like my fool of a brother when he was a child, but now I see some of your mother in him. Where is my brother?"

Toury raised her eyebrows at Aschen, and he shrugged his shoulders as if to say he had no idea where to begin.

Toury started to retell her tale from the moment her aunt lost consciousness. The servants brought in food. Edwina cursed Toury's parents throughout the tale, praised her bravery but also called it foolishness, and then doted on her newfound nephew, so much so that Toury retreated from the room with a smile. He may have lost his parents—or left them, to be honest—but he'd just gained a doting aunt who would mold him into a little gentleman worthy of the Hematite estate...if Alex didn't dissolve it. She wasn't sure how far the sins of the father passed onto the son in Fyr, but she knew Alex would not punish her brother. He was as innocent as she was to her parents' schemes, and Alex had never held it against her. She knew now was not the time to ask Alex about her brother or his own, but she sought Alex out anyway, needing to see that he was still alive and his skin was warm.

She dreamed no more of necromancers or rebels coming to kidnap her. Her nightmares were now of Alex cold, pale, and dead, his blood leeching out onto the floor and her wedding dress soaking it up until it turned blood red. Last night was the first night she'd woken to have him in her arms, and she'd been able to relax and fall back asleep. Would their entire lives be like this? Would she fear he would die every single minute they were apart? Or would they get the peace in the kingdom that he dreamed of? She couldn't live like this, but she knew she couldn't live without him. The second idea outweighed the first, as always.

36

A PROPOSITION

When Alex woke, it was midday, and he was still exhausted. He felt as if his body had been trampled by horse hooves. He ached to the bone; every muscle protested movement. After a hot shower didn't help, he caved into going to the infirmary. The healing properties of the stones helped him tremendously, but he knew he might need another day to gain back the amount of energy he'd expended. What he had done was unheard of, so he had no clue how long it would take for him to feel whole again.

He went to his study, thinking to summon Cobalt to see where they'd go from here, but Cobalt was already in there, pacing; Mary sitting at Alex's desk; and his mother hovering, reading correspondence.

"What's going on?" he asked, a little wary. Where was Toury? Why was Mary in his seat?

"We decided not to lose any time, Alex," Mary said apologetically. "Mother is still a queen and second in command until you get married. She named me Lady of the Castle until you woke up." She stood up and motioned for him to sit in his chair. She wore the Prince Medallion. It would go to Toury once they were married and she was with child. He shook the idea from his head. There were more immediate concerns than rescheduling a wedding.

The next question that came out was, "Where's Toury?"

"She's with her aunt," his mother said. "She was able to heal her aunt enough for the woman to wake. Toury is fine, no lingering effects from her ordeal or using her powers so much. Much has occurred in twelve hours. Please, sit."

He looked to Cobalt, not at all liking being left in the dark about his kingdom.

"Right, so, Your Majesty. While the rebels were following us, I had sent off a missive with a runner, asking for aid from Lord Jasper who was in—"

"Aberdane, rounding up necromancers." Alex's impatience didn't want a long-winded story.

"Yes, and he and his men came to help us straightaway, but they arrived too late. They were, however, successful in cutting off the rebel army. They killed some, managed ten prisoners, and some got away. He sent a few spies to follow them in hopes to find the rebel stronghold. It's somewhere in Mineria as we suspected. Your soldiers are awaiting your command. The prisoners were questioned. Some wanting a pardon talked quite a lot. We didn't get their leader or his identity—'the commander' they call him—but we got the whereabouts of the Hematites off the, um...baseborn who helped Toury."

Everyone in the room shifted uncomfortably, and his mother huffed out an annoyed breath. What to do with this brother was a problem he wanted to push off.

Thankfully, Cobalt moved on. "Mary ordered an elite task force to take them unawares. The daughter and a few people staying there got away, but we have Toury's parents. Mary brought them back herself—to not risk an escape. They're in the dungeon."

Alex sighed. This was a mess. The woman he loved had parents with strong rebel ties, and the people of his kingdom would all know. Worse, he may have to have them killed, something she'd never forgive him for, even if she did understand that anyone who'd attempt to murder the king must be executed. There always was something coming between them. It infuriated him.

"What will you do with them?" Mary asked, her voice expressing her concern over the entire situation.

"I don't know," he growled.

"You marry her," his mother said, "immediately."

It instantly clicked. Alex wanted to jump up and hug his mother. It was a way out of him making a ruling. If the Hematites were actual family, he could opt out of the decision and leave it to the guilds.

"Let's keep their capture quiet then, just for a couple days," Alex mused, tapping his fingers on the desk thoughtfully. "Anything else?" he asked Cobalt, hoping to change the subject.

"The rebels have been hit hard today, but we don't know how many, how they communicate, nor where they are located. They seem to be scattered."

"But most in Mineria," Alex thought aloud. "The mines. Have them check the abandoned mines."

"There's more." Mary said.

"Your cousin Henry has finally returned with lots of interesting information, but it needs corroboration," Cobalt said.

Mary scoffed. "Alex, he left his post to go under. He was with the rebels. He knows a lot. Ignore Cobalt. He's never liked Henry."

"I don't trust him." Cobalt gritted his teeth.

"That can wait. I'll speak with him later." Alex just wanted to stop their argument without choosing sides. He had always trusted Henry, but now he was wary of everyone. He stood. "Am I caught up to speed? Completely?"

Cobalt nodded.

"I'm off then."

"There's so much to do," Mary protested.

"And you're doing a fine job. You two continue to orchestrate the capture of the rebels. If you have questions, search me out. I'm off to break this news to Toury, then question the Hematites myself, and convince her somehow to get married right away."

Alex decided to do it in that order. He went to the dungeons with Toury, her face as stoic as his. She didn't even react when her parents came to the bars.

"Kneel to His Majesty," the guard boomed.

Her father knelt down right away, but the mother hesitated before she curtsied. "I am a noble. I will not kneel," Toury's mother said. She looked remarkably like an older version of Toury, but the eyes were wrong, and her expression was worn, miserable.

"Sweetling, kneel. Now is not the time." The father had those grey eyes, but they didn't have the vibrant effect Toury's had with his paler skin and large nose.

"She curtsied, which is enough. Rise," Alex said. "I've never been one to make people grovel. The kneeling law will be abolished. All people of Fyr will merely need to show respect to their sovereign, not that they are lesser."

Hematite rose. Alex's father had decreed the man no longer a lord in name or owner of property, but hadn't decreed anything against the aunt and knew nothing about future children.

"Where is my son?" Toury's mother demanded.

"He is fine. He helped me escape. He's turned his back on you," Toury ground out, keeping her emotions just barely under the surface.

"You poisoned him against us," her mother said, losing her bravery and breaking down with a sob.

"No, you did. I never even got to speak to him alone. He's only eight, but he recognizes how his parents will sell their children's lives for revenge on a dead man."

"No, you did this," the woman continued, almost delirious in her denials.

"Those were his sentiments. He was afraid you'd hand him over to the others and he'd be killed. He was eager to get away from you."

The woman wailed as if Toury were physically torturing her and then slumped against the wall.

"She's right. They were never alone, Angelica. She never had time to persuade the boy of anything," the father said, sounding defeated. "Your Majesty, what will happen to my children?"

"That is for Her Majesty to decide," Alex said, nodding to Toury.

She could not mask her surprise at being called that. He winked at her, hoping she'd play along and pretend they were married already. The mother spat at the ground. The father leaned his head onto the bars with a groan. Alex got the reaction he expected, so he dropped pretenses.

"Not yet, but there is an authority in the castle, the license was already signed, and I'm not risking a public wedding after you destroyed our first. Tonight perhaps?" He directed his question to Toury, whose eyes lit up, and she suppressed a smile. She blushed and nodded.

"I told you we should've had one of the men despoil her to prevent this," the mother hissed.

Toury's little smile flew from her face so quickly, her mother's words being more effective than a physical slap. "Despoil me? Much like Prince Alfred despoiled you? The sad part is, you don't even realize you've become the monsters you think you are fighting."

"I'd never let a man hurt my daughter," Hematite said. He gave his lifemate a sad, condemning look. "What happens to us?"

Alex shrugged. "If I marry your daughter tonight, you will be my family. I can claim an unfair bias, which takes it out of my hands and allows the guilds to decide."

"They will burn us. Will you let us suffer that fate, Daughter?" the mother demanded.

"This is what you wanted," Toury said with such strength and ease that he was amazed. "You wanted King Alex dead so the guilds would rule. It seems poetic justice to have them decide your fate."

"Now, I still have influence, obviously. Whatever I suggest, they most likely will agree with: snuffing, banishment, a quick death..." He paused.

"But you want something in return," the man said quietly.

"You said you saw who did it. Who cursed them?" Toury entreated.

"You tell me, and you could be cleared of the charges my father had laid upon you, and the guilds might be more lenient. You don't, and they'll think you are guilty of cursing the royal family, murdering a protected creature, causing a mass murder, and trying to murder me. I cannot see them letting you live if they believe all that. We already know banishment won't stop you, so if you want a chance to live, you need to strike a deal."

"Don't do it, Aschen! We'll take it to the grave. He'll kill us anyway!"

"You need more incentive?" Alex pressed. "The title Lord Hematite has been eradicated from this sphere by my father. I can reinstate it by making the younger Aschen Hematite a lord. Instead of a baron, as the brother of the queen, he could be a duke."

He watched the transformation of the mother's face. She loved that child, a clear favorite, the only child kept.

"Our other child?" the man asked.

"Forget Racine! She left us to be captured and saved her own hide," the woman protested.

"I want to leave this world knowing their fates."

"She is with the rebels. She will suffer the rebels' fate," Alex said. There was no way Racine would be pardoned by any guild for her ruthlessness. There was no love between the sisters, which could be seen in Toury's lack of protest.

"I'm done here. Are you?" Toury asked.

He nodded. She wanted to leave. Her nerves were wrought, and she was tired of hiding them under her mask of stoicism. "You have until morning to think about this. I'll be back to see what you say to my proposition."

"Wait!" Hematite called. "Tourmaline."

Toury turned reluctantly to her father.

"I believed that what had been was still going on. I see Sapphirian eyes, and I think of Alfred." The man's fists coiled in anger. He took a deep breath and focused on his daughter. "He's not Alfred."

The mother scoffed at that comment.

"You breaking the curse makes me see it all had to happen this way. If he makes you happy, I can say that any regret I have was worth your happiness." Her father bowed his head then, overtaken by emotion.

Toury's eyes began to glisten. Alex held out his arm for her to take. She slipped it through his, and they left the dungeons.

37
MAJESTY

As soon as they were in their chambers, Toury dismissed Madge for the time being. She didn't want anyone around right now, for she was a pot of unstable emotions and fatigue. Alex dismissed David, then did his typical partial disrobing of himself, cuffs and collar undone, the medallion off his neck.

She plopped on the settee, unable to even bother with her laces. "Did you mean that, or was it for show?"

"Mean what?" He looked at her, confused. "I said a lot in there."

"Are we marrying tonight?"

"Oh, that." He sighed, running his hand through his hair, messing it up, looking adorably unlike a king. "I said that to get a reaction, to see where the land lay with them. Your father is remorseful, which is good, as he's the one who did try to kill me. They may be more lenient. Your mother..." He continued with a whistle, most likely unable to say the cruel words needed to describe her. "I'm glad she didn't raise you, Toury. You are ten times the person she is. I know my uncle wronged her, and there's no excuse for what he did, but you would never let hate consume you like that. You are the strongest and most forgiving woman I know."

Toury blinked away tears. A compliment wrapped up in an insult about her mother was strange, and yet she saw the positive in what he was saying. It was honest, and Toury did not see herself in her parents.

"Please," Alex begged. He sat beside her, and she melted into his warm embrace. "Don't cry. I will try to convince the guilds to spare their lives."

"I'm glad the decision can't be yours if we marry, but I don't want to get married tonight if that's the only reason."

"Only reason?" He pulled back, staring at her, stunned. He leaned his forehead against hers, letting out a shaky breath. "When I awoke and was told they'd taken you, Toury..." His voice cracked.

"Stop," she pleaded, taking his face in her hands and kissing his lips. "I cannot relive those moments. I was afraid you would die. Promise me we won't part."

"I can't." He looked at her sadly. "You know I can't promise that. We've got to find out who is behind all this. I need to protect you and my kingdom, and I need you safe here."

"Alex, you can't take everything on your own. You promised a partnership."

"And I will honor that, I promise. I let you walk into battle yesterday, even though just the very thought of it horrified me."

"When, when will we be equal? When will you let me help you?"

"You help me so much already, Toury. You've saved my life again and again, but since we promised honesty at all times, you cannot risk yourself in any way until my heir is born. You and I are together for life, Toury, and even if the worst should happen, I could not take another queen. It's only you. We have to continue the Sapphirian line, which means no more risks until we have a child, which is another reason we must marry."

"The risks find me."

"We are already supposed to be married. We don't have to marry tonight. Whenever you feel recovered from your ordeal, we'll elope. Just you and me with the authority. He already has the signed marriage license and is still here. We just need to say our vows in front of him, and it's official."

"But your mother will be upset. She was so invigorated by planning the wedding."

"It was her idea for us to marry in haste, and she can throw us a party later, when things are safe and settled."

"And Mary?"

"She will delay us. Mary will want a proper dress, flowers—all that wedding stuff—I think you know by now Sapphirian women never do things by halves. I want it to be you and me, no impediments. We can have the whole thing all over again in style when things are settled if you like. I just want to marry you before the day is over before anyone or anything can stop us again."

Her heart leaping with excitement, Toury took up his hand in hers. "Tonight?"

"Right now, if you like. I can put off some debriefing until tomorrow. Let's go." The idea shifted something in him. He was grinning, and his eyes shone with that luminescent twinkle she noticed must be love.

The same rush of elation passed through her, burning away her concerns and worries. She was going to finally get married. She playfully smacked his shoulder. "At least give me time to put on my best dress."

He was suspicious that she might be fishing for a way out of it.

She shot him a dirty look back. "Just a few moments," she amended.

"Done." He kissed her and left with a torn expression, obviously not wanting to part with her for five minutes. She understood the sentiment.

Due to her excitement, she rang for Madge instantly and rushed the servant through readying her. Then Madge led her to a part of the castle on the first floor she had never been to, an old temple or chapel with interesting antiquated architecture. The room had stale air in it, as if rarely used. Dragons were carved in the stone along the walls, with words she couldn't understand in the old language. A large chandelier hung down from the center with those common tear-drop bulbs that looked like white flames. Around that, the domed ceiling had a dragon profile with its wings wrapped around it in a circle that she recognized; it was the same dragon pattern as on Alex's King Medallion.

She and Alex were almost alone, with Madge and David sitting in pews as witnesses and guards. They would not be interrupted. The entire time, she half expected more rebels or necromancers to attack, but nothing dire happened. It was a short, formal-sounding ceremony that consisted of handfasting, where there was some metaphor about their lives being tied together in a knot, by using a chord of fabric to symbolize their union, but the words were lost to Toury. Her heart was thumping loudly in her ears, and she only had eyes for Alex, who only had eyes for her. Neither looked away from each other the entire time, and Alex tried being serious, but a smirk kept alighting his lips, which made her smile. They were named lifemates, and Alex kissed her chastely.

She had thought it was over, but the authority brought out her circlet on a pillow. Apparently, she was being coronated today as well. The authority said something in the old language that Alex repeated. Then with pride in his eyes, Alex placed the circlet on her head. The authority bowed to her, calling her "Majesty," and her head whirled with realization. She had always wanted Alex; being queen was something she thought was a perk and a role that would eventually come with being with him. She was Queen of Fyr. The idea was staggering. She almost tripped when Alex took her arm, leading her from the room. Then he scooped her up in his arms and kissed her more passionately than he'd allowed himself in front of a religious official, in a temple where the god and goddess could be watching.

He transported them back to his room, carrying her over the threshold in his own magical way. Despite the hunger in his eyes, he placed her gently down on the bed and lay down next to her. He touched her cheek, running his hand down her face, memorizing her every feature. "My lifemate," he whispered in awe.

She broke into a smile, allowing him to simply behold her, nervous yet desirous of what she figured would happen next. He removed the circlet from her head and placed it down on the table by his bed. She pulled off his medallion and placed it next to her crown. Seeing those together was a symbol of who they were and what they would be. Then they simply stared at each other for a couple minutes, Alex pulling pins from her hair slowly, making a pile of hairpins between them. The sun was setting, and it cast an orange glow across him, making him seem like the very element he controlled. When he was finished, she moved the pile onto the table while he ran his hands through her hair.

"You did wear your best dress." Alex quietly pointed out she did not wear a fine gown, but the purple one he had bought for her the day they met and caused quite a scandal by doing so.

"It is my best. It means the most."

Alex captured her lips in his, showing how much her words moved him.

A knock sounded on the bedroom door.

Alex pulled away, and his soft eyes cut to hard. "I just dismissed you for the rest of the day! I said to leave us be. Our schedules are cleared!" Alex barked.

Toury couldn't help but smile. He wanted to make her his lifemate truly and so badly, he was ready to rip off the servants' heads.

"Your Majesty, you know I'd only disturb you for emergencies," David said through the door.

"Come in then. We're decent," Alex ordered.

Despite being fully clothed, Toury was still a little embarrassed, so she sat up on the edge of the bed, trying to emulate a regal manner.

David walked in, his head down, his expression solemn. "My apologies, Your Majesties. There's been an attack in the dungeons."

There it was again, the weird title she'd have to get used to. Then the servant's words clicked into place. Were her parents involved?

Alex stood bolt upright instantly. "Have the prisoners escaped?"

"No, Your Majesty. The attack was on the prisoners."

"Someone attacked the prisoners? My god and goddess, the Hematites?"

"Yes."

"Why?" Toury burst out, her emotions betraying her.

Alex looked at her, his eyes full of worry. "Because someone wants to silence them. The cursemaker or someone acting on his behalf." He asked David, "My guards?"

"Five dead, sir. All the ones guarding that ward. No other guards saw anyone enter."

Alex let out a gruff breath. "It had to be an attack from within. Seal the castle immediately. No one gets out. Have Madge gather up all the Hematites and the royal family and protect them in the dower's safeaway. I'll meet you there."

"Wait," Toury said, her mind trying to process what was happening. "Are they—is my family alive?"

David did not meet her gaze. "Sorry to inform you, Your Majesty," he directed the title to her. "But your father did not survive. Your mother is hanging on in the infirmary."

Whatever expression he read upon her face filled Alex's gaze with pain and sympathy. "We will go to her, and then, Toury, I need you to stay safe."

She nodded and allowed Alex to guide her. She was a queen now, and her first hour as sovereign, her wedding day, would be horrifically etched into her mind forever.

38

AN END'S BEGINNING

Alex's heart was aching as if this woman lying in the infirmary were his own mother. It wasn't because he cared about her, because she was a cruel shell of a person who wanted him dead. It was because it was tearing up the woman he loved. Toury's mother's tawny flesh, which had given Toury her beautiful tan, was paling, making her green in appearance. She was a horrible person, had dragged his Toury through hot coals emotionally, but he knew it still was horrific to see one's estranged mother die. The healers were trying to staunch the blood, but Angelica Hematite kept bleeding out from the looks of it.

"Let me try." Toury knelt down by her mother.

"No," her mother choked out. "Let...me speak." Blood bubbled in her mouth. This wasn't something even someone as talented as Toury could heal.

"Mother," Toury pleaded.

Alex placed his hand on her shoulder for comfort, but her pain was his pain, and he swallowed to dislodge the lump growing in his throat. He couldn't do anything for her, and that made things even worse. "Who did this to you?" Alex asked gently. Time was of the essence, and Toury's pleas would only swallow up the time her mother had left.

Angelica turned her head slightly to meet his gaze and then closed her eyes. "I hate those eyes."

He ignored her barb. "Do not die in vain; avenge yourself and your lifemate. Who killed him?"

"Aschen," the woman began to cry. "I'm coming."

"No," Toury begged. Her body shook under his hand from her sobbing.

"My uncle wronged you. I will let all who comment on your rebellion against the crown know why. I don't want a world full of people like him. I want what you want. So, please. Fix this. Tell me who hurt you, and tell me the cursemaker's name. I beg you. Give your daughter a chance to avenge this."

"Your uncle." She laughed. "You should not keep uncles around, my boy..." She paused to gasp. "Or you might lose your head."

Alex's stomach dropped. He let go of Toury and turned away. There was a reason she wouldn't heal, despite all the healers' efforts. He digested the information for a moment, and then asked Toury to stop, for she was trying to heal her mother now, but it was making the woman moan in pain. Toury's tearstained face peered up at him, and her bloodstained hands shook.

"You cannot heal her."

"I have to try." Toury trembled.

"No, Toury, what I mean is that nothing will work."

"I don't understand."

"The emerald stone has many positive qualities—bringing friendship, happiness, loyalty,—" he scoffed at that "—but mostly deals with the heart. My guess is that if emerald power turns dark, it inverses the power. That is all taken away. One problem with stone power is when they can heal parts of the body, inversely, they can harm. My guess is your mother's heart will push the blood out of her body until there's none left, and there's no magic, save emerald that can stop it."

"Then call one of them. It might not be too late."

"Noble lines are dying out. There is only...my uncle."

It clicked right away. She stood up and fell into his arms, her mother's blood smearing on him.

Her mother spent her last moments laughing.

"I will kill him," Alex vowed to Toury and her mother simultaneously.

"Good." Her mother gasped for air, much like a fish out of water. "He was the architect behind the curse. He made her do it. Aschen saw them, both of them, over your cradle." She lolled back and took a deep splintered breath.

"Who?" Toury asked.

"My aunt," Alex breathed out. "They are necromancers, Toury, or at least she is. My father had thought the cursemaker used light magic, blamed your father, but he was wrong. It was fire. The inverse of fire magic could create a dark curse that could snuff or control it."

The woman went silent, her breaths shorter, and then they stopped. Toury simply turned her face away into his shoulder and held herself together, surprising him. He got the message, though. He transported her out of there.

They reappeared in their sitting room, and he left her to Madge's care, while David relayed a servant's message: his uncle was nowhere in the castle, his belongings gone as well. A feeling of dread creeping over him, he ordered the alert to be lowered but to continue searching the grounds.

Alex changed out of his bloodstained clothes, burning them all in the fireplace. His second wedding attire covered in blood. The dress that meant so much to Toury stained with blood. When would this end?

Alex returned to the sitting room and poured them firewhiskeys. He thought she'd be in shock and get upset when he wanted to talk about everything, but Toury surprised him. She wanted to talk it out, needed to. She spoke about her parents; he, about his family, how they both had been betrayed by them. There was no blame, no anger at each other, being equally innocent in all of this. There were promises of never betraying each other, never trusting anyone but themselves, the two of them and no one else. Then he told her what he dreaded most. He had to leave. He had to go after his uncle. It had to be him, and he had to kill him.

He sighed, pulling her into his arms. "I'd hate to leave you like this."

"I am the queen. I will make you proud, but you must do something first. Some might challenge me while you're gone if we're not properly wed," she told him, trying to sound official, but even through her grief, her coy tone came through.

He marveled at her strength of character, her vivacity, and her ability to be positive through horrible times. He had made the right choice. Then her words clicked in his head, making his blood stir.

"You stressed to me that your line is imperative. It must carry on. As much as I don't want you to go, this isn't a ploy to make you stay. If anything happened to me, you wouldn't continue your line, so the same goes for you."

"I won't die, Toury. David won't allow me." He tried to make a joke, but she didn't smile. No, how could she smile at a time like this? He couldn't imagine finding your parents to realize they abandoned you again for their cause and then lose them completely and forever. She had hoped that they could have reconciled or at least lived somewhere other than Fyr.

She grabbed his collar tightly in her hands in frustration. "Alex, you never know what will happen. I beg you not to go. I should remind you of a promise—"

He cut her off with a kiss. "I know. God and goddess, yet again, I'm forced between duty and you."

"What do you mean?"

"Only a royal can arrest and execute another royal. He's not a royal by blood, but still qualifies under the law. I need you to read the royal book of edicts, unchangeable laws." He pulled it off his bookshelf and dropped it on his desk with a thud. "This all applies to you now too. I have to be present, and please don't suggest Mary, because I am tempted to say yes, and if anything happens to her..."

"You speak of duties. You and I have a duty to the throne, and you won't leave until that is fulfilled."

Such a simple request. They were both so fertile, but it could take a month or more. Sure, the healers with their stones could tell them a bit earlier than when Toury could discover on her own whether she'd conceived, but what would he have them do? Test her every time they...

His uncle could escape the sphere—from his grasp forever. The power-hungry man could make plans, find alliances, get his necromancers and maybe the rebels alike to attack Alex's family. He had to act fast, and yet Toury was right. He was expected to continue and have descendants, and by the god and goddess, he wanted to beget them. He had waited so long to be with Toury.

"It is our duty, after all," he said quietly, claiming her lips with his. "We have to make this marriage binding." He walked her backward until she fell onto his bed. She pulled him down with her.

There was no hesitancy yet no overconsuming rush and no hindrances. They took their time until the fire and light in their blood were ready to boil over. Then, as mates for life, they finally became one and let the fire and light merge. It was a much more powerful meld than any kiss had ever been—even that powerful curse-breaking kiss or her healing light magic.

When they came back to Fyr, utterly changed forever, they fell asleep in each other's arms.

When Alex woke, he stoked up the fire with a clear mind for firebranding. He stared into the flames in hopes to see something of his future. As soon as he could see beyond a doubt that a child was on the way, he could go and take out this threat to his throne and family. He and Mary had played a game when they were young, much like when other kids toss a Sapphirian to see king's head or dragon's tail. "If it were in the flames game." If he saw anything in the flames, he would go. If nothing was there pertaining to his heir, he'd stay until he saw a sure future. As much as he had to leave in search of his uncle—because Toury, Mary, and he would never be safe as long as the man was free, trying to usurp the crown for his son—Toury was right. He needed that Prince Medallion or Princess Circlet to carry on first.

It did not take long to see snippets of the future. He saw things that made his heart melt and things utterly terrifying, but he got his answer. He just didn't know exactly when.

Alex slipped out of bed, trying not to wake her. Toury might not forgive him right away for not saying goodbye, but he knew if he woke her, he'd never be able to leave. Alex pulled down the covers and ran his hands down her body, resting them on her lower abdomen. He kissed her belly, which made her squirm and sigh in her sleep, and then he pulled away and covered her, mentally stoking the fire to keep her warm in his absence.

He would return, transport every week, maybe every day, to check in. Part of it was to selfishly ensure the child he saw in the flames would become a reality, but a huge part of it was a compromise. He feared what rampage his queen would wreak upon him if he outright abandoned her the day after their wedding for however long it would take to find his uncle. He penned her a letter, hoping it was enough for her to forgive him. Hopefully, she would understand that he was trying to protect their future.

Alex watched her sleep for a moment before he slipped out the door, on a mission to protect his family, a family that might already be increasing by one. There was so much to do, and the softness he felt around his lifemate, lulled by love and affection, faded away as he fixated on revenge. By the time he walked down to the prince room, the kindhearted man was gone, and the Draca stood in his stead.

Anyone who dared to threaten his queen, the Draca would reduce to ash.

COMPLETE THE STORY!

CELESTIAL SPHERES BOOK #3
BLADESUNG

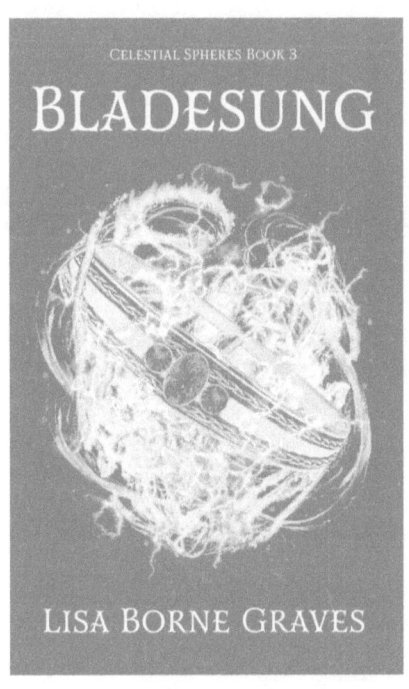

ABOUT THE AUTHOR

LISA BORNE GRAVES

Lisa Borne Graves is a YA author, English Lecturer, wife, and supermom of one wild child. Originally from the Philadelphia area, she relocated to the Deep South and found her true place of inspiration. Her love for all literature led her to branch out from the academic arena to spin her own tales. Lisa has a voracious appetite for books, British television, and pizza. Her inability to sit still makes her enjoy life to its fullest, and she can be found at the beach, pool, or on some crazy adventure.

Follow her online:

lisabornegraves.com
Twitter: @lisabornegraves
Facebook: @lisabornegravesauthor
Instagram: @lisabornegraves

ALSO BY LISA BORNE GRAVES

THE IMMORTAL TRANSCRIPTS I

QUIVER

What would you do if you could live forever? Could you hide it from the one you truly loved, especially if her life depended on it?

Thanks to his dysfunctional Olympian family, Archer Ambrose finds out firsthand how difficult this can be. He never falls in love but bestows it on others—until he meets Callie.

When Callie Syches moves to the Upper East Side to prepare for her father's impending death, she doesn't expect to meet the boy of her dreams. She also never believed her father's harebrained theory about myths, but her uncanny ability to "see" uncovers godly secrets Callie can hardly fathom.

With an immortal family demanding absolute obedience, how far will Archer go to protect his love from the storm the gods will unleash upon them?

In this reinvention of Cupid and Psyche, experience an electrifying series where familial and romantic bonds are at war, and knowledge could mean the end of everything...or a new beginning.

books2read.com/quiver

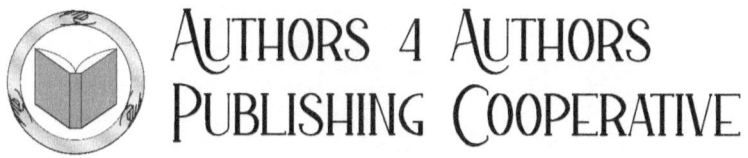

Authors 4 Authors Publishing Cooperative

A publishing company for authors, run by authors, blending the best of traditional and independent publishing

We specialize in speculative fiction: science fiction, fantasy, paranormal, and romance. Get lost in another world!

Check out our collection at https://books2read.com/rl/a4a or visit Authors4AuthorsPublishing.com/books

For updates, scan the QR code or visit our website to join our semi-monthly newsletter!

Want more romantic fantasy? We recommend:

KISS OF TREASON
by Brandi Spencer

Two forbidden lovers share the rare gift to heal others with a kiss—but at a cost. Odelia's life has been a lie. When the queen tries to remove her from the palace, Odelia uncovers the truth. Now she must decide whether to forsake her people or embrace a destiny that would pit her against the current heir to the throne...her best friend. Though her only hope of avoiding a civil war lies in winning his heart, revealing her secrets too soon could cost both their lives. And a kiss might not be strong enough to save them...

books2read.com/kisstreason